D0989209

OFF BY ONE

Jonathan Ackley

Copyright © 2022 Jonathan Ackley

All rights reserved.

OZYMANDIAS

I met a traveller from an antique land,
Who said—"Two vast and trunkless legs of stone
Stand in the desert. . . . Near them, on the sand,
Half sunk a shattered visage lies, whose frown,
And wrinkled lip, and sneer of cold command,
Tell that its sculptor well those passions read
Which yet survive, stamped on these lifeless things,
The hand that mocked them, and the heart that fed;
And on the pedestal, these words appear:
My name is Ozymandias, King of Kings;
Look on my Works, ye Mighty, and despair!
Nothing beside remains. Round the decay
Of that colossal Wreck, boundless and bare
The lone and level sands stretch far away."

Percy Bysshe Shelley

GAME MAKER'S PROVERB

Give a man a game and he will be happy for a day.
Teach a man to make games and he will never be
happy again.

CHAPTER ONE

IN THE STRATOSPHERE

January 5, 1994

The last thing Melvin Smart could remember, it was daytime and he was in his hotel room, packing his bag. He'd just finished his mining tariff review meetings with the Morozov group and was preparing for his flight home.

Now it was nighttime, it was cold and he was confused. He'd raised himself to his feet with great difficulty, falling several times and cracking his teeth on the concrete. He sensed he was drunk, but it was a drunk like he'd never felt before. Melvin felt completely rewired. Trying to move his hand, he instead kicked out with his leg. When he tried to turn his head, his whole body spun in place. Twice more he almost fell. Unable to take in his situation as a whole, he decided to focus on individual details and see if he could put them together.

"It's windy," he thought. "It's dark. I can see buildings. I can see a pyramid. It's got light coming out the top. Right! I'm in Las Vegas. But where in Vegas?"

Unable to concentrate and stand at the same time, Melvin lost his balance and stumbled forwards towards the sheer drop. The fire and police at the base gasped, but he caught himself at the last second. They'd been trying to reach him but the motors of the tower's construction elevator had burned out. The fire department was devising a plan to lower a rescuer from the big crane next to the tower.

Melvin looked down. The eleven hundred-foot drop shocked him. The resulting adrenaline helped him focus. His memory was coming back. He'd been in his room packing when a man grabbed him. Melvin couldn't remember the man's face. He hadn't seen it. But there had been a second man, a big man with dark hair pulled back into a ponytail. He'd had a syringe.

Melvin thought he might talk himself through the situation.

"I've been drugged and I'm really high," he thought then laughed at the pun. "If I got up here…there's got to be a way down…so there's probably a ladder or an elevator somewhere."

Very slowly, he turned his head to the right and the world spun around him. He could tell that any rapid movement would throw off his equilibrium. Fighting to keep his head level, he finally turned far enough to see his goal. The elevator! He just needed to rotate about ninety degrees and walk about twenty feet. Then he'd press the elevator call button and get in when it arrived. He'd be safe. Melvin planned his next move carefully. He visualized pivoting in place, putting all his weight on his left foot and stepping backward with his right. Just as he had turned his head, he would do it very, very slowly. Plan firmly in his mind, Melvin began to move. He shifted his weight.

"So far, so good," he thought.

He instructed his leg to take the step back and with great conviction, took a huge step forward off the tower. He had no fear as he fell, just confusion. There were spinning lights, a roar in his ears and a feeling someone was pushing on his head and chest. Then he felt nothing.

CHAPTER TWO

SHOCKWAVE

6 Months Earlier - July 18, 1993
Sakha Republic, Russia
Siberia, 200 Miles South of Siktyakh along the Lena River

Though small and thin, Olga didn't break a sweat as she hauled the cables, cases and metal rods through the larch forest to the installation point. Her sinewy arm muscles showed clearly beneath her taut skin.

Olga's snow-white hair, shaved short on the sides, blended perfectly with her pale complexion. If not for her dark-brown eyes, one would have thought she lacked any pigment at all.

Crouching low, she set a heavy battery pack on the ground next to her computer specialist, Flexx.

Flexx was a stupid name, thought Olga. It wasn't a name for a grown Russian man and it certainly didn't match the six-foot-four, 245-pound lump sitting at her feet. She watched his pasty cheeks redden in the Siberian summer sun.

He connected the batteries to an instrument case then switched on the computer inside.

"Flexx. A hacker name," thought Olga and unconsciously scoffed aloud.

She grabbed a long, steel sensor rod and pounded it into the ground with an oversized mallet. Chores complete, Olga turned and hauled her tools back to the pickup truck.

Flexx punched three keys on the computer's keyboard and watched a stream of data roll across its amber screen. Satisfied that the sensor system was up and running, he trudged back to the pickup, sat down and swung his legs up into the cab.

Olga climbed in and started the engine. The cab bounced on oversized tires as the truck sped over logs and rock outcroppings. Flexx hadn't buckled his seatbelt and cursed loudly as he hit his head on the roof.

"We're in a hurry, remember," laughed Olga, speaking in Russian.

"Yeah, yeah."

Twenty minutes later they were out of the woods, finally stopping on a plateau overlooking the grassy flood plain of the river *Lena*.

It was late summer and the hard, dry earth made the meadow a perfect landing spot for a small, single-engine plane. Olga waved to the aircraft, catching the attention of the pilot who leaned casually against the fuselage. Seeing her signal, the man crushed his cigarette with his boot and made preparations for takeoff.

Olga and Flexx jumped from the truck and hurried down the embankment. Reaching the aircraft, they climbed into the fuselage, sealed the cabin and sat down in the seats behind the cockpit. Soon, they were airborne.

Flexx looked down to see a small family of Siberian musk deer, a mother and two fawns, browsing at the edge of the woods. At the riverbank, he saw a shaggy brown bear wading into a shallow for a drink. Flexx pointed excitedly at the bear, trying to catch Olga's attention. She ignored him. Olga had seen plenty of bears.

Without warning, the plane rose rapidly. Flexx grabbed his armrests while Olga laughed at him. The craft leveled out and they climbed above the hills, revealing the panoramic view ahead. They saw a small city, now a ghost town of rotting water towers, factory buildings, houses and stores. Before the diamond mine had closed in the 1960s, the town had been home to 40,000 people. But today, the secret Soviet city had been completely abandoned.

Again, the plane ascended abruptly and leveled, giving Olga and Flexx a view of the Bogatyye open-pit mine just beyond the town. A giant funnel in the ground, a mile across at the top, the mine spiraled deep into the earth. Huge abandoned earth-moving machines appeared as tiny dots within the cone, dwarfed by the giant scar in the planet.

The plane banked quickly to the right, flying over the town but well outside the edge of the pit. Confused by the change in bearing, Flexx looked at Olga, who had been checking her watch. Understanding Flexx's implied question, she said, "He won't fly over the pit. It's too dangerous. The Bogatyye mine is so large it creates its own weather.

Look down now."

Flexx looked out his side window. He had a view of the forest while Olga looked across the pit to the grassland beyond. They heard a booming sound from beneath them, loud and long, yet deep and muffled. Flexx's eyes widened as he saw a circular wave of force radiate from the pit mine's center. It rolled through the earth as a ring of water moving outward from a rock dropped in a still pond.

Olga had the best view of the town. She watched the waves lift the buildings a dozen feet in the air then drop them. On impact, some of the taller structures toppled, splintering into pieces.

On Flexx's side, the woodland pines first flexed inward toward the mine then quickly snapped away. The tremor passed through the forest, until it looked to Flexx as though the wilderness rippled like a field of wheat in a strong wind. Surprised nuthatches, tits and even a golden eagle zoomed upward, taking refuge in the sky.

"Good job," said Olga, playfully punching Flexx in the arm. "Site 2 will be a success. Tomorrow we'll come back to collect the equipment."

Flexx wondered if the deer and bear had survived the shockwave. He found it an interesting question, but the answer didn't concern him much either way.

CHAPTER THREE

PEACEMAKER

Owen left Ike's body lying face up in the street. The young man entered the hotel, brandishing his weapon, a revolver with three shots remaining.

"Three shots might be enough," he thought.

He was sure there would be another attack, but Owen was ready. From his position on the ground floor, Owen looked up at the three doors along the hotel's interior-facing second-story balcony. Sanchez was waiting behind one of those doors. Taking a guess, Owen aimed his gun at the one in the center. He took a step forward.

The door on the right burst open and Sanchez emerged, blasting wildly with his rifle.

With the measured confidence of a trained gunman, Owen adjusted swiftly and fired a shot. It hit the target. Sanchez roared in anger and pain but didn't drop.

"Damn," Owen cursed and spent a second shot which finally brought the man down.

Only one bullet left. He would have to save it for Ambrose.

Holstering his gun, Owen took up his enormous Bowie knife. Stalking across the hotel lobby, he reached the opening to the bar. Pausing for a moment, he took a few deep breaths to slow his heart rate then entered.

Owen spun left and lunged. The swift attack caught Levi by surprise and Owen drove his "Arkansas Toothpick" into the barman. Levi never had a chance to let loose with his sawed-off shotgun.

Running for cover, Owen ducked behind the bar. Had he been slower by half a second, he'd have been gunned down.

General Ambrose fired his weapons so rapidly, the shots sounded like beating snare drums. Although Ambrose' firepower seemed unlimited, especially when compared with Owen's single bullet, the young man knew a secret the general did not.

Crouching low, Owen pressed a panel on the bar's back wall. The "click" told him he'd unlocked the hidden passage. That's when everything went wrong.

First came a deep rattling sound. This escalated to a high, hideous whine. Random colors flashed everywhere. There was an explosion of inexplicable, flashing alphanumeric characters. This went on for several seconds before the entire computer locked up, hard.

The monitor went black.

"Shit," Owen muttered, shutting off the power to the CPU. The terrible screech faded away.

It could not be denied. Famed game designer and programmer, Owen Nickerson, had a crash bug in *Peacemaker*, his new western-themed 3D shooter.

"Oh, bless your heart, Owen. You owe a dollar to the Swear Jar," cooed the slim man leaning over the lead programmer's shoulder.

"Can it, Mitch," scolded the lead programmer.

"I told you losers we would break your damn game," Ryan announced, proudly. "It crashes at every secret door. The bar. The fort. The courthouse. I already talked to Jarrod. He says you have to fix it."

Test lead Ryan, stood nearby Owen's programming workstation, grinning. The young man practically sparkled with energy, humor and good-natured aggression. He had high, hollow cheekbones, dark brown skin, neatly trimmed hair and a button-up checked shirt. Ryan was a jerk, but that's why Owen loved him. Nice testers didn't find all the bugs.

"By the way, Mitch," Ryan continued, "nice outfit today."

Mitch was dressed from head to toe in gold. Every item on his body looked as if King Midas had touched it. Boat shoes, socks, pants, canvas belt and dress shirt all matched.

"What's special about it?" asked Owen. "He dresses like that every day."

"No, Owen," Ryan corrected. "Mitch dresses in a single, bright color every day. But I've never before seen him in this particular shade."

"I'm glad one of y'all noticed," Mitch drawled. "It was to celebrate the game going 'gold' today. But I guess that's not going to happen."

"Oh, we're going to release the gold candidate today," Owen

declared. "The bug is new to this build. That means it's in one of... err...one of forty-five files. I can't believe we made that many changes before going into QA? Son of a bitch!"

Throwing a mild tantrum, Owen kicked out and dented the sheetrock wall behind his workstation. The blow shook the high shelf holding his collection of vintage action figures and toppled a 24-inch tall Shogun Warrior robot. The toy fell backward, striking the wall. This jarred its firing mechanism and fired a gleaming, plastic fist into the air.

Mesmerized, the three spectators watched as the projectile arced gracefully upward. When it came down, it struck Owen in the dead center of his forehead.

"Oh, my god!" laughed Mitch. "That was amazing!"

Frustrated, Owen stood abruptly and pushed his seat backward. One of the chair's cheap casters caught on a bubble in the office's gray, marinara-stained carpet. It toppled with a crash. The unexpected violence of the gesture made it seem absurdly melodramatic.

"You think this is funny, Mitch?" snarled Owen.

"You gotta admit, Owen. It's a *little* funny," Mitch answered.

"Really? The money we made from *Apoplexy* is trailing off. Now it is just an old game in the discount pile. Will you think it's funny if *Peacemaker* doesn't launch for Christmas and we go bankrupt? Will it be funny when the company shuts down and all your friends are unemployed?"

Mitch tried asking Owen to lighten up, but the game designer just talked over his protests.

"I don't think it's funny," Owen said, glaring. "Wait! I have an idea. Why don't you be helpful for once? Why don't you just sit down at my workstation and find the bug? Go ahead, Mitch. Come on. I'm waiting."

Mitch gaped.

"Are - are you - are you serious?" stammered Mitch.

Owen nodded.

"But the bug has to be in the engine or the game logic. You can't expect me to debug code I've never seen."

Owen stabbed a finger at his subordinate's chest, "And *that* is why I have you working in tools!"

"Oh, wow!" Ryan said, shaking his head. "I'm sorry, guys. I've made a terrible mistake."

"What now?" Owen demanded.

Ryan remained placid.

He answered, "You see, Owen - I put up a sign in the test pit. It tells the team which Owen they should expect on any given day. This morning I set it to, 'Game-Making Automaton,'but now I see that it should be set to 'Full-On Pissy Diva.'"

Owen tried responding, but Ryan's words had short-circuited his brain. He froze, momentarily. Finally, he looked to the floor and chuckled.

He sighed then turned to Mitch.

"Sorry," he said. "The pressure just got to me and I took it out on you."

"No, no. I get it," said the tools programmer. "Like always, I forgive you. But y'all have to tell me one thing."

"What's that?"

Mitch gestured toward Ryan, saying, "How does he always get away with talking to you like that?"

"Oh, I can tell you," said the lead tester, smiling. "It's because Owen knows that without my professional brilliance and unassailable gameplay instincts, the world would be referring to his last game as 'Crapoplexy.'"

Owen gave Mitch a chagrined look and a shrug. Then he righted his chair and sat back down at his workstation.

Opening all forty-five suspect files in his text editor, Owen scrutinized the game code. He hadn't had a haircut in months, which made debugging all the more challenging. Just to see his computer screen, Owen had to pause every few seconds to brush aside the sandy blonde forelock that continually fell in front of his dark green eyes.

Mitch leaned in to see what Owen was doing. The lead programmer scanned each file so rapidly that Mitch could barely make out a single line of code.

"I will never know how y'all do that," said Mitch in astonishment.

Owen closed the last document and his eyes. He leaned back in his chair, forcing Mitch to move aside and out of the way. In his mind, Owen walked through each of the hundred different logic paths. Seconds later, his eyes popped open.

Reopening one of the files, Owen pointed to the screen. "Right here. Cole accesses my array. But... I start at 0. He starts at 1."

"Off-by-one error," Mitch concurred. "He's reading from unallocated memory."

"I hope Cole gets here soon," said Owen. "I don't want to make

her hands and feet. Fighting through the pain, she strained to create slack. Pulling so hard on the cord that it cut her skin, Martina eventually freed her hands. Making quick work of her leg bindings, she rose.

She listened for noises in the next room, but there were none. All she heard was the muffled and indistinct sound of a voice amplified by a distant loudspeaker.

Cracking open the closet door, she peeked out. There was nothing. It was a vacant hotel room. It had no bed, no dresser and no television. Stepping out of the closet, she tiptoed to the center of the room. It was deathly quiet. She worried that each step would alert the kidnapper of her escape.

Needing to determine her location she went to the hotel room's window. Looking out, Martina could tell she was up high, at least 10 floors. She had a view of the Las Vegas strip and the Flamingo Hotel.

She thought to herself, "OK. That means I'm in the north tower of... the *Dunes*. Wait! What day is it? What time is it? Oh, no!"

Martina turned and sprinted for the door to the hallway.

* * *

"... FIRE!"

Morozov, Ilizarov and the rest of the partygoers held their collective breaths as they gazed toward the Treasure Island Hotel. In the distance, fiery explosions burst from the pirate ship's guns. A second later, plumes of flame shot up from the base of the Dunes' north tower. The shockwave rattled the windows of the Flamingo.

The pirates fired another volley. This time a cannonball "hit" the hotel's famous sign. A shower of firework sparks fell from the minaret, before dynamite at its base blew, causing it to fall toward the hotel. As it toppled, the demolition team ignited the forty-two hundred gallons of aviation fuel hidden within the tower itself. This created a black and orange fireball that engulfed the hotel, rising 50 feet above the structure's roof while explosive charges went off inside, severing its load-bearing structures.

The fiery cloud dissipated, leaving the building visible once more. The flash from the explosions left the spectators' pupils contracted, capable of seeing only the dark mass of the doomed building and the flames burning in its windows. There was a suspenseful pause, then the building crumbled, falling away from the strip and landing in billows of smoke and dust.

Everyone around Leonid Morozov cheered and screamed with excitement. He just smirked and muttered, "Good riddance."

CHAPTER FIVE

TEAM BUILDING

October 27, 1993
San Rafael, CA

The rush Owen had received from emergency bug fixing left him full of adrenaline, like a runner after a sprint. Hoping a walk home would burn off his nervous energy, he left the office, paced to D Street then climbed the steep driveway to his apartment building.

His space was small—just two rooms and a kitchenette. A ratty brown loveseat took up a corner, across from Owen's high-end videocassette recorder and low-end television. A computer monitor and keyboard rested on a bookshelf, braced between towers of stacked cinderblocks. Almost every flat surface in the apartment was covered with action figures.

The apartment did have one or two major drawbacks. Mindy, the resident of the room below, was a drummer. Moreover, she was a blind drummer and as such, possessed exceptionally sensitive hearing. Owen's slightest step on the floor could result in screams from below, with Mindy chastising him for his "Clomping Yeti Feet."

The second issue Owen had with Mindy was her habit of playing heavy metal drum solos in the middle of the night. In a way, being stuck at the office during game development crunch mode was something of a relief to him. Unlike home, he could sleep at work.

Owen flopped onto his bed. He'd only lain down to rest momentarily when the drumming started. He couldn't place the song, but he was sure the beats were John Bonham's.

Unable to rest, he got up and prepared for that night's team event.

Owen was already down the steps to the carport when he

remembered he was going to a Halloween party. He needed a costume! A few weeks before, Owen had planned an elaborate costume but had then been too distracted by work to follow through.

Running back inside, he steeled himself against the pounding of the drums as he scrounged for an outfit.

"Yes!" he thought as he slipped into a black, hooded sweatshirt and grabbed the large, stuffed killer whale he'd won at the Marin County Fair. He crammed the back of the whale into his hood so the orca's friendly face stuck out over his forehead.

And so Owen, in his low-rent whale costume, headed to Larkspur, two exits south of his apartment, in his silver Toyota Corolla. He had lived in the North Bay for over two years but had spent most of it indoors so basic navigation remained a bit of a challenge. He over-shot Larkspur and wound up at the front of the gargantuan walls of San Quentin Prison. Its arrival gates open, San Quentin seemed to invite him to enter.

The wheels on Owen's Corolla squealed as he spun the car 180 degrees. A strange paranoia overcame Owen. Could prison guards arrest traffic violators? He ducked his head down, just in case officers fired at the fleeing vehicle. He got away. This time. All the guards saw was a killer whale making an illegal U-turn in a compact car.

Soon after, Owen arrived at the shopping mall. The game-maker was half an hour early for dinner, so he decided to pass the time in a nearby bookshop. It was spacious, had a lot of books and a small dais where a local author was signing copies of her book about San Francisco's 1915 Panama-Pacific International Exposition. He studied the oversized displays of the book's illustrations. In one picture a man gave fair visitors rides over the bay in his rickety, hand-built airplane.

Owen thought hopefully, "Maybe now that the game's done, I'll have time to read a book."

As he browsed through the store's spy novels, co-workers tracked him down. Viv and Miles entered together. Upon seeing Owen's costume, they both screamed, "Free Willy!"

For Halloween, Viv and Miles had coordinated costumes. Miles came as a giant, double-sided vinyl record. Its painted, cardstock records hung like a sandwich board from his shoulder straps. Viv looked fabulous as Parliament's outrageous bassist, Bootsy Collins.

Ordinarily a curvy five foot three inches tall, Viv appeared five-nine in platform shoes and even taller in her glitter-covered, green, construction paper hat. Star-shaped sunglasses and a star-shaped

As usual, she brought a cheer from her Coliseum Arts peers.

"As for me," Jarrod announced, "my vacation begins *before* it ships. I trust this great game team to bring it home, so *tomorrow* I'm going to take my long-awaited trip to the Bahamas."

"Where in the Bahamas?" asked Owen.

"Nassau."

Being English, Cole had more knowledge of the Bahamas than his American collaborators.

"New Providence is a little rough, yes? Crime and all?"

"I suppose that's true of most of the Caribbean, but where I'm staying has a private beach, so I'm sure I'll be all right."

Viv was excited by the whole prospect.

"Are you taking a cruise?" she asked

"No. Just flying in and out."

"How long will you be gone?"

"Just a week and a half and then back here to release the shareware version."

"A week and a half? Sounds wonderful!" Viv imagined a poolside bar where one could order frozen tropical drinks without leaving the water. "Who are you taking?"

"No one. I'm just going to decompress all by myself," answered Jarrod. "And besides, half of the trip will be in Georgia with our logistics partners, setting up the mail forwarding service and getting the packaging and fulfillment company ready."

"Now it makes sense. A real vacation seemed out of character," said Owen, jabbing Jarrod in the side.

"Just stop," said Jarrod seriously. "Viv, how 'bout you?"

"I don't want to do much. Maybe…maybe I'll do some painting. I've got a new romance novel. Maybe I'll watch TV. There's a *Perry Mason* marathon this weekend. He's my favorite."

"Well, that's oddly compelling. How about you, Miles? Anything fun?" Owen asked before taking a deep drink.

"I'm working on a personal project."

Viv turned to Miles, "What project? You never told me about it!"

"I didn't tell you," said Miles, "because it's a surprise."

"What is it?" she pressed.

"It's… a surprise." Miles smiled. He changed the subject. "Cole? What are you going to do?"

Cole had been waiting for this moment all night. Grinning, he hit a button on his costume, causing Optimus Prime to say, "We hunt for what remains of our Decepticon foes!"

"Riiiight," laughed Owen. "How about you, Mitch?"

"First, I'm going to quit smoking!" Mitch announced proudly.

Then team cheered enthusiastically.

Mitch continued, "Then I'm going to visit my dad in Virginia. Since the big box store moved in down the road, he's been having a hard time with his hardware store. He had to lay off his guys, so I thought I'd go back and help him out."

"Oh, you sweet thing! That's so nice. I bet your dad will love that," Maxine said sympathetically.

"Free Willy?" Viv addressed Owen, giving him a wink that made his heart skip. "Question to you. What will *you* do with your time off?"

He thought for a moment then answered, "I was thinking I might go down to San Diego. I used to surf at Cardiff. It's pretty sweet."

"You know," said Viv, "I've never been to San Di . . . "

"Now, Owen," interrupted Jenn. "I was thinking about our schedule for the new game. It's just…it's just *so* tight. You just finished your little cowboy game and I get that, but if we're going to deconstruct the 3D shooter genre for the sequel to *Apoplexy*—and I mean just tear it down to its essence and rebuild it to a sublime fusion of interaction and narratology—then we don't have much time to finish the design. So why not spend the next few weeks with me?"

Viv looked side-eyed at Jenn, seething.

Owen pushed the Orca back a little into the sweatshirt's hood so he could scratch his head. He quickly calculated the time allotted for the next project and everything he wanted to accomplish.

"Wow. I guess you're right, Jenn. Good catch," he said. "I'll just take a couple of days then see you in the office on Monday."

CHAPTER SIX

THE RED EYE

November 14, 1993
Boryspil International Airport
Kyiv, Ukraine

Captain Ted Donahue pulled back on the yoke and the sleek U.S. Air Force C-20H twinjet responded, rising quickly and smoothly. Below, snow-blanketed Kyiv's landscape, but weather reports predicted clear skies to their destination, Ramstein Air Base in southwest Germany. There, the European NATO officials would debark the modified Gulfstream IV, the plane would refuel, then Captain Ted and his co-pilot would ferry their 11 State Department VIPs back to Andrews Air Force Base in Washington, D.C.

When the plane reached 6000 feet, a shrill alarm sounded in the cockpit. Quickly, Captain Donahue scanned his console. On a panel to his left, he saw red and green lights flashing together, signaling an incoming missile alert. Infrared cameras on the underside of the plane's fuselage had detected an ascending surface-to-air missile. Once ignited, the rocket's solid-fuel engines would propel the warhead to two and a half times the speed of sound.

As military pilots, Donahue and his co-pilot had been trained for rocket attacks, but it had never been a major focus of their simulations. It took the captain a few moments to process the meaning of the emergency signal before he reacted. It didn't look good. The Gulfstream was fast, but there was no way the C-20 could outrun the attack.

Donahue reached out his left hand, grasping a protective switch cover below the alarm lights. He pulled up hard on the hinged plate, breaking the thin security wire securing it and exposing the toggle switch for the plane's anti-missile systems.

"Hands off yoke. Now!" The captain screamed to be heard over the alarm.

The co-pilot released the plane's controls and Donahue flipped the toggle, activating the defensive autopilot.

The Stinger Missile saw only the heat radiating from the plane's turbofans. To the rocket's control system, the target appeared as a simple, white blob on a dark background. A deep red filter covering the camera at the missile's tip ensured only heat radiation would reach the guidance sensor. The Stinger had a good lock and the white target blob grew larger and larger in the missile's view.

The Gulfstream rattled as the autopilot wrenched the plane from its original course with a brutality no human pilot would ever consider. The plane's AI was attempting to match the missile's horizontal vector in a bid to buy a few extra milliseconds before impact. The plane's engines shrieked as the autopilot revved them to full throttle. The craft's nose tilted up, reaching 30 degrees above the line of the horizon. The extreme angle terrified the passengers, as everyone worried the craft would stall and plummet.

Captain Donahue comprehended the autopilot's logic. A Stinger missile couldn't hit a target above 10,000 feet. But the aircraft would never reach that altitude in time. He figured they had just a few seconds left to live.

Donahue heard a sequence of rattles and hisses as minor tremors rolled through the plane. These announced the release of the plane's anti-missile flares. Each flare burned at 2000 degrees, twice the temperature of molten lava. Burning hotter than the Gulfstream's engines, the hope was that the Stinger would chase the strongest heat source.

Moments earlier, the missile's targeting system had shown only a single, relatively dim target. Once the flares were airborne, there were eight bright targets along with the faint original. Even so, the rocket remained locked on the turbojet. It wasn't running first-generation targeting software. It had some smarts. The missile still registered the jet as the primary target. In a few seconds, a cone of exploding shrapnel would obliterate the plane and all aboard.

Executing its final counter-move, the plane's artificial intelligence banked hard left with such unexpected severity that several passengers struck their heads against the aircraft's windows.

This maneuver placed the brightly burning flares directly between the missile and the plane. Within the Stinger's infrared sensor, the plane's signature merged with the flare's overwhelming heat, causing the missile to conflate the two objects.

Donahue held his breath, knowing there was still a good chance the plane would be too close to the missile when it detonated. He feared the blast wouldn't kill them instantly, but would instead disable the plane, leaving all aboard wide-awake as they plummeted to their deaths. Fortunately, the captain never heard the explosion.

The flares and the onboard missile defense system had been so effective that the Stinger had blown up several hundred yards away. Captain Donahue switched off the missile defense system and piloted the Gulfstream above 10,000 feet. The attackers wouldn't get a second chance to shoot down his plane.

"Boryspil Departure Control, this is U.S. Air Force Golf Bravo Zero Four Three. We have come under surface-to-air missile attack, approximately 20 miles south-southeast of your location."

* * *

Far below, a furious figure in black screamed orders to his accomplices. The Stinger missile had missed and the authorities would soon arrive. Capture meant execution.

The ragged band scrambled into to their beat-up vehicles. Cursing, they sped away, filled with disappointment and rage. They had taken an expensive gamble and had lost.

CHAPTER SEVEN

THE HOLIDAY SPIRIT

When Jarrod returned from his Caribbean trip, he asked Owen for an update. The lead programmer announced his findings with great seriousness, "While the testers found no bugs in the game that would prevent its launch, there was one important discovery that I feel must be mentioned."

"Oh?" asked Jarrod, concerned. "What's that?"

"Because you returned from a weeklong Caribbean vacation without any semblance of a tan, we the team must officially conclude that you, Jarrod Young, are in fact, the *whitest* man on earth."

"Owen Nickerson, you get the hell out of my office!" Jarrod snapped, trying but failing to keep a straight face.

The next day, Jarrod hired a bonded courier to hand-carry *Peacemaker*'s Gold Release CDs to the disc duplicator in Finland. When they'd shipped *Apoplexy*, the ever-frugal CEO had discovered a Finnish manufacturer charging a fraction of the going U.S. rate. The savings far outweighed the cost of a courier and airfare.

Then it was time for Max to work her magic. Owen gave her a disc containing a demo version of Peacemaker that included 3 of its 15 playable levels. She took this demo disc to the corner of the common room and sat down at the company's Internet-connected marketing computer.

For security reasons, the marketing computer was configured to sit outside the company's internal network. Even if a hacker broke in, he couldn't access the sensitive data stored in the Coliseum Arts system.

Max loaded the disc and uploaded the game demo to a number of the world's most popular electronic bulletin boards. From these, a hundred thousand players would download the free version and many of these would burn copies for friends.

Those liking the demo would send Coliseum Arts a check for a copy of the complete game.

As they watched the progress bar tracking the upload, Max proclaimed expansively, "Farewell, *Peacemaker*. Child of our hearts! Offspring of our imaginations! Bring your blessings of joy and amusement to the people of the world."

And with that, the shareware version of *Peacemaker* launched in early November, just in time for the Christmas sales season.

For the next month, Jenn and Owen worked intensely on the design for the sequel to *Apoplexy*. The story they invented for the game had an unsettled, dream-within-a-dream structure. Was the protagonist an innocent man unjustly committed to a madhouse or was he a mad man who thought he was an innocent man unjustly committed to a madhouse or...?

While the rest of the Coliseum Arts team took off most of December in exchange for the unpaid overtime worked during the *Peacemaker* production, Miles continued to come into the office. Crammed inside his soundproof office full of recording equipment, with its thick glass window facing the programmers, he toiled away at his pet project. Owen thought he looked like a DJ in a radio booth.

When Mitch returned to the office in mid-December, Owen pitched him the new game concept and the tools programmer didn't hold back his enthusiasm.

As they chatted, Owen learned that Mitch couldn't afford another trip to Virginia and had planned on celebrating Christmas alone. This gave Owen an idea. His own parents were spending the week on a Christmas Cruise to Cabo San Lucas and their Santa Cruz area beach house would be free.

Owen could invite Mitch to spend the holiday with him in Aptos. There, they could work a little on the new game and Owen could try and atone for his behavior toward Mitch on the last day of the *Peacemaker* project. He pitched the idea and Mitch accepted immediately.

On Christmas, they climbed into Owen's car and drove south, taking the scenic route along Highway 1 through San Francisco, Half Moon Bay and Santa Cruz.

Arriving at his parent's beach house, Owen leapt from the car, threw open the front door and bounded up the entry stairs to the two-story, Nantucket-style home's living area. Mitch followed in similar fashion and his heavy steps rattled the wood-framed building.

At the top of the stairs was a living room, crowded with overstuffed couches, upholstered in faded, floral-patterns. These filled most of the floor space, making it nearly impossible to cross the room without stumbling over an ottoman or two. In the corner sat an ungainly, faux-wood paneled, projection TV. Beside which stood a decaying but festively decorated artificial tree.

"Check it out," called Owen, pulling aside the glass door and stepping outside onto a weathered, wooden deck. Mitch followed.

From the lookout, they could see the frigid Monterey Bay. Its gray waters so closely matched the overcast skies that it was impossible to identify the position of the horizon.

For a time they gazed, silently, watching the seabirds struggle to stay aloft in the bay's buffeting winter winds.

Finally, Owen returned inside to order a Christmas pizza. When he returned to the deck, he brought Mitch a warm coat from the hall closet. It didn't match Mitch's 'Christmas Tree Green' outfit, but was gratefully accepted, nonetheless.

They chatted for an hour before Mitch excused himself to call his father in Virginia from the kitchen phone. The conversation started jovially, but it quickly became apparent to Owen that things were not well in Martinsville. Giving Mitch some privacy, he took a walk to the beach. Returning after sunset, he thought they might rent a movie but noticed that his friend was exhausted.

"Time for bed," said Owen. "You'll take my room."

Owen led Mitch to the bedroom, opened the door and said goodnight.

Stepping in, Mitch noticed an out-of-date IBM 286 sitting on a deteriorating pressboard desk. While he'd expected to find a computer in Owen's room, he hadn't expected the numerous surfboards. He counted four, ranging in length from six to ten feet.

Each rainbow-colored board featured numerous decorative decals. Teenager Owen had coated each with stickers of cartoon sharks, seal lions, killer whales, "Hang Loose" shakas and the Yin and Yang symbols.

Mitch noticed the arm of a neoprene wetsuit peeking out from behind the open bedroom door. Wanting to get a closer look, he pushed the door shut, slamming it accidentally.

The impact disturbed a nearby long board. It listed right, slid along the wall and crashed into the desk, knocking a picture frame to the

When is dinner? I'm hungry."

Ludmilla didn't answer her brother. She was too angry. Instead, she sat at the edge of her bed, repeatedly pounding a hand-embroidered pillow with her fist.

CHAPTER NINE

OUT WITH THE NEW

At Maxine's insistence, Jarrod had approved a New Year's office party for the Coliseum Arts team. It was a potluck and along with food, each attendee had to make an additional contribution to the party, choosing a job from a list on the wall.

Mitch and Maxine chose "entertainment." Max brought the music, lighting and karaoke, while Mitch volunteered to provide the electronic entertainment. Dressed all in Burgundy, he spent the hours before the party setting up each work computer with a copy of one of Coliseum Arts' games. Having already spent thousands of hours playing each game, not a single partygoer wound up taking advantage of Mitch's hard work.

Everyone breathed a sigh of relief when Miles and Viv jumped at handling the decorations. Not only did the pair transform the office into a shiny, wintery fairyland, they also arrived in matching costumes. Viv was the 'Old Year.' She wore a gray wig, drooping white bathrobe and a long, glued-on beard. Miles came as "Baby New Year,' shirtless and wearing a diaper made out of a bedsheet. Everyone, including Miles, agreed the costume was disturbing and he quickly changed into the sharp, silver sharkskin suit he wore when gigging with his bar bands.

Owen volunteered to bring alcohol. And while his sparkling wine purchases weren't embarrassing, he did make the mistake of acquiring large amounts of boxed wine. Close as they were to the Napa Valley, this sort of crime against grape might have warranted punishment by guillotine. Fortunately, Jenn's foresight saved the day. Seeing Owen's name next to "alcohol" on the sign-up sheet, she knew it was imperative she bring several bottles of the good stuff.

Throughout the night, Viv partook heartily of the good stuff, becoming quite tipsy. Noticing this, Max decided to keep an eye on her. Viv spent a long stretch of party staring at Owen. A drink or two later, she moved to stand a little too close to him. Another drink and she was laughing too loudly at his jokes.

"Pardon me, my loves," said Max, draping her arm firmly around Viv's shoulders. "I have a special chore and I need this dear girl's help."

She escorted Viv to the powder room. As the young artist struggled to fix her makeup, Maxine made conversation.

"Did I mention that I spoke with the editor of *PC Gaming World* this week? Off the record, he told me that *Peacemaker* is the frontrunner for this year's 'Highlight Award' for *Achievement in Art Direction*."

Without looking away from the mirror, Viv just said, "OK."

"It's a big deal, my love," Max continued. "It means they've recognized you as one of the best in the business."

Viv nodded, sighed and finally turned to let loose her frustrations.

"Max, why won't Owen notice me?"

"Well, my dear, you have a few things working against you," she answered. "First, he's a man and you must know that they're notoriously clueless. Second, he's a programmer, which makes him doubly so. And third: he probably thinks you want to be with Miles."

"Miles and I are just friends," Viv sighed.

"Does Miles know that?" asked Max, already knowing the answer.

Viv looked at her feet, looking ashamed and a little woozy.

Ignoring Max's implication, she said, "It's so weird. Owen never dates anyone. He only cares about work and his stupid games. He spends all his time with *Jenn*."

"Games and love are all mixed up inside Owen," Max answered. "He told me that he once loved a girl and they played games together, all the time. It was the thing they shared."

Viv's mascara had begun to run.

"What happened to her?" she asked.

"She died," said Max. "in a car accident, right before they left for college. I think all the love and attention he once gave her now just goes into his games."

"That's so sad," replied Viv.

"Yes, it's very sad. But that was years ago," said Max. "Owen's a man now, or at least he should be. It's high time he moved on. But before that happens, my lovely Vivian, you'll have to make things right with Miles."

"I know," said Viv. She sobbed into her hands, wishing she had gone easy on the boxed wine. And the tequila.

"One last thing, my love," said Max. "I can see that something is upsetting you, but I don't think it's because you're having trouble finding a boyfriend."

"Then why am I always feeling sad? What's wrong with me?" asked Viv.

"My dearest, I really don't know," replied Max. "You'll need to figure that out for yourself. But when you do, I have faith that you'll know how to make yourself happy. Trust me, Vivian. I'm an excellent judge of character."

Viv laughed weakly, wiped her eyes and embraced her friend.

Max comforted her for a few minutes more, then left Viv to clean herself up before returning to the party.

When midnight came, the team shot off explosive confetti launchers and drank champagne. Cole stood on a desk and led the group in singing Auld Lange Syne. The few couples in romantic relationships kissed passionately while everyone else just gave hugs.

Miles looked around hopefully but was disappointed. Viv missed the big moment, arriving in the common room five minutes too late. Without embarrassment, she loudly announced to the room that she'd been in the toilet, throwing up. This was a sign to Miles that it was time to take Viv home.

CHAPTER TEN

THE MAN IN ST. PETERSBURG

January 2, 1994
Helsinki, Finland

Early in the morning, Flexx left his apartment block and trudged down the wet sidewalks of the Finnish capital. It was cold, but at least it wasn't Moscow cold. The walk he'd planned was just a few blocks—his black leather jacket would keep him reasonably warm.

There was a public phone near his building, but Flexx needed one farther from his apartment. The previous day he'd identified a good one. The phone booth was in an alley near the Helsinki Lutheran Cathedral. The call box looked like a little green minaret, with a cross on the top.

Reaching the booth, Flexx swore under his breath. He'd forgotten that while the phone box had an enclosed top, its base was an open lattice, providing his feet no protection from the wind. He sighed and shuffled inside.

Taking out his phone card, he lifted the receiver and dialed several long numbers.

He waited in suspense for a ring tone. Calls to St. Petersburg often failed to get through. He stamped his frozen feet, restoring just a little bit of feeling. Finally, it rang and a man answered.

"Ilizarov," announced the voice.

"Yes, uh. Hello, Doctor," fumbled the caller. "I am Flexx. I believe Alvar Morozov may have mentioned me. He gave me your number."

"Yes," answered Dr. Ilizarov.

"I have an opportunity and Alvar mentioned that it was the sort of thing that might interest you. Did he tell you anything about it?" asked

41

Flexx.

"Yes."

"Well, good. That's good," said Flexx unsteadily. "Does it sound like something you'd be interested in? I can get the software. Alvar told me that you know people with the hardware."

"For my part yes, I would be interested in your merchandise," Dr. Ilizarov replied.

Flexx felt his swagger return. He thought cutting a major business deal would be harder.

Ilizarov continued. "But I must tell you that my business partner is not in favor of such things. While I am an investor in the business, it is my partner who makes the final decisions."

"Well, if he's in charge," said Flexx, "then I'm sure he's not stupid. The product is amazing. Nobody else can get it. He'll make millions!"

"No, he is not stupid. I will present him with the opportunity, but please do not be surprised when the answer is 'No,'" replied Ilizarov.

"I could come to him. You know… we could talk to him together," Flexx suggested. "I mean... come on. This deal is unbelievable."

"I believe it is best if I approach him first," said the doctor. "I'm sure you understand. I must insist that you not approach my partner."

But Flexx did not understand.

"That's bullshit, man! It's like I'm giving him free money. We could be the sole supplier to the market. Look, I don't know how long Phrenetiq will be willing to wait. We are talking about Stinger missiles here!"

The line went dead on Ilizarov's end.

"Hello? Hello? Are you still there?" Flexx yelled into the mouthpiece. "Hello?!"

CHAPTER ELEVEN

SIGNIFICANT PENALTY

After a few days of recuperation from the New Years' festivities, Owen, Jarrod and Max prepared for their trip to Vegas for Winter CES, the *Consumer Electronics Expo*.

One week a year, the huge conference took over the entire city of Las Vegas. Created to introduce new televisions, radios and CD players, the Expo had recently expanded its horizons. Now videogames were in the spotlight and Max was poised to take full advantage of the PR opportunities.

The day before the trip, Jarrod sat in his office, making entries in his planner. To make the CES trip worth the expense, he needed to maximize his meeting time. When he looked up, he noticed Mitch, dressed all in bright blue, waiting outside his door.

"Yes?" Jarrod asked.

Mitch stepped inside. "Jarrod," he said. "I'm sure you know that my father is having some trouble with his business."

"OK?"

Right," said Mitch, a bit flustered. "He just needs a small loan to, you know, pay off some debts. His shop needs some repairs to bring it to code. Then he can keep his insurance. It's a big Catch-22 thing."

"Right. And?"

Mitch realized he needed to just spell it out, "I know it's going to be a few months before we start getting money back from *Peacemaker*, but I was wondering if I could get an advance on the royalties. Just ten-thousand is all I'd need."

"Look, Mitch," Jarrod tried hard to sound a little sympathetic, "I'd really like to help you, but we're running a business here. Until I get a look at our actual profits, I can't calculate your bonus."

Mitch dug in. "I know, but don't you think we'll sell more than the first game? Lots more people have computers now."

"Coliseum Arts is your employer, Mitch. It's not a bank."

"Come on, Jarrod, please! If things don't get better soon, my dad might lose his business. Maybe his house," Mitch pleaded.

"It's my job to keep Coliseum Arts financially solvent by not making the same kinds of mistakes your father has made," said the CEO flatly.

"What do you know about it?" Mitch yelled. "You don't know what he's been through?"

"Mitch," said Jarrod coldly, "Come into the office."

From his desk, Owen could hear Jarrod's raised voice through the office door but couldn't make out the words. Several minutes later, Mitch stormed out, slamming the door behind and leaving for the day.

Owen poked his head into Jarrod's office.

"Stop right there, Owen," said the CEO sternly. "When we started this company together, we had two rules. I wouldn't interfere with your game making and you would let me run the business."

"I know, but…"

"Have I *ever* told you how to make your games? Have I *ever* told you to make a change you didn't want to make?"

"No," Owen admitted.

"Then you need to let me worry about the money." Jarrod switched his demeanor to something friendlier, "OK?"

"I just don't know why you're not being more flexible. Surely the profits from—"

"There may not *be* any profits, Owen," Jarrod interrupted.

"What are you talking about? *Peacemaker* is our best game ever."

"Yes, I know," said Jarrod. "And I have no doubt that people are going to love it. But it's been cracked."

"Cracked? The full game?"

"The full game," answered Jarrod. "I downloaded it last night from a gamer board. The cracker drew his name on the title screen, 'Cracked by Flexx' along with the date. November 17. That's before we even got any product back from the disc duplicator."

Owen was stunned. Flexx was a legendary cracker who operated out of Finland. As a cash-poor high schooler, many of the games in Owen's collection had come to him courtesy of the mysterious Flexx.

Owen asked, "Was it a pre-release build of the game or the final version?"

"Final version. Now, I don't think anyone from our team did it. It's more likely the courier we sent with the disc gave a copy to Flexx on his way to the Helsinki duplication factory."

"That's unbelievable," Owen stammered.

"Believe it. And please, don't repeat any of this to the team. Not yet," said Jarrod. "So I hope you understand why I won't give Mitch an advance on royalties. We're not likely to sell a whole lot of games when people can download our product for free."

CHAPTER TWELVE

MEDIA DAY

January 5, 1994
Las Vegas, NV

A panicked email from Max caused Owen to begin his trip to the Consumer Electronics Expo a little later than he'd planned. Her batch of *Peacemaker* demo discs hadn't arrived in time for the show and she needed him to make a few Public Relations copies for her to hand out. Happy to help, he came to work.

While waiting for the duplication process to complete, Owen created some disc labels using a pixelated picture of an old movie cowboy he'd found on his hard drive. He was no artist and wound up disappointed by the result.

The hole at the center of each disc ended up smack dab in the middle of Gene Autry's forehead. It looked like the poor cowpoke had lost a gunfight. But Owen figured it was still better than just writing the word *Peacemaker* on the discs in black felt pen.

Demo discs in hand, Owen began his early-morning drive south to the Oakland airport. He parked in the lot directly in front of the terminal and hauled his large, soft-sided gray-blue suitcase from the trunk to the airline check-in counter.

Owen bounced a little on the balls of his feet. It was his first trip to Las Vegas. Max and Jarrod met him at the gate so they could board together.

The flight was an hour and a half from Oakland.

Owen was happy he had a window seat. An infrequent traveler, even trips on budget airlines made him feel like a jet setter. As his excitement grew, so did the air turbulence. Owen grabbed the arm of his seat with one hand and Max's hand with the other.

"Oh, you poor little bunny," Maxine whispered.

"This turbulence? This is nothing," Jarrod sneered dismissively, looking at him over his magazine.

"Really?" asked Owen.

"Sure. The real ride starts right before we arrive."

Jarrod was prophetic. As the plane passed over the Spring Mountain Range west of Las Vegas, it felt as if a giant rat terrier had caught the plane in its mouth and shaken it. When they landed, Owen was a bundle of nerves.

They waited forty minutes at the baggage carousel for their luggage then twenty more for a taxi before finally heading into the city.

Unbroken gray clouds blanketed the sky and wind gusts made the desert feel colder than the reported 57 degrees. As they took a taxi into town, they noticed a construction site with tall outer walls that couldn't quite hide the blocks of concrete and twisted steel on the far side.

Jarrod pointed at the wreckage, saying, "That's what's left of the north tower of the old Dunes hotel. They blew it up in October."

"They blew it up? Why?" asked Owen.

"They're going to build a new casino there called *the Bellaggio*. It's going to be really high-end. I also heard that when they started clearing away the wreckage from the Dunes, they found a woman's body," answered Jarrod.

"That's crap. It's just a rumor," said their taxi driver bluntly, as he pulled to a stop.

"Sorry," said Jarrod, paying the man as the others exited the town car.

Owen was giddy, having immediately forgotten the terrors of the flight. "I can't believe you got us in here!"

"Ta-da!" sung Max, framing the casino with her arms. "Here it is my precious boys! Circus Circus!"

"They filmed *Diamonds Are Forever* at this hotel!" said Owen, grinning. "You know?"

"We know," Jarrod and Max sighed together. They'd heard Owen mention the fact a dozen times before.

The seductive sound of slot machine bells greeted the three visitors as they entered the cool, dim atmosphere of the casino.

Owen raced to check in and soon was upstairs in his room. Setting down his bag, he glanced out the window at the unfinished, concrete tower of the Stratosphere Hotel, still missing its observation sphere. He jumped in the air, came down on the bed feet first, bounced back down to the floor then headed for the casino to play the slots.

He planned to meet up with Max and Jarrod in the convention center for a briefing before their big interviews. Jarrod had already gone ahead to meet with a U.S. Army colonel. He'd said a friend from the Cal Business School asked him to take the meeting as a favor.

Owen spent 12 dollars on a drink and lost 40 more at slots and video poker before giving up and catching a cab to the expo. Along the way, his taxi driver happily told Owen stories of the old days of Vegas, the *real* Vegas, back when the mob kept things neat and orderly.

When he arrived at the convention, it was still hours before the meet-up, so Owen spent his time walking the cavernous exhibit halls. Maroon-carpeted walkways crisscrossed the rooms, allowing conventioneers easy access to every booth.

Some exhibitor spaces were multi-storied extravaganzas the size of small houses. Others were just card tables and flyers. Most areas of the show floor were loud to the point of pain; a terrible mix of overlapping music, voices and videogame explosions.

Many booths had giveaways and Owen was quick to grab all the free booth tchotchkes he could. Usually, these were logo-emblazoned pens or reusable plastic coffee cups. At the *Incredible Universe* booth, he walked away with a flashlight keying. While pleased with this plastic treasure, Owen had already overloaded his current keychain, so he hooked the flashlight to a belt loop and continued his quest for free junk.

He wandered the floor but found little to hold his interest. He visited the IBM booth and found that they'd merged a cellular phone with a touch screen computer to create a strange device they called *Simon*. Owen doubted the idea would catch on.

He found Nintendo's announcement of a partnership with the super-computing company Silicon Graphics more interesting. The two companies would work together to create a new gaming machine they called, "Project Reality." SGI provided the high-end graphics power behind the special-effects movie blockbusters of the day. If they could make Nintendo games look like *Terminator 2* and *Jurassic Park*, then Owen was in full support.

Finally, it was time to meet his co-workers. He found Max and Jarrod at the back of the convention's dining area. Maxine looked phenomenal in a bright yellow taffeta dress. She wore her golden hair in a beautiful "up-do" bouffant. As usual, wherever Max went she was the center of attention.

"Let me have a look at my two dress-up dolls," she said, sizing up her co-workers.

Jarrod looked very professional in his blue suit and dark red "power tie."

"Jarrod my beauty, you look like a model. I'm so proud," she gushed.

Without looking at Owen, she reached into her lemon-colored purse and pulled out a neatly folded, lavender business shirt.

"Owen. Put this on," she ordered.

Obediently, Owen took the shirt to the restroom and changed.

When he returned, Owen asked Jarrod how his meeting with the colonel went.

"Good. Interesting," he responded cryptically.

"All right my sugar-cakes," said Max. "It's almost time for your interviews. I want you to know that I love you like my own children. I really do. But you two are without a doubt, the worst interviewees I've ever seen."

Jarrod and Owen looked at her in shock.

"Jarrod," continued Max, "the world does not care about the details of your business. Just tell them that the game is great and when and how they can get it."

Owen snickered.

"You, young man!" Max waved a finger in front of his face. "ALL I want you to say is: *Peacemaker* is our best game yet. That's it. Keep saying the name. '*Peacemaker.*' '*Peacemaker.*' Over-and-over. Both of you got it?"

"Sure. Got it."

"OK. Got it. Yep."

They were scheduled to perform their interviews back to back. Max stood next to the video camera, hoping she would be visible to her boys during their turns.

First under the lights was Jarrod. He sat in a black director's chair, angled toward the interviewer, Victoria Ochoa. He was scowling.

Max waved at him, trying to get his attention. She gave an exaggerated smile in the hopes that Jarrod would get the idea. He didn't.

The interview began and immediately went off the rails. Jarrod expressed his concern as a businessman that the games business was 'hits-driven.' It was impossible to predict a hit.

He said that the safe money was to be made as a publisher, distributing other people's games and taking a cut of their revenue.

Silently, Max mouthed the word, "NO."

Her coaching did no good.

Jarrod's next point of discussion was Coliseum Arts' shareware infrastructure. Max held her heart.

"So in our first game, *Apoplexy*, buyers sent their orders right to the fulfillment house to get their game discs. That worked well initially, but…" Jarrod paused for effect, "… there turned out to be a problem. We had so many orders that the fulfillment house reached capacity. Suddenly gamers had to wait months to receive their discs. That's not good! So, in our new shareware system, orders first go to a mail forwarding service. You see, if our first fulfillment company reaches capacity, we can have the mail service split the orders between the two *different* companies."

"In the name of our lady, Dolly Parton," Max whispered to herself, "please stop talking, Jarrod. *Please* stop talking."

The CEO did not. He seemed convinced the world needed to know *all* the details of shareware entertainment software shipping strategies.

"We're thinking of including multiplayer Internet support soon," Jarrod rambled. "I don't know if the market is big enough to justify the investment, so we've put a check box on all our purchase forms. If the customers can connect to the Internet, we'll know!"

The reporter did a good job of nodding and smiling respectfully, though Ms. Ochoa knew she would use almost nothing from the interview.

Jarrod climbed down from his chair and looked to Max for approval. She gave two over-enthusiastic thumbs up and Jarrod smiled with relief. Next, it was Owen's turn to sit in the interview chair.

"Are you OK?" the reporter asked. "Do you need some water or anything?"

"I'm good," said Owen, but he wasn't. Ms. Ochoa was so transcendently TV-beautiful it flustered him.

"OK," she turned to her cameraman and said, "Anytime."

A red light on the video camera went on.

"Owen, can you please state your name for the camera?"

"Owen Nickerson."

"Perfect, thank you." The reporter went into her broadcast voice, "Good evening, this is Victoria Ochoa reporting from Winter CES, here at the Las Vegas Convention Center in Las Vegas, Nevada.

Owen smiled. He wondered why she had to say, "Las Vegas" twice.

Ms. Ochoa turned with a warm smile to Owen and began her interview. "Owen, your last game *Apoplexy* has been heavily criticized for its heavy use of violence. In the game, players shoot and maim unarmed, innocent people who are suffering from mental health issues. Don't you feel that as a game designer you have a responsibility to not put children in the role of mindless, psychotic killers? Don't games like those created by Coliseum Arts actually contribute to the spread of mental illness by desensitizing players to violence and training kids to believe that senseless violent outbursts will lead to reward rather than punishment?"

Stunned, Owen froze for what seemed like an hour. He looked around for Max, but couldn't see past the glare of the camera lights

Owen coughed, "Oh, uh. Well, you don't *have* to shoot the inmates."

"But you do earn extra points for shooting them?" she pressed.

"Yes," he said quietly.

Ms. Ochoa sensed Owen was going to back into his shell, so she tried to pull him out again. "What can you tell me about your new game, *The Peacemaker*?"

Owen sighed with relief. He could do this. "It's just '*Peacemaker*' actually."

Max ran to the news producer. She was livid.

"What the Hell is this?" Max demanded. The producer just smiled and placed a finger to his lips.

"OK, tell me about *Peacemaker*," Ms. Ochoa prompted.

"Well, it's a western, like those Clint Eastwood spaghetti westerns," said Owen. "You play a gunfighter who's trying to reform. He comes to a town that's been taken over by the cattle baron, Masterson and his men."

"Tell me about his men," Ms. Ochoa said, giving Owen another smile.

"They're all based on old west archetypes." Owen gushed, "There's Ambrose, who's a disgraced Southern Civil War general, Sanchez is a bandit and Red Bear who's a renegade Ind—Native American."

The reporter asked a little flatly, "And the goal of the game is to kill them and save the town?"

"Yes," said Owen.

"How?"

"Oh, there are tons of different weapons! Of course, there's the Colt

Peacemaker, the Bowie knife, nitroglycerine bottles and on the later levels, you even get to shoot a Gatling gun."

Ms. Ochoa leaned forward. "I'm sure you realize that the line between archetype and stereotype can be quite fine. Do you recognize that the goal of *Peacemaker* is to bring about peace by murdering, largely, people of color?"

Owen reassured her, "I'm just bringing characters and settings people love from classic movies and letting them take part in the story. It's a part of American mythology."

Ms. Ochoa pressed on.

"Don't you believe it's time to destroy the myth that a heroic white man came to the west to protect their own from the dangerous Red Indians? A people who, in reality, were murdered and unfairly displaced by the whites who grabbed the best lands of the North American continent."

Owen tried to recover from Ms. Ochoa's body blows, but she hammered away.

"It's a game where you literally look through the eyes of the killer. A game where children are taught to gun down people who look or speak differently from themselves—"

Owen cut her off, "I'm sorry, but you're wrong. A game can't teach someone to kill. Have you seen a keyboard? Have you seen a mouse? Do they look anything like guns? Do the U.S. Special Forces operate their black-ops teams by pressing the 'up' arrow key?"

The reporter interrupted before Owen could continue his thought. "In March, Senators Joseph Lieberman and Herbert Kohl will hold their second hearing on the harmful effects of videogames on children. In the first hearing, they discussed *Mortal Kombat*, *Night Trap* and Coliseum Arts' own game, *Apoplexy*. Do you have any thoughts about that?"

"Yes, I do." Owen was warming up. He and his development team had hours of discussion on the topic over lunches. He knew exactly what to say.

"First, you in the media need to actually know what you're talking about. Computer games aren't videogames. Computer gamers are totally different. Children play Sega and Nintendo videogames. Adults, not kids, play computer games. We're not infecting the minds of America's youth. Really, this is all about free speech!"

"Making murder into entertainment is free speech?"

"It's ridiculous that someone from your network would even

criticize us. There's no violence on TV, is that it? You hypocrites got great ratings out of Operation Desert Storm, didn't you? I just make art. Art doesn't kill anyone. It's clear to me that you and Joe Lieberman don't play games. You don't know anything about them, but you're going to use your pulpit to condemn them. You and Joe Lieberman don't like what I do. That's OK with me. But I *know* that the games I make help society."

This statement caught Miss Ochoa flat-footed, "You believe they *help* society?"

"People are struggling in this world," Owen said sincerely. "They feel like they've lost control over their lives. These are the weak, the sick and the poor. Maybe they've given up trying to change the world. Maybe they're resigned to live in sadness. Maybe they're planning to do something much worse. But when people play games, they learn that they can make a difference. They can do anything, be anyone. They can build gleaming cities, save a planet or beat the stock market and become a billionaire. A game can give the disabled the freedom to travel the world. You see, our games give people hope… a belief that if they keep trying they can change their world and make it better. But if we let the government censor our games, then the good that comes with them will just disappear!"

Ms. Ochoa smiled and turned to the camera. "Thank you, Owen Nickerson."

"Thank you," said Owen, then suddenly remembered Max's instructions and rushed out the words, "The game is called *Peacemaker!*"

The interview over, Owen shot out of his chair. His adrenaline was through the roof. He was pumped! He got to have his say and on network television, too.

"Hey!" Owen approached Max. He smiled. "How'd I do?"

CHAPTER THIRTEEN

ELEVATOR, GOING UP

Maxine gave the TV news producer the tongue lashing of the year. He'd betrayed her boys, interviewed them both under false pretenses and now she was going to make sure she spoke her mind. She made him feel it, too. Every time he turned to walk away, she blocked his path. Max was vengeance in a yellow dress, trapping the panicked producer and letting loose all manner of threats and insults.

Jarrod just set his jaw in a grimace. He took a deep breath and said, "Owen, I guess we messed up. Maybe we should go gambling. Or drinking."

But before they could decide their next course of action, a tall man with a heavy, Russian accent interrupted.

"Excuse please," he began, "I overhear your interview. You are Owen Nickerson who make the game *Apoplexy*?"

Owen smiled and nodded. He noticed the Russian wore his long, dark hair pulled back in a ponytail. He sported dark sunglasses, even though they were indoors.

"I am big computer game fan. I love your *Apoplexy* game very, very much," the stranger gushed. "I play it all the time. It gets me pumped."

"Well, that's fantastic to hear," said Owen, shaking the man's hand.

The Russian leaned in and whispered to Owen in confidence, "Sometimes, I play game two, maybe three days straight. No sleep. I just play *Apoplexy*."

"That's amazing," Owen replied. "But take it easy. I don't want you getting sick."

"Sick? Oh, fuck that!" yelled the man.

This caused Max to cease her harangue and turn their way.

"It won't make me sick," said the Russian. "I even take a computer with me. Everywhere I go I have computer. It's in my hotel room right fucking now. I could show it to you. I played *Apoplexy* all night last night. *All night!* Look at me! Huh? I'm great! Damn right."

Realizing Owen was again in trouble, Max left the news producer and rushed to the young man's defense.

"Well... that's good," said Owen, trying to end the conversation, but the man wasn't quite done.

"I wonder will you sign my conference guide," asked the Russian.

"Uh... OK. Sure," answered Owen and the man handed him his guide and a pen. "What's your name?"

It was then that Owen noticed the broad scar running the length of the man's left jawline. It looked awful, like someone had scrubbed it repeatedly with a cheese grater. To avoid staring at the old wound, Owen looked down at the conference guide.

The man didn't answer the question, so Owen just wrote, "Glad you like *Apoplexy*! Take care, Owen Nickerson."

He reread his message and realized it sounded strange. He'd written it in pen so it was too late to change. He handed the guide back to its owner.

Owen hoped the conversation was over, but the Russian wanted more. "What also I want to know is this—"

"We're done here," said Max, placing herself between the stranger and her game designer.

"I'm talking with the man, right now," protested the Russian.

"You were. Now you're done," she answered, staring directly into the man's eyes. He backed down.

"Bitch!" the stranger spat, then turned and walked off into the convention crowd.

"Thank you," Owen said to Maxine.

"Don't worry about it," replied Max. "Public Relations is a full-contact sport."

They returned to Circus Circus where Owen dropped off his homemade demo discs in Max's room. Max laughed when she saw poor, head-wound Gene Autry on the label.

The team played the slot machines for a while before eating a delicious but inexpensive prime rib dinner. The men wanted to prove themselves at the poker tables, but Max announced she still had work to do in her room.

"Goodbye, my sweet angels," she said, hugging each before leaving them to lose their money.

* * *

After half an hour of work, Max felt energized. The meal and highly oxygenated casino air had left her refreshed and she decided to explore the city. It felt electric!

By the time she'd escaped the maze-like casino floor, the sun had set. Although the majority of the strip lay to the south, Max decided to first take a short walk north to see the historic 1952 hotel, the *Sahara Las Vegas*.

It seemed ridiculous that the boys would intentionally miss seeing the resort that was once home to Johnny Carson, Buddy Hackett, Louis Prima and Jerry Lewis. How could they gamble when they were so close to history?

She approached the corner of the Sahara and Las Vegas boulevards. Max prepared to cross Las Vegas and explore the *Sahara Casino* but noticed something going on at the base of the incomplete Stratosphere tower. Police and fire department vehicles surrounded the flat-topped, 1100-foot high tripod of gray concrete.

"Maybe it's a fire," she thought.

This wouldn't be unprecedented, as she'd read that a fire had damaged the structure the previous August. Intrigued, she kept moving north towards it. It was well lit and she made out new details as they approached. The globe that would serve as the *Stratosphere's* visitor center had yet to be installed. The building looked like a gigantic tripod missing its camera.

As she approached, she found a line of policemen blocking the south end of the street. Max stopped among a small crowd of onlookers perhaps 20 feet from the barricade.

An officer waved them away, saying "Nothing to see. Please head back the way you came."

This wasn't exactly truthful.

Max saw something moving all the way up at the tower's top. It was a person. Whoever it was careened around the edges of the lookout, braving a 10-second fall to the ground below. Suddenly recognizing the situation, Max turned back toward the south end of the strip. She had no desire to watch a suicide.

But as she turned, Max recognized someone in the crowd—the tall, scar-faced Russian who'd asked Owen for his autograph. The man no longer wore sunglasses, but there could be no mistaking that face and the scar. He was huffing and puffing as if recovering from running a Marathon.

As she stared, the man turned and their eyes locked. There was a look of recognition on the Russian's face. Max didn't like the look.

Walking swiftly away, he disappeared into a dark side alley.

* * *

Atop the unfinished Stratosphere tower, a drugged and confused Melvin Smart staggered toward his death.

CHAPTER FOURTEEN

KICK-OFF

As the sun rose, Jarrod and Owen met at the casino exit and waited for
Maxine. Fifteen minutes later Max still hadn't arrived, so Jarrod left
Owen with the bags and called her room from a courtesy phone. No
answer. Jarrod thought perhaps she might be in the elevator on the
way down, so he returned to the rendezvous point. Ten minutes after
that, he started to worry they might miss their flight back to Oakland.

This time it was Owen's turn to check, so he decided to go to her
room in person. He race-walked across the casino. In the elevator, he
grew impatient at its slow progress and found himself stamping on the
car floor.

Finally, the elevator doors opened and he sprinted down the hotel
corridor to Max's room. First, he knocked. Then he called. Then he
pounded and called. Owen listened at the door but heard no shower
noise. Max wasn't in her room.

When Owen reached Jarrod again, he was out of breath and panted
as he gave his report.

"Maybe she's already gone to the airport," suggested the CEO.

A quick taxi ride took them to McCarran International where they
dropped their bags, passed through security and arrived at the orange-
carpeted boarding gate. Max wasn't there. The men were becoming
extremely nervous. They checked the airline information desk and
found that their colleague hadn't checked in.

Abandoning their flight, the pair spent a couple of hours driving
through the city streets in a rental car. With computer-accurate recall,
Owen recounted the list of the Las Vegas landmarks that had
interested Max. They visited each but found no trace of their friend.

Finally, Owen suggested they return to the hotel and check again.

This time both went inside. Jarrod found a manager who led them back to Max's room.

The manager turned the lock with his passkey, cracked the door and announced himself, "Hotel staff! Hello?"

There was no answer, so they entered.

"Please don't touch anything," cautioned the manager.

Max's toiletries still sat on the bathroom counter. A crumpled wet towel on its white-tiled floor let them know that the maid service hadn't yet cleaned.

Her suitcase lay open on the professionally made bed. There was nothing unusual inside, just clothes and a few of Owen's hand-labeled demo discs. From this, the three concluded that she hadn't slept in the room.

The manager had seen enough.

"Gentlemen," he said, "please exit the room and come with me. I'm just going to make a few calls."

Owen and Jarrod spent the rest of the afternoon in a small, uncomfortable casino office, giving statements to a police detective. At the end of the emotionally exhausting day, with no more help to give, Owen and Jarrod flew home.

Max's disappearance left the Coliseum Arts team in shock and disbelief. The office felt the loss of her flamboyant energy. There was an unspoken sense of fear for their missing friend and while the team tried to remain hopeful and positive, they couldn't always hold their emotions in check.

In the weeks that followed, many took sick days. Three or four times a week, Viv would leave her desk and hide in the bathroom where she would break down and cry for a few minutes before returning to work.

Over the next few days, Jarrod received a few updates from the Las Vegas police. One of the casino's many security cameras caught video of Max being escorted from the building through a rear loading dock by a man wearing a dark, hooded sweatshirt and dark sunglasses. The disguise was effective. All that could be gathered from the footage was that the kidnapper was Caucasian. The man had hustled Max into a white car that had been stolen just a couple of hours before. Then they'd driven off.

The police followed many leads and even interrogated the producer of Owen's television interview, but they found only dead ends.

As time passed, the police reports grew more and more infrequent, until finally, a detective told Jarrod that there was little hope of ever finding Max alive. The CEO chose not to share this opinion with the rest of his team.

Slowly and sadly, work recommenced, but the team's unsettled emotional state made the game's dark, violent and gruesome tone too much to take. Reflexively, the artists began to slip in humorous elements.

Viv created a three-legged creature. The monster wore two matched shoes and one bunny slipper. There was a machine gun that had a loop-the-loop barrel and a mad doctor who could attack the hero with a demented seven-iron. Miles composed a soundtrack best described as bubblegum-pop as heard through a demon's ears. He called it "Elevator (to Hell) Music."

Jenn was not amused with Viv's comedic take on the material and complained to Owen, but he defended the artistic contributions of his teammate.

"This is a collaboration," he explained. "We've got to stay open to new ideas."

Jenn gave up, but not without first grousing, "I thought we were trying to make art, but I guess not. We began the project aiming for Hieronymus Bosch but instead we're getting *Abbott and Costello Meet Frankenstein*."

On April 1st, Jarrod received a phone call. The Coliseum Arts CES interviews would air the following Friday, about three months after they were recorded. He let the team know and a few suggested having a work gathering to watch. They couldn't bring themselves to call it a party.

Most of the CES coverage had played during convention week. New products, companies and technologies needed immediate reporting. But Owen's interview was part of a much bigger story on the dangers videogames posed to children.

To the news organizations, the story had everything: money, governmental power, sex, violence, helpless children, the First Amendment and American Senators patriotically waving red and blue plastic guns.

For the Friday news broadcast, the team stayed late. The talking heads covered the news of the day in just 15 minutes, reserving the last half of the broadcast for a 'special report.'

Viv set the television on mute and led the team in a silent prayer for Maxine's safety. Afterward, they spent a few minutes composing themselves and when the gaming report began, Viv switched the sound back on.

Everyone clapped when Jarrod appeared on the screen, but the CEO was only allowed to introduce Coliseum Arts and then never appeared again.

On the other hand, Ms. Ochoa used most of Owen's interview, particularly the ranting parts. Conflict made for good television and the Coliseum Arts team laughed and cheered! It didn't matter that Owen looked like an insane zealot. He was their insane zealot, raving about the artist's right to freedom of expression.

Only Viv didn't laugh. Owen glanced over at her. She cocked her head and gave him a wink. All Owen could do was respond with a goofy grin and a shoulder shrug.

When the gathering ended, Jenn approached Owen as he picked up the empty cups and chip bowls.

"I'm not sure that was the best way to get your point across," she said. Owen's heart sank a bit, but then she put her hand on his arm, "But I love your passion."

Viv slammed down her beer and quickly left the room.

CHAPTER FIFTEEN

ON A FROZEN SEA

April 19, 1994
City 42
Novaya Zemlya Archipelago, Russia

Olga swung her leg over the snowmobile seat and brought her spike-soled boots down heavily on the yard-thick ice that covered the frozen fjord. Removing her goggles, she wiped the lenses clear with her heavy black gloves, momentarily exposing her dark eyes to the freezing winds swirling through the inlet. Quickly replacing her eye protection, Olga blinked repeatedly until she could see again.

Wrapped in her fur-lined parka, she stood at the very center of the bay. To the east and west were the fjord's steep canyon walls. Each resembled an ebony pyramid rising a thousand feet above the ice.

Through the arctic night, Olga looked northward towards the endless white sheet that was the Kara Sea. She could barely see past the mouth of this glacier-cut harbor. The little light there was came from snowmobile headlights and the glow of the aging Soviet city at the bay's south end.

Olga led a troop of five men, all wearing white and tan cold-weather outfits. The suits still bore the icon of the Hammer and Sickle, symbols of the recently defunct Soviet Union.

She shouted to be heard over the snowmobile engines and the shrieking wind. Motioning to one of her men, she gave him an order in Russian. He nodded. Leaning his assault rifle against the handlebars of his snowmobile, he walked to the rear of the vehicle where a tow bar extended back to a sledge, heavily burdened with equipment.

He unclipped two carabiners and pulled back the tarpaulin

protecting the sledge's contents. With both hands, he pulled out a gasoline-powered auger. Olga pointed to a spot on the ice. Dragging the auger into position, the man reached out to grab the motor's pull cord. But before he could start the power drill, there were shouts.

Olga's team looked north, out towards the vast frozen sea. Struggling to see through the darkness and clouds of blowing ice-crystals, she made her hands into blinders, blocking out the glare of the snowmobile's headlights. Her eyes soon adjusted and she could make out a large object in the distance. It was moving towards her team.

The extreme cold slowed Olga's thought processes and hindered her ability to recognize the approaching threat. For a moment it just looked like an undulating, white mass. But when she saw the coal-black eyes and nose, she knew her opponent. A polar bear had lumbered within 30 yards of Olga's party.

"Big boy!" Olga shouted.

It was an enormous male, 10-feet tall and weighing well over a thousand pounds. The curious bear became cautious, ceased his approach and grunted. Swinging his massive head back and forth, he studied the humans and their strange goings-on.

One of the lookouts called out to Olga. He presented his firearm and asked, "Do you want us to scare him off?"

"No," she yelled. "Kill it!"

Immediately obeying, two of the team aimed at the animal and taking turns, let loose with four bursts from their machine guns. The light of the muzzle flashes reflected off the sleet and ice, giving a momentary illusion of daylight.

With a deep, sad cry, the polar bear lay down and died.

"Now... drill," Olga ordered.

One of the men pull-started the auger and its drill bit began to spin. Within fifteen minutes it had twice punctured the sheet-ice, creating eight-inch wide holes, each providing a tunnel to the unfrozen seawater.

Olga yanked a large, yellow plastic case from her sledge and lugged it to the ice-holes. Placing it on the ice, she snapped open its clasps with her gloved thumbs, revealing a hydrophone, a device used for underwater communication. Olga switched on the battery-powered transceiver. It lit up while simultaneously emitting an audible "Pop!"

She connected the hydrophone's microphone and speaker and lowered each through a hole in the ice.

On top of the hydrophone was a small, red button. Placing her left index finger on it, Olga took a deep breath and began to tap. With each button press, the underwater speaker broadcast an electronic tone across the bay.

"Dot. Dash. Dash. Dot. Dot. Dash."

Olga sent her coded message then waited.

In just a few seconds she'd received an answer.

"Get ready!" she shouted to her men. "They are coming up!"

Olga dragged up the microphone and speaker, disconnected the hydrophone from its cables and secured it in her sledge.

Opening her snowmobile's saddlebag, she removed a flare gun. This she loaded and fired into the sky. The signal flare left a bright red trail that rose hundreds of feet into the air before disappearing into the thick, low-lying clouds.

She turned and looked back at City 42. During the daytime, Olga found it hideous. Viewed in full sunlight, City 42's Soviet Brutalist architecture, utilitarian factory buildings and vapor-belching smokestacks appeared as insults to the natural landscape.

But at night she could gaze at the city's ten thousand industrial lights as they sparkled in the darkness. She could see the dramatic red and blue flames flicker from the tops of towering chimneys. She admired the glow of supernatural green radiating from the windows of its administrative offices. Even in the cold, she smiled in admiration. To Olga, City 42 was the most beautiful city in the world.

She was equally confident that her agents at City 42's under-mountain facility must have seen her signal flare. Soon they would swing open the factory's thirty-foot high steel doors and send a flatbed truck through the town. It would roll past the gymnasium, the ice-covered busts of Lenin and Marx and finally the concrete boat ramp. From there, the truck would drive down onto the frozen fjord.

She heard a sharp cracking from behind. Spinning in place, she found her men facing out toward the Kara Sea. Olga and her men ran to the snowmobiles, turning them and pointing their headlights north.

A hundred yards away, a massive chunk of ice lifted high into the air. Through the blackness, Olga made out the conning tower of a surfacing Russian Navy submarine.

As she watched, the hull of the Oscar-class nuclear vessel breached the ice, bending the sheet upwards and creating a 500 foot-long, 60 foot-wide submarine-shaped contour.

Olga gunned her snowmobile's engine. She and her team raced past the polar bear's corpse and toward the submersible. As they approached, a hatch on top of the sub opened and a sailor emerged. He began clearing large ice blocks from the conning tower with a long steel pole. As he did so, the City 42 team arrived just below.

The first mate climbed up to the conning tower. Looking down, he directed Olga's team to locate the deck-level hatch hidden beneath the ice on the submarine's nose. At once, two of Olga's men removed long-bladed chainsaws from their sledges, fired them up and began slicing through the ice to free the hatch. Olga glanced back at the city. She saw the twin headlights of a delivery truck approaching.

In just a few minutes, the forward hatch opened and a platoon of armed soldiers spread out across the length of the boat. They held their guns at the ready, in case Olga or her men tried anything unexpected. Next emerged the senior officers dressed in their heavy blue coats. They climbed down onto the frozen fjord one at a time.

The sailors' upturned collars and pulled-down hats prevented Olga from recognizing any faces. She could only identify the captain by the gold insignias and stripes of rank on his uniform.

Not wishing to waste time with formal introductions, Olga gave the sub commander a quick wave then stalked to her sledge. She removed a heavy canvas duffel bag, shouldered it and struggled against the wind to carry it to the sub. A junior officer stepped forward to help, but the captain threw out his arm, striking the man in the chest and holding him in place.

Olga staggered towards the officers and placed the duffel at the captain's feet. Just at that moment, a flatbed truck pulled to a stop beside the enormous ship.

Seizing the bag, the captain ordered his men to transfer the truck's cargo to the submarine. The sailors pulled a tarp off the truck's bed to reveal a few wooden crates and a much larger steel object – 15 feet long, 4 in diameter, with a smooth green casing and a sharp red tip.

A Navy engineer from the sub climbed onto the truck and examined its freight. He carried a portable Geiger counter and with its wand-like radiation sensor scanned the crates and the metal device. Satisfied, the engineer signaled "all clear" to his commander.

The captain shouted some brief commands as more crewmen emerged from the sub. A group of submariners swarmed the truck, unfastening the ties that held the cargo in place. Others nearby assembled a small, rolling handcart. Ordinarily, they would use this to load the warship's torpedoes, but it was also perfectly suited to safely move the strange and heavy steel capsule.

"Please tell your sailors to be careful, Captain," said Olga, only half-joking. "I need it safely delivered to Site 3, not to the bottom of the Barents Sea."

The captain smiled and nodded, saying, "Don't worry, Doctor. We'll have drinks when I see you next, in Murmansk."

In just a half an hour, the sailors had the device safely aboard the ship. A few minutes later, the submarine once again held its full complement of crew.

Olga's men helped close the forward hatch then scrambled back to their snowmobiles. The Russian Navy captain waved to her from the conning tower then descended below decks.

The exchange had gone as well as she could have hoped. Olga cupped her hands around her face, exhaling heavily in an attempt to warm her frozen nose. She wanted to stay and watch the great vessel dive, but could no longer stand the biting cold. Olga climbed aboard her snowmobile and turned it south. Opening up the throttle, she tore across the ice at full speed. Soon she would be back at City 42. Soon she would be home.

CHAPTER SIXTEEN

THE COMPUTER GAME DEVELOPERS CONFERENCE

In the two weeks that followed the broadcast of Owen's CES interview, Coliseum Arts had become an office of people who seemed to do nothing but stare at glowing boxes. But soon would come a break in the monotony. It was almost time for the Computer Game Developers Conference.

Owen grew excited. He and 2000 other gamers would crowd the Westin San Jose Hotel. The conference rooms and banquets halls would fill for lectures, tutorials and roundtable discussions about the serious business of games. There would also be an exhibit floor where companies could showcase their upcoming products. But for Owen, the main draw of the CGDC was the legendary, all-night party circuit.

While Jarrod was skeptical about the value of sending his whole company to the conference for educational reasons, he was keen to sign up developers to his new shareware publishing system. To advance this goal, he would bring the entire team and assign everyone to shifts manning the Coliseum Arts sales booth.

Everyone tried to arrive early at the conference. They checked in and received name badges and canvas totes laden with a conference schedule, demo discs and an enormous book—the "Conference Proceedings." On its cover was a robot playing checkers.

The Coliseum booth didn't open until late in the afternoon and the team members had time to pick their first conference sessions of the day. Owen, Miles, Viv, Mitch and Cole chose the obvious favorite, "Violence in Videogames." The Coliseum developers were a little late to the roundtable and when they opened the conference room door, it made an attention-grabbing screech. The discussion came to a halt and the attendees turned to examine the newcomers.

Recognizing Owen from his anti-censorship TV rant, the room burst into applause. Owen grinned and waved at the crowd. A few seconds later, the group calmed down and the roundtable continued.

Following the session, the team stood in line for free box lunches. Sitting in the sparsely decorated banquet hall, they had a chance to take out their schedules and choose their next talks.

"I was thinking I'd go to one of the art sessions," said Miles to Viv. "I'd like to learn more about what you do, so…*Pixel Painting for Palletized Graphics.*"

"Owen, how about you?" asked Viv.

"I don't know. I mean I'm getting paid to be here so I should go to at least one talk on programming," he said, "I guess I'll go to 'Programming in Mode Y.'"

"I was looking at that, too. Who's giving it?" asked Mitch.

"Dogg," answered Owen.

"No way!" said Mitch, impressed.

Griffin "Dogg" Dobbs was a high-end programmer and technical author. Dogg's book series *Graphics Jewels* was pretty much the starting point for every developer building a game engine. Owen had no doubt that he had at least some of Mr. Dobbs' routines running somewhere in each of the Coliseum Arts games.

"I'm in," said Mitch. "Cole?"

"No, actually I'm going to go to the roundtable on 'Women in Gaming.'"

"Really?" Viv asked Cole.

"Yes, really! A man can't go to a discussion on the topic?" Cole exclaimed in mock anger.

"OK. OK. Good for you," said Viv.

Miles asked Viv if she'd picked a session.

"I like your idea, Miles," Viv replied.

Miles responded with a grin.

Then she said, "Like you, I'm also going to go to a session I usually wouldn't. I'm going to go to 'Programming in Mode Y.'"

The table was stunned and Miles ceased smiling. This wasn't a beginner's talk suitable for an artist. It was a highly technical tutorial about low-level graphics-card programming.

Mitch couldn't withhold his smile and asked, "Don't you think y'all should—you know—learn how to program first?

spare any team members right now. They're all working to finish *Apoplexy II*."

Jarrod responded excitedly, "That's the beauty of it. Dogg is an approved military contractor. He's already got security clearances. We're going to give him an office at Coliseum and give him access to our build directory."

"Jarrod, hold on," Owen was trying to hide his high level of pissed-offish-ness. "We're going to make engine changes all the time. We can't just take a copy of the game today, give it to Dogg and tell him to use it. It's got bugs and half-implemented features."

"That's fine," Dogg broke in. "I'm not going to touch any of your code. I'll just need you to change your project set up a little bit, so it can call an external DLL of mine."

Owen considered the proposal. A Dynamic Link Library or "DLL" was just some computer code that lived in a file, separate from the main application. Owen reasoned that, because the final version of *Apoplexy II* wouldn't include Dogg's DLL, Jarrod's plan probably wouldn't hurt his game's development.

What troubled Owen was that he couldn't tell what Dogg's program would do. If the work *were* for military training, Dogg would have to create all-new interactive content. He would need a development team of his own. As good as Dogg was, he was just a single coder.

"What part of my game code would call yours?" asked Owen.

Dogg replied without hesitating, "I can't answer that until we have a contract."

Owen said that he wanted to talk with Jarrod. Dogg shook Owen's hand and left the partners alone.

"Do we really want to be military contractors, Jarrod?" Owen asked. "There's got to be a lot of strange stuff that comes with that."

"Owen, at first I was just considering it because it looked interesting. Now it's become essential to the company's survival."

"What do you mean by that?" asked Owen.

"I got the sales report from our fulfillment company in Georgia. *Peacemaker* is tanking. When the game leaked, it killed our sales," said Jarrod, looking pained. "In a couple of months, we won't be able to make payroll. That's why we need this government contract. We have got to have that money."

Owen looked at the floor and nodded, "OK. We should do it. And besides... how cool is it to have a secret military project!"

Jarrod looked relieved.

"Well, great! We get to stay in business," he said, then admonished his partner. "Please don't mention the leak to Dogg. I don't want the military thinking we have security issues."

CHAPTER SEVENTEEN

SMART BOMBS

April 24, 1994
Helsinki, Finland

Flexx sat in his undecorated apartment, typing madly. He had Phrenetiq on the line. As the Russian typed, he struck the computer keys so hard the keyboard inched its way across the glass-topped table. Every sentence or two, he had to move it back.

It had been weeks since they'd communicated and Flexx was nervous. He needed to make sure the hacker didn't sell his stolen software to anyone else.

> *Flexx>* Are you there?
> *Phrenetiq>* Any word from your clients?
> *Flexx> Not yet*

Flexx was lying. He'd spoken with Dr. Ilizarov the week before and the answer from Leonid Morozov had been an emphatic, 'No.'

Without the Morozov syndicate's connections, Flexx had no access to buyers of black-market weapons. But as long as Dr. Ilizarov remained in favor of the plan, Flexx would keep trying.

> *Flexx>* Still working on the deal. Can you wait?
> *Phrenetiq>* Why should I wait? I have other options.

The hacker sucked air in through his teeth, making a hissing sound.

> *Flexx>* You need to wait because my partners have the best

connections.

Flexx> We can sell your guidance software to every paramilitary group that bought the leftover Stinger missiles from the Soviet-Afghan war.

Flexx hoped this boast would impress Phrenetiq. He waited for a response but received none. Trying again, he typed.

Flexx> Lots of the Stinger-RMPs the Americans sold to the Saudis are missing.
Flexx> We know where they went.
Flexx> Those militias HAVE to upgrade those weapons. With the ones they have, the simplest counter-measures will beat their Stinger's targeting software.
Flexx> We'll have customers lining up for your new missile guidance program.
Flexx> That's why my partners will be able to pay you more than anyone else. You should wait. No doubt.

Again there was a pause.

Phrenetiq> If your organization can pay more, I will wait.

When Phrenetiq logged off, Flexx screamed and his voice echoed across his apartment, "Fuck, shit, crap, damn, fuckity-fuck!"

He thought, "This would all be so *easy* if Ilizarov were in charge, instead of Morozov."

Placing his elbows on the table, he leaned forward and ran his hands back through his deep brown hair. It was all so frustrating! Here he had a direct connection to a hacker inside a major U.S. defense company but no way to sell his goods.

Flexx vowed not to let the deal die. In the meantime, he'd continue working for Olga.

The thought of Olga made Flexx cringe. If she were to discover his solo business dealings, how would she feel? More importantly, how would she react?

CHAPTER EIGHTEEN

THE CRAWLS

April 24, 1994
Santa Clara, California

By the second day, the conference was in full swing. The Coliseum Arts team enjoyed their morning lectures, but made sure to arrive early for good seats at Jenn's 1 p.m. talk, "Hitting the Target: Auteur vs. Agency in Interactive Narrative."

Because of her previous industry lectures, Jenn was a popular draw and her double-size conference room was packed to standing room only. Like a Broadway show, the lights dimmed and music swelled. To warm up the crowd, Jenn improvised a light show using a high-powered flashlight and a lava lamp. Then she cooked a sausage on a stick over the blue flame of a Sterno can. This was a metaphor of some kind, although afterward, no one could remember for what.

The climax of Jenn's show involved lasers and a smoke machine, for which she received a standing ovation and a lecture from the Fire Marshall.

Afterward, Owen attended a few more lectures but his mind was on "The Crawls."

First up was the "Booth Crawl," a social event, which took place on the Exhibition floor. It began at six. Most exhibitors brought in bottled beer on ice, but some of the larger, more established companies, like Electronic Arts, gave out wine and snacks, too.

Owen "crawled" the Expo alone. Approaching a medium-sized booth, a black-clad ninja offered him beers of above-average quality. As the faux assassin skulked away, Owen spotted Viv and waved.

As she approached, Owen asked, "Where's Miles? What's he up to?"

Viv replied, "He's getting set up. The game composers are having a jam session later at the Hotel Crawl. Miles is playing."

When he looked up, Owen realized they'd wandered in front of the Magazine Publisher's expo booth. Here publishing companies showed off their wide array of gaming magazines.

While Viv stopped to enjoy the displays of magazine cover art, Owen browsed. Several curved desks made up the booth, giving it a circular shape. Drifting around the perimeter, Owen found himself in a small slice of the pie devoted to the international game magazines. Not speaking any languages besides English, Owen saw little of interest until he noticed *Peacemaker* on one of the covers. The magazine was *Pelit*, a Finnish gaming publication. Owen thumbed through the pages until he found the cover story on his game.

He furrowed his brow and thought for a moment, arriving at a plan.

"Hey!" Owen called out to a man stacking magazines behind the desk.

The man in the booth spoke with a German accent, "Hallo!"

"I'm...I'm Owen Nickerson, from Coliseum Arts."

"Oh, yes! Coliseum. Wonderful games. It's a pleasure to meet you. · I'm Gerhard."

Looking for Owen, Viv rounded the booth.

Owen asked Gerhard, "I was wondering, is there anyone here from *Pelit*? The Finnish magazine?"

The German thought a moment, "Let me just check. One second."

Gerhard disappeared through the back curtain into the circular center of the booth. A minute later he emerged, pulling back the curtain with his forearm to allow a lovely young woman to step out. He pointed to Owen and went back to stacking his magazines.

"What's this?" asked Viv.

"Something just occurred to me," said Owen, but he didn't take his eyes off the approaching Finn.

"Hello. I'm Astrid Hahl from *Pelit* magazine. Gerhard said you wanted to talk?"

Astrid spoke English with a flat, Finnish accent. She was five feet seven inches and wore her long hair with bangs. Astrid's face was pretty but two striking features overwhelmed all the others—her satin black hair and luminous pale blue eyes. Neither Owen nor Viv could resist staring.

"Yes," said Owen. He had to reset his brain to regain his train of thought. "I was wondering. Have you heard of a Finnish software cracker named Flexx?"

Astrid looked at Owen's shoes, rather than his eyes, "Why may I ask?"

"I'm Owen Nickerson from Coliseum Arts. He cracked a…"

Owen glanced at Viv and stopped. Thinking of a more suitable answer, he continued, "I just want to know more about him."

Astrid looked up, studying Owen's face. Finally, she said, "Please come around."

She walked Owen and Viv to a break in the booth's circle of desks.

Owen stopped and addressed Viv. "Actually, I need to do this alone. I hope that's OK."

It was clear from the expression on Viv's face that it was *not* OK.

"Whatever," she replied with annoyance and thumbed through a magazine.

Astrid escorted him through the curtains to the break area. She gestured toward one of two flimsy white folding chairs.

Astrid spoke immediately, "I am a reporter. I have interviewed Flexx."

"No way," Owen leaned forward, smiling.

"Yes. Way!" Astrid bugged her eyes and leaned forward, too. This unexpected change from Finnish reserve to cartoonishness made Owen laugh.

Astrid continued, "I am working on an investigative article about software piracy."

"Oh, wow. That's amazing," gushed Owen. "Can you tell me anything about him? When did you talk to him?"

"We spoke in December."

"Did he tell you anything about how he got our game, *Peacemaker*?"

"Flexx never mentioned it," she said simply.

"Never mentioned how he got it?"

"He never mentioned your *Peacemaker* game at all." Astrid was emotionless and definitive.

Owen paused. His energy drained away and he said, "Oh. OK. Well, thank you for your time."

"Just one question for my article, if that's all right," Astrid asked before Owen could leave. It didn't sound like she cared if it was really all right with him.

"Sure," he answered, "What's your question?"

"How does it feel to know that someone stole your game?"

Owen exhaled and looked up at the ceiling. "How does it feel? Well, it doesn't feel good. I mean we worked on the game for a year and a half. The team really put themselves into *Peacemaker*. To think that someone would just give it away...it's a complete betrayal."

"Thank you," said Astrid.

She stood, indicating the conclusion of the interview. Owen followed her example and rose, looking disappointed.

The reporter considered Owen's expression.

"Hold on," she said, picking up a white purse. From it, Astrid removed a business card. She stepped forward, standing so close to Owen she had to tip her head back to look up at his face. Taking his hand, she pressed her card into his palm. Owen held his breath.

Astrid whispered into his ear, "Here is my card. You can email me if you have any more questions." Astrid switched her personality back to its default setting. "I need to go now. Goodbye."

She turned and walked out, leaving Owen standing in the booth's break room. When he returned to the show floor, he was happy to find that Viv had waited.

* * *

The "Hotel Crawl" was the biggest spectacle of the Computer Game Developers Conferences. Gamers partied on every floor of the Westin tower. The biggest game companies rented the largest executive and honeymoon suites, transforming them into opulent hospitality lounges. Inside, guests sipped mixed drinks while reclining in comfortable chairs, listening to soothing music and snacking on warm appetizers.

Executives from the smallest companies simply pushed their luggage into a closet and voila! They had a 'mini-suite.' In these rooms, folks just sat on the beds, chatted and drank beer. Gaming rigs often sat in a corner allowing visitors to try out a company's latest and greatest.

Viv and Owen walked the long corridor that separated the convention space from the hotel tower. At its end, they found a mass of people waiting in front of the elevators—the preferred route to the Hotel Crawl. Unwilling to wait for a ride, the pair located a stairwell and climbed to the top floor. They would work their way down, party by party.

Owen was thrilled to explore the evening with the beautiful Viv. She acted like a hospitality-suite passkey, granting them entrance to all but the most exclusive party rooms.

Each floor's music was so loud that Owen had to assume that there were only conference participants at the hotel. Unaffiliated individuals staying at the Westin San Jose on the night of the crawl would have spent an angry, sleepless night screaming at the hotel managers and an army of drunken nerds.

Viv enjoyed herself at first, especially the free drinks, but soon grew bored with never-ending videogame discussions. By floor four she'd had enough of the hospitality lounges.

She yelled in Owen's ear, "Let's find Miles' jam session!" He nodded.

They found the game composers' band playing in a multi-purpose room two flights down. The most conspicuous performer was William "The Thin Man," Cody. The skinny Texas musician stood downstage, playing lead guitar, wearing a silver 10-gallon hat and an outrageous maroon cowboy outfit covered in gigantic, silver spots.

Backing the Thin Man were in-house musicians from Broderbund, LucasArts and a drummer from MicroProse. Miles sat to the left side of the stage. He was playing a system of electronic keyboards so complex it looked like a NASA control panel. Cody led the group on stage with Motown standards like *Mustang Sally* and *Heard it Through the Grapevine*. The room looked hot and crowded.

"Maybe we should just stay out here," suggested Owen. "Crowds really aren't my thing."

"Come on," urged Viv. "Time to live a little, Owen. You walk through and I'll follow. All the way to the back wall, OK?" She pushed Owen into the room, keeping her hands on his back as she steered him through the crowd like a naval icebreaker.

Owen breathed a sigh of relief as they reached the back wall. They didn't have a great view of the band, but at least there was a little space and something to lean against. As he enjoyed the show, Owen turned and caught Viv staring his way. Suddenly, he had the look of a doomed snowshoe rabbit, transfixed by a mink's hungry gaze.

As the Thin Man started the band in a cover of *Rockin' Pneumonia and the Boogie Woogie Flu*, Viv swung around in front of Owen. She grabbed the front of his shirt then pushed him hard against the back wall. He had no idea what was happening. Standing on her toes, Viv leaned forward and kissed Owen full on the lips. He froze momentarily but quickly recovered.

Surprised and confused but thrilled, he kissed her back.

CHAPTER NINETEEN

BUMPS IN THE ROAD

Though the Coliseum Arts team remained upset and unnerved by Maxine's disappearance, many held out hope that she might still be found safe. There were many theories. Perhaps she'd fulfilled a childhood dream and joined a Las Vegas chorus line. Or perhaps she'd met a man, fallen in love, got married and run off to Mexico. While these possibilities were far-fetched, her friends clung to them. The alternative explanation was just too horrible to believe.

The distracting preliminaries of game development out of the way, Mitch and Cole got into a programming groove. All day, they did nothing but stare at their screens and type.

Mitch took pride in the new project. Each night before leaving, the tools programmer proudly sent Owen a list of his day's achievements. Owen was openly impressed and this sent Mitch's self-worth through the roof. Cole's typically jovial attitude didn't change. Ryan's didn't change either—he was never in a good mood.

One particularly lovely spring day, Viv took Miles out to Phyllis' Giant Burger on San Rafael's "Miracle Mile." Phyllis' Giant was their special-occasion destination. She bought him a Mt. Tam burger with onion rings and a chocolate shake. It was warm, so they sat at an outdoor table under a red umbrella.

Viv smiled as Miles took his first bite.

"I have some news," Viv began, "and I wanted to tell you before I tell the rest of the office."

"You're not quitting, are you?" said Miles, his mouth still full. He looked concerned.

"No. Definitely not," Viv assured. Miles set down his burger.

"OK, what is it?"

"I don't want this to change things between us," Viv continued, but too slowly for Miles.

"Tell me," he spoke firmly but didn't raise his voice.

"Owen and I are dating," she said, then paused, waiting for a reaction. Miles' lanky body contracted, somehow folding in on itself. He placed his hands flat on the table and looked down at his tray.

"But there's no way you can't know how I feel about you," Miles said, staring down. "It couldn't be any clearer."

"Miles—" she began, but he interrupted.

"Oh, my god," he said, astonished. "At New Years. You left the room at midnight. You were afraid I would try to kiss you."

He stood up with a jerk, avoiding eye contact.

"Take me back to the office," he said curtly.

Viv looked up with concern, "Miles, you know I love you."

Miles snatched up his tray and dumped it into a nearby garbage drum. His milkshake slipped off, splattering on the ground.

"I want to go back to the office," he demanded.

Viv drove and Miles stared out the passenger window. The car was still rolling into its parking space behind Coliseum Arts when Miles jumped out and ran into the building. When Viv ascended the stairs and walked through the programmer's area, she saw that Miles had shut his door and window blinds.

Afterward, Owen seldom saw the composer. Miles avoided him, each day walking rapidly to his office and closing and locking the door. At the end of the day, he would leave just as quickly. Miles skipped most team meetings and all social gatherings. When asked for creative input, Miles simply said, "Whatever you want. Just tell me what to do."

The rest of the game team approved of Coliseum Arts' newest couple. They hoped that Viv's laid-back attitude might take some of the edge off Owen's hyper-intensity.

As the season progressed, the spring sun cast so much glare on the programmers' screens that they couldn't see to code. One day, Mitch and Owen arrived early to solve the problem. With duct tape and black plastic garbage bags, they blacked out all the external windows in the programmers' area.

Jenn hadn't been consulted on the plan and was furious to find her window-adjacent desk in darkness. Immediately, she cut a large hole in the window plastic near her desk. It helped a bit.

Still, the office seemed transformed. Once bright and happy, the game makers of Coliseum Arts now worked in perpetual twilight.

CHAPTER TWENTY

DOGG'S ARRIVAL

Jarrod finalized the Army contract and prepared the facility for Dogg's arrival. Due to Army requirements, Dogg needed his computers stored in a secure, lockable space. This meant he couldn't sit in the programmer or artist areas. The common area was out as well. Miles needed his office for audio recording and the test pit was already full to the gills. The only office left was Jarrod's. The CEO would have to subdivide his space, giving Dogg half.

It took workmen two weeks to frame a new wall, add sheetrock, install a door, run wires and finish the job with a coat of white paint. During the first week, the construction noise aggravated Owen and Mitch so badly it put a dent in their productivity. As usual, Cole avoided the distractions by working from home.

When the work was finally complete, Dogg pushed his desk underneath the new plate glass window. Through it, he could see the programmers and they could see him. But from outside the office, no one could catch a glimpse of the top-secret work on Dogg's computer screen.

As always, Cole's output was solid. Every Monday he drove up from San Francisco, arriving at the office carrying his computer. He'd plug in, turn on and copy files to Owen's machine. Owen would merge these with his previous week's work.

The lead programmer didn't love this process of merging code files. Mistakes were common. But he also didn't consider it a huge issue. Cole was a great game programmer and merge bugs were usually found and fixed in less than an hour.

Although it was only early May, the delays caused by the office construction made Owen aware that *Apoplexy II's* September launch date was much, much closer than he wished. Leading by example, he ramped up his work intensity. The other programmers followed suit.

But every night, they still fell further and further behind schedule. Each workday lasted five minutes longer than the one before and the programmers began to resent anything that distracted them from their coding. The morning of Dogg's arrival, Owen nearly snapped when Jarrod tapped him on the shoulder.

"What?" he asked, annoyed.

"We're taking Dogg out to a welcome lunch," said Jarrod. "You need to come. Even Cole drove up for it."

Owen didn't look up. He just stared at one of his three screens and said, "I have a bug. I will ruin lunch."

One of the things that made Owen great at his job was his inability to tolerate imperfection. When he had a bug he couldn't fix, Owen couldn't sleep, let alone socialize. The CEO knew this to be true and that at lunch, Owen would be a carbuncle of suppressed anger.

Jarrod thought about the problem for a second. He knew *one* way to defuse his friend's mood.

"Bamyan," said Jarrod, confidently.

Owen pressed the 'off' button on his computer and stood up. Grabbing his jacket, he said, "I'm ready. Let's go."

Bamyan Afghan Cuisine was arguably the best restaurant in town. Inarguably, it had the worst location, hidden at the back of a strip mall. How it stayed alive was a topic of many team discussions.

When they arrived at 12:30 p.m., the sprawling restaurant had no other customers.

The large dining room held 20 circular tables, each capable of holding 10 people. A mural covered the entire left wall of the restaurant. It depicted Afghan men competing in a polo-like game in which they wrestled over a goat carcass.

The hostess greeted the Coliseum Arts team as friends. She called a pair of waiters from the kitchen to push two tables together.

The game team of seventeen enjoyed the staff's full attention. Dogg tried to order the kebab but was quickly overruled. Ryan insisted that he must have what everyone else was having—qabili murgh. The plates arrived, heaped with chicken and yellow saffron rice, sweetened with cooked raisins and shredded carrots.

Jarrod raised his glass of cola in a toast, "Welcome to Coliseum Arts, Dogg!"

Everyone drank except Jenn, who raised her glass but then placed it on the table.

"So, *Dogg*," she emphasized his nickname, "What can you tell us about yourself?"

"Not much," he smiled, "I'm the only one here with security clearance."

Jenn wasn't deterred, "Right. Tell us what you're working on."

"I can't," he smiled back.

"We know it's for the Army," Jenn pressed.

"Ooops. Somebody's been talking," Dogg joked lightly.

"I've been wondering—"

"Have you?" interrupted Dogg.

"When you do work for the military, do you have any problem knowing that your work might be used to kill people?" asked Jenn sweetly.

Jarrod tried to intercede, but Dogg waved him off, good-naturedly.

"You mean do I have a problem knowing I'm helping the people who defend our country? No, I don't have a problem with that at all. Do you?"

"Governments don't have a great track record of keeping their weapons to themselves."

"Who told you I was working on a weapon?" asked Dogg. "Don't you think it's much more likely I'm working on data encryption, a communication system, or a training tool?"

"Are you working on those?"

"I can't say."

"All three of those things can be greater weapons than a machine gun," Jenn said. "A well-trained soldier defeats an untrained one. A German encryption machine helped the Nazis take over Europe, North Africa and much of Russia."

"Well, sure," said Dogg, "and the technologists who helped crack the Enigma machine probably saved hundreds of thousands of lives. But I'm not really interested in the argument. It's moot."

Jenn paused. It was one of the few times Owen had seen her genuinely nonplussed.

Dogg continued, "Technology is agnostic. Hitler has missiles. He fires them at London. NASA has missiles and men walk on the moon. Are you going to blame that on the inventor of the rocket for Hitler or praise him for the moon shot? There *will* be technological advancements. Do you want to stop those advancements?"

Now Jenn felt she had something to hang her hat on.

"I think we can slow down those advancements until society understands the power of those technologies and what can go wrong," she said. "It should wait until it understands how to use its new toys."

Dogg continued conversationally, "That's for someone else to think about. I'm not a priest and I'm not a philosopher. My responsibility is to my family. For them, I must work to put clothes on their backs, food on the table and gas in the car. If what I do helps protect America, that's great too. But it's not why I do what I do."

Jenn decided to press him. She started, "But what…"

"Look," Dogg interrupted her again. "Do you have any guilt over all the kids who got sedentary and fat while sitting on their butts playing your videogames? No? I didn't think so." Then he said to Ryan, "You know, that qabili murgh was *great!*"

Owen led the rest of the lunch conversation, purposely lightening the mood. By 2:30 they were all back in the office, fat and happy.

Owen was impatient to return to his bug fixing, but Dogg asked him to help carry some hardware up from his car. By the time Owen reached the alley, Mitch and Cole were already unloading the contents of Dogg's Jeep.

Dogg brought his own U.S. military-approved machines - all big, all heavy. The last piece of equipment in the car was a thick, translucent green glass plate. It lay flat of the floor of the Jeep's cargo space. At its top, two sturdy metal brackets stuck up at 90-degree angles.

Owen called out to Dogg as he walked into the building, "What is this? Some kind of monster glare guard?"

Dogg didn't hear him and kept walking. It looked like a glare guard. The brackets probably hooked to a monitor's top, leaving the emerald-tinted glass hanging down in front of the view-screen.

Owen tried lifting the glass plate on his own and nearly injured his back. It weighed a ton. Mitch arrived and together they muscled the odd, green screen guard up to Dogg's space.

It took Owen several more hours to get Dogg's machines connected to the company network. Once they were up and running, Dogg insisted Owen make the game engine changes he needed. They looked over the code.

"Right here," said Dogg, pointing to Owen's screen "I need you to call a stub function for my DLL right here."

"Are you kidding? You want me to add it into the graphics rendering code?" asked Owen incredulously. "That's the most delicate routine in the whole system!"

Dogg responded with an arrogance bred from technical mastery, "Oh, please. It's not going to affect your precious little game. If it doesn't find my file, it'll run your code just as you wrote it."

The contractor had one more instruction. "Set up your project to look for a file called, 'DSASP4.dll'."

"DSASP4," Owen repeated. "OK."

He turned to go back to his desk then had a thought. Turning back around, Owen asked, "What does DSASP4 stand for? I mean, if you can tell me."

"Oh, sure. I can tell you," said Dogg, "It stands for 'Dogg's Super Awesome Secret Project 4'."

CHAPTER TWENTY-ONE
GREETINGS FROM FINLAND

By the end of May, the team worked long hours, but it couldn't be considered "crunch mode" yet. Viv and Owen spent lunches and evenings together. Soon, they spent mornings together as well. Owen felt that each day was like one long date, filled with game development. What could be better? He thought Viv looked happy, too, although he suspected she couldn't care less about *Apoplexy II*.

Miles, on the other hand, continued to brood in his office, refusing to speak with Viv or even look at Owen.

The sales reports from Georgia were discouraging. *Peacemaker* had been their best game to date, but Jarrod estimated that, because of the leak, revenue wouldn't reach 60 percent of *Apoplexy's*. No one would receive any royalties from *Peacemaker*. In an emotional meeting, Owen had to break the news to Mitch.

If his teammates were going to put their hearts and souls into *Apoplexy II*, Owen would have to do everything he could to make sure the game could not leak.

On May 29th Owen had a sudden inspiration and he pulled his Computer Game Developers Conference tote from under his desk. Rummaging through the bag, he found Astrid Hahl's business card. He opened his e-mail program and sent her a hastily worded message.

> *Hello Astrid, this is Owen Nickerson.*
> *We met at the developer's conference back in April. I asked you about Flexx and how he cracked my game. I'm still trying to figure out how he got it.*
> *How is your article going? Have you heard anything more from*

him? Any information?
Thanks,
Owen

To his surprise, Owen received a reply by the following day. It read:

I will ask.

The next day, Astrid forwarded Owen a chain of emails. In it, Astrid told Flexx that Owen wanted to speak with him. Flexx had replied:

Dear Owen,
I am a big fan of your games. I played Apoplexy for like, 1000 hours.
I don't know if you meant to do this, but did you know if you shoot
correctly, you can write words on the walls with the inmates' blood?
So cool! Please keep up the good work. I really look forward to the
sequel!
|=13><><

Everything about the response confused Owen. It was just another fan-boy letter. And what was that last line about? He called Mitch over for a translation.

"That thing at the bottom says, 'FLEXX'. It's this super annoying way hackers write. It's called 'Leet' as in, short for 'elite.' The pipe symbol and the equals sign together make an 'F,' the 1 is an 'L,' then the 3 is an 'E' and each greater-than- less-than pairs make the 'Xs'."

"Wow. That *is* super annoying," Owen agreed.

He asked Mitch if Flexx's email address could be tracked back to the location of its server computer. Mitch laughed. Owen was great at programming 3D game engines, but he had a lot to learn about the Internet.

"Probably not," said Mitch, "Even if you could, I don't think the Finnish police would help. Do you?"

On the surface, Flexx's message looked innocuous, but the line, 'I'm really looking forward to the sequel!' stuck in Owen's head. The more he thought about it, the more he worried. It was almost a given that Flexx was going to try and crack *Apoplexy II*. Then he would give it away free.

Owen's jaw clenched and he made up his mind to outsmart the hacker.

Owen marched toward Jarrod's office but he didn't make it. As he walked, a small boy with dark skin and wavy, brown hair unexpectedly ran across his path. Contorting himself to avoid knocking the child down, Owen nearly fell himself.

The boy pounded on Dogg's locked office door, yelling "Dad!"

It opened immediately and Dogg scooped up the kid, who looked to be around six years old.

"Hey, Stevie," said Dogg, carrying the boy back to the common room, "You gotta be quiet, OK? People are working here and they need quiet."

Loudly, Stevie promised he'd be quiet.

"You want to color, Stevie?" asked Dogg, "Let's go get your crayons and your coloring books."

With Stevie squared away, Dogg returned to his office. As he passed, Owen asked, "Your son?"

"Did he give it away when he called me dad?" Dogg laughed. "My wife's mom is sick, so Monique's off to Vermont to take care of her. Stevie will be with me in the office whenever I can't get daycare. I cleared it with Jarrod."

"OK. Sure," said Owen, but he didn't like the idea of a kid running around the office.

Things were getting too complicated for Owen. No game he'd ever made had been like this. Every day, there were too many distractions and variables out of his control. He needed a few minutes of quiet. Owen shut off his computer, left the office and headed outside. He walked around the block, through the park and back to work.

As Owen re-entered the office and passed little Stevie, he heard Mitch swearing, angrily and creatively. Walking into the programmer space he found his tools guy smashing a keyboard on the desk.

"Dude," shushed Owen, "There's a little kid in the next room. Easy on the language… and the keyboard."

Mitch breathed deeply for a few seconds. Turning toward Owen he made his announcement.

"The file server just crashed hard. We just lost all the data we had on the network."

CHAPTER TWENTY-TWO

THE GAMERS

June 1, 1994
St. Petersburg, Russia

"Oh my god, I love coming here! This house amazing!" yelled Flexx in his native Russian.

He looked up and admired the mural painted on the ceiling of the Morozov mansion entryway. Angels. Nice! Leaning back, he held out his arms out for balance. Turning slowly, he took in every bit of the massive picture with its embellishments of gold leaf.

The hacker turned to Olga excitedly but was disappointed to find she showed no interest in the opulent, 18th-century architecture.

"Olga, you must look," said Flexx pointing towards the roof. "They've got a painting of heaven. Look!"

With a sigh, Olga reluctantly glanced up.

"There. I saw it," she said.

Flexx noticed the white marble floor. He stomped his boots and the echo rolled down the long hallways to either side. When the noise subsided, he did it again.

"Stop it, at once!" Olga scolded with a whisper that implied a threat.

In the Russian oligarch's palatial home, Flexx looked particularly out of place. He wore his military-style khaki pants and a skull-emblazoned black T-shirt.

Flexx ran to the back of the room, beneath a large oval window.

"Look!" he said, gesturing to a spot on the floor. "Alvar showed me this last time we were here. During the battle of Leningrad, a German shell landed right there, but it didn't explode."

"Ah, yes. Alvar," Olga muttered under her breath. "The idiot brother."

Flexx and Olga heard the steps of hard-soled shoes approaching from the south wing. The steps grew louder until Leonid Morozov arrived at the entryway.

He greeted Olga and they shook hands. Flexx jogged over to the pair, but Leonid gave him no notice.

"Doctor," said Leonid to Olga, "when do you—"

"Sorry, but where's Alvar?" Flexx asked.

Leonid Morozov wasn't used to being interrupted. He wasn't sure how to respond.

"What? Oh. Alvar?" stammered Leonid. "He's in the office in the north wing."

"I brought my gaming machine today," Flexx boasted. He waved his hand toward the rolling pushcart near the front door. "It's the full kit. I got my tower PC, monitor, speakers. Everything."

"That's… fine," said Leonid. "Just take it down the hall to the office. It's the last door on the left."

Flexx tromped to the cart. Grabbing it by the handle he wrestled it across the floor until it faced the north hallway. Olga and Leonid watched impatiently as he rolled it away.

As the sound of the rolling wheels faded, Olga and Leonid were free to speak.

Leonid completed his original question. "When do you think you can procure a device for Site Four?"

"How can you be ready for Site Four?" Olga asked. "The Site Three device is still sitting in Murmansk. I can't just have another one lying around in some Hong Kong or Los Angeles warehouse."

He scoffed at her concern. "Trust me. Site Four will be ready soon. We had just a few bureaucratic issues but they're out of the way now."

"So I'll be able to conduct the test… when?" she pressed.

"By next spring, I believe," assured Leonid.

"All right. But you need to keep me informed," said Olga, staring directly into the man's eyes. "Pulling it off in the United States will be much tougher than in Siberia."

"Yes, much tougher," announced Dr. Ilizarov, entering from the gilded hallway of the north wing. Mikhail Morozov followed.

Ilizarov added, "One might even say, 'insane.'"

"Good day, Dr. Ilizarov. Good day, Mikhail," said Olga, smiling suddenly.

Olga was not immune to Mikhail's remarkable good looks and surreptitiously scrutinized the young man's form from top to bottom; delicate features, high cheekbones, strong jaw, shining black hair. She bit her lower lip.

Struggling to maintain his air of geniality, Leonid Morozov dismissed Ilizarov's assertion.

"'Difficult' is not the same as 'insane.' You see, my dear Olga, my business partner here would have me sell your goods. He wants me to be a retailer! Can you imagine?"

"What you choose to do with the devices I provide is not my concern," she replied, hoping to end the digression. The tycoon didn't catch the hint

"With the data we collect from Site Four, I can develop a massive U.S. mining operation," said Leonid, who then turned towards the doctor. "Question for you, Ilizarov. Why did the United States mobs give up on Las Vegas?"

Ilizarov smiled a thin smile and guessed sarcastically, "Oh, I don't know. They got arrested?"

Leonid shook his head, "No. They didn't have enough capital to compete with the authorities. With my mystifying ability to discover rich, untapped mining sites, I'll have more money than the U.S. Government. Why buy a store, when I can own a city?"

He pursed his lips in a smile and winked at Olga.

Ilizarov replied with a single word. "Risky."

"I'm in charge. It's *my* risk to take," snapped Morozov. "Mine and Mikhail's!"

The doctor turned to Mikhail and asked, "What do you think, my boy?"

"My father built this empire from such risks," Mikhail answered proudly. "I stand with him."

The industrialist beamed, "Good boy."

"You two are a perfect pair," said Ilizarov dismissively. "And I also say that there is nothing wrong with Flexx's proposal."

Olga snapped to attention.

"Flexx's proposal?" she asked, sharply. "What is Flexx's proposal?"

Confused, Ilizarov cocked his head to the side.

"You don't know about his proposal to sell Stinger missile targeting systems? Flexx has a source inside a U.S. defense company. I assumed you knew since Flexx works for you."

"Ah, yes. I'd forgotten," she lied, gritting out a smile. "But since my employers, the Morozovs, say 'no' then I must say 'no' to the idea as well."

She turned to Leonid saying, "As to the Site Four project, please transfer the usual up-front fee and I will send word to City 42. They will begin work on the new device. Let me know if there's a delay. I have other customers who are eager to buy."

"Surely," Leonid said, warmly.

Olga had one last request for Leonid. "The next time I come here, I'd prefer to come alone."

Leonid threw up his hands, "Ah! I know what you mean, Olga. But Alvar likes Flexx. He asked him to come. They're good friends. They play their stupid game."

"Flexx is good with computers," Olga admitted, "but he's unprofessional. Sloppy."

"What can I do? How can I say no to my brother?" Morozov said with a smile.

* * *

In the north wing of the mansion, Flexx assembled his 'gaming rig.'

As Flexx worked, Alvar sat at the desk, paying him no attention. He and Alvar had to share this particular piece of furniture, but it was so wide, they each had plenty of room.

Alvar was about equal in height to Flexx's 6'-4", but was older, leaner and more muscular. His hair was pulled back into its usual ponytail. The younger Morozov brother played a solo computer game. He appeared transfixed.

Flexx crawled under the desk and connected the two machines with an orange cable.

"We should be good now," said Flexx. "Whenever you're ready, we can play each other head to head."

"Hold on," replied Alvar. "I need to finish the level."

While Alvar was blasting *Apoplexy's* monstrous horrors to bits, Flexx dragged one of the room's heavily ornamented wooden chairs over to his gaming station.

"Done!" Alvar announced. "Let's play."

He hit a few keys to start the multi-player game.

"Did you know I met the designer of this game once? I got his autograph," Alvar bragged.

"No way!" Flexx was impressed. "Where? In America?"

"Yes. I was going to ask him if I could Beta-test the next game, but some bitch interrupted me," said Alvar. "The game is starting. Let's go!"

Flexx and Alvar were masters of *Apoplexy*. Flexx had more natural ability but Alvar led in "hours played" by a wide margin. Though he made no surprising or inspired moves, Alvar made no mistakes. And while Flexx talked, laughed and yowled throughout the battle, Alvar just stared intently at the screen and worked his game controls.

For an hour, they played each other hard, with Flexx earning a slight advantage.

As the contest's intensity rose, so did Alvar's heartbeat. His reddish face drained, becoming ash white. His breathing accelerated and his chest expanded and contracted in spasms. He wheezed. Eyes dilated, Alvar lost his peripheral vision.

His breathing became so loud it caught Flexx's attention.

"Alvar, are you OK? Alvar?" asked Flexx.

Alvar made no verbal response. His answer was a well-aimed shotgun blast to the face of Flexx's game character.

The heavy breathing intensified, becoming a series of alarming wheezes. Concerned, Flexx stopped playing and rose from his chair.

"Hey!" he called. Again, there was no reaction from Alvar.

Flexx reached out and touched his friend on the wrist.

Alvar's attack was so fast, Flexx had no chance to defend himself. His arm bent behind his back, the hacker's head slamming into the oak desktop. When the pain from the impact subsided, he pried his eyes open.

Flexx saw the muzzle of a pistol pressed against his nose. Behind the gun was Alvar's grimacing face. This angle gave Flexx a good look at the massive scar that ran along Alvar's left jawline.

Alvar pushed down on Flexx with his right arm while grasping the gun in his left. He cocked the pistol's hammer with his thumb. Alvar's sneer changed to a deranged grin.

Flexx closed his eyes, doubting he'd ever open them again. Then a voice called out, "Alvar! *Alvar!* Stop!"

It was Leonid Morozov's voice. He entered the cavernous office, followed by Olga, Mikhail and Ilizarov.

"What are you doing, Alvar? What is going on here?" demanded Leonid.

Alvar gave Flexx's arm one final, painful wrench then released him. He set down his gun on the desk and backed away, hands raised above his shoulders. His breathing slowed.

"It's... it's nothing. It's fine," panted Alvar. "We were just playing a game, Leonid. That's all. It's just a game."

Flexx straightened himself up and shook out his sore shoulder. The hacker threw a glance at Alvar. The hitman gave Flexx a wink.

"That's right," said Flexx, swaggering up to Alvar and casually throwing his arm around the man's shoulders. "Everything is good. It was just a game."

CHAPTER TWENTY-THREE
CRUNCH MODE

To the programmers, the crash of the development server was annoying but not catastrophic. Each had copies of the code on their personal machines.

The far more serious blow was to the artists who relied on the server to store their models and textures. Owen checked the last tape backups to find that they'd failed. The last good one they had was three weeks old.

Suddenly, Viv and the small team of *Apoplexy II* artists found themselves far behind schedule and fuming with frustration.

Team morale was already low. They'd already been working some overtime and looked drained. The crash of the network server did nothing to help the mood. It seemed like another signal from the universe that *Apoplexy II* was a cursed project.

Owen asked Cole to drive in from San Francisco, not just for another code merge, but also for a full team meeting. The crew gathered in the common area, standing or slumping into the old, overly soft couches. Dogg skipped the meeting, but Stevie sat on a seat between Viv and Owen.

Jarrod kicked it off, "I want you all to know how much I appreciate your hard work during the first phase of *Apoplexy II*. It's really shaping up. I'm hearing great things out of test."

"It is crashing *much* better now," said Ryan, gushing with positivity.

Jarrod smiled and rolled on, "We've had some big successes, but we've also had unexpected setbacks. We've lost some programmer and artist time, but we have commitments to meet, the most important of these being our launch date. Along with our continuing shareware strategy, both Target and Wal-Mart are so excited about *Apoplexy II* that they've agreed to carry the game for Christmas. Both will give us prime advertising space in their circulars the week before Thanksgiving. It's a huge opportunity for us. But to get it, we can't miss our September ship date. We just can't."

Jarrod's expression turned grim.

"To hit that date, we are starting crunch mode on Monday. I know, it's much earlier than we had planned. But we've got to do it. That means everyone here is expected to work every day and evening, also on weekends and holidays."

The team did the math. Crunch would run from the second week of June until Quality Assurance in early September. At first blush, three months of crunch didn't seem too bad. Friends at other companies told stories of crunch lasting six or even twelve months.

The more experienced team members had a more negative reaction. In their opinion, the project duration was already too short and the game scope too ambitious. They would be trying to pack six months of work into three.

Owen could feel his colleagues' disappointment. He knew Jarrod's explanation hadn't helped. You didn't motivate artists by talking about retail advertising.

He addressed the room, saying, "I know that starting crunch mode this early is upsetting. It is for me, too. But we all know what's at stake here. Even though it's still early, it's clear that *Apoplexy II* is a breakthrough game. We're doing things no one has done before, both technically and artistically. With this game, we have the opportunity to achieve something few will – create a world. We owe it to our players to make our world as bold and rich as possible. And we owe it to ourselves."

Jenn led the team in applauding, although a few at the back of the room heard Miles say, "It sounds like we're making coffee."

"Thank you, Owen. OK, next point of business," continued Jarrod, "A few of us have known for a while now, but we've kept it a secret. It is time to let you all know, last fall *Peacemaker* got leaked to a cracker who posted it up to the Internet."

The announcement shocked the room. Soon everyone was whispering.

Jarrod asked the group to calm down then said, "We don't know who leaked it. We're pretty sure it wasn't from anyone inside the company. However, just to be safe, I've asked Owen to recommend some reasonable steps to protect our intellectual property. Owen?"

Owen squirmed a little. The security ideas had been his, but he didn't really want to take the credit – or blame.

"OK," he began. "So, the idea we're adopting is something that the military calls 'compartmentalization' or 'need to know.' We're only going to give those who really need it access to the complete game build."

Mitch nodded.

Owen continued, "When I rebuilt the development server, I split it up into three different partitions: Game Developers, Artists and Tools Programming."

Mitch froze.

Owen continued his explanation, "Because we're the ones working on the game code directly, only Cole and I will have access to all three data sets. Test will check out serially numbered game disks. These will be checked back in at the end of a shift. "

Cole nodded. It seemed reasonable to him, until Owen added, "We're also going to start locking down our data. That means that no one will be allowed to take development computers out of the Coliseum Arts office."

Mitch raised his hand, but started talking before Owen called on him, "I really think all the programmers should have access to the game build."

"Because the tools don't ship with the final game, it makes sense to keep tools code separate from the game code," replied Owen, "Also we're shutting off access to the Internet for all desktop machines."

"Owen, what are all y'all thinking?" Mitch was almost shouting. His tone was angry. Tears gathered at the corners of his eyes.

"If you need to get online to check your email or what have you, everyone has permission to use the marketing computer, " Jarrod interjected, "Look, if we're going to execute the 'need to know' model well, then we need to isolate the data properly. I don't want anyone to feel like they're under suspicion or that they're being picked on. This is just our new process and we're going to try it out."

Cole jumped in, "How can you say we shouldn't feel like we're under suspicion? I can't work from home now? Owen, this is shite."

Mitch fumed. He stood up and walked towards Owen until they stood nose to nose. Before he could say anything, Jarrod stepped in, saying, "Let's end this meeting now. The programmers can have a separate department meeting of their own if they feel the need."

Cole, Mitch and Owen all followed Jarrod to his office. The door shut, but everyone still heard what was said.

"How can you not trust us?" Mitch pleaded. "We wouldn't do anything to hurt the company!"

"Mitch," said Jarrod firmly, "This isn't about you. It's just a new protocol."

"Absolutely it's about me! One of the protocols is there to protect this company from me. Specifically. I'm the only programmer without access to the game code. Do you know how that makes me feel?"

Jarrod continued to fight emotion with logic, "Look, Mitch, you of all people should appreciate this. You won't be getting a bonus because *Peacemaker* leaked. If you want to have the money to help your dad out with his—"

"Don't you mention my father," Mitch demanded. "I asked you for help and you didn't give me any! How do I even know there *was* a leak? Maybe it was just a scam by you guys to cheat us out of our bonuses!"

Jarrod's eyes went cold.

"You should think *three* times before another word comes out of your mouth," said the CEO threateningly. "We are done."

"If Maxine were still here," said Cole, "she would *never* let you do this."

CHAPTER TWENTY-FOUR

STEVIE AND THE SECRET PROJECT

Cole's words hit Owen hard. He returned to his desk and tried to take his mind off the argument by programming for a while.

"If I were on the other side, I wouldn't take the code lock-out personally," thought Owen, trying to convince himself.

He hit the hotkeys to save his file then ran the game to test his changes.

Pressing the 'up' arrow key, he moved the game's hero, Brock Masters, deeper into the level. As he slid the computer mouse to look left, Stevie slid under Owen's arms, climbed up and sat in his lap. At first, the programmer was truly surprised. He paused his playing and wondered what Stevie wanted. Stevie just kept looking at the screen, never back at Owen.

"I guess he wants to see the game," thought Owen. He pressed down the 'up' key again. Brock rounded a corner, confronting a huge, hideous re-animated corpse monster! It screamed its baleful cry and approached, flailing its four arms. Down went the left-mouse button. Brock's hundred round, fully automatic mini-cannon shot a stream of bullets, kicking up fountains of blood that covered the walls.

"Let's see your game do that, Carmack!" thought Owen, taking pride in his belief that he'd bested an engine-programming nemesis.

As the suffering undead creature howled in agony, Owen wondered if the violence would be too much for Stevie.

Stevie started chuckling. The chuckles started slowly but soon grew to an uncontrollable cackle. It would be almost a minute of laughing before he had enough surplus air to say, "The monster is funny!"

Owen paused again and Stevie paused his laughing. All went quiet for a second. Without warning, Owen shot a quick burst of three bullets and the zombie shrieked again. This was too much for Stevie. He laughed so hard he fell to the floor and rolled around, chortling. Owen turned around to grin at the rest of the office. Cole smiled. Mitch and Jenn did not.

Dogg opened his office door quickly, causing the keys that hung from the doorknob to jingle musically. The six-foot-eight-inch graphics master looked down at his son with a little smile. Stevie still laughed uncontrollably. Dogg addressed Owen matter-of-factly, "I've seen Stevie do this before, Owen. This is your responsibility. If he vomits, you're the one cleaning it up."

The first week of crunch mode went as well as anyone might expect. This wasn't the team's first game. They knew how to power through the long hours.

Although they all worked hard, Jarrod didn't want to burn his team out early. He'd seen too many bad things happen.

During the extended crunch of *Peacemaker*, an exhausted art tech had made a bad decision and climbed on his motorcycle in an attempt to drive home. On the way, he fell asleep and crashed his bike while riding south on 101. Thankfully, he had been lucky and the surgeons were able to save his leg, but he never returned to Coliseum Arts, blaming his crash on being over-worked.

This time around, Jarrod would be more conservative with crunch. The art tech could have sued the company for big bucks. That hadn't happened and Jarrod considered it a narrow escape. He gave the team strict instructions not to come in before 8 a.m. and or stay later than 11 p.m.

The only person not crunching was Dogg, as he wasn't working on the game. Dogg only worked on "Dogg's Super Awesome Secret Project 4" and had no interest in unpaid overtime. It was certain Dogg was using the *Apoplexy II* game for something, but for what, no one knew.

When Owen made a new build, it automatically copied to Dogg's network directory and that was the only interaction between the game team and the military contractor.

To everyone's surprise, the best part about going to work each day was Stevie. His light mood and calming presence brought a joy long-missed to the stressed-out office. Most days, Stevie sat quietly on the couch or lay on the floor in the good light of the common room, reading and coloring. His father printed educational worksheets, which Stevie completed with enthusiasm.

It became common practice to get Stevie's opinion on the game in development. While not always useful, Stevie's feedback was always quotable. Viv showed him one of her new monster designs, a creature covered in red horns. The monster's mouth sat on its forehead and pus oozed from its numerous seeping goiters. Stevie considered Viv's artistic creation.

"His name is…Banana Boat Bunny Guy," declared Stevie. And that's how the name appeared in the *Apoplexy II* strategy guide.

Every week, two U.S. Army soldiers visited the office. They wore dark blue uniforms, adorned with insignias and ribbons. Using the marketing machine, Mitch scoured the Internet for pictures of military uniforms until he determined the Army folk were probably intelligence officers. Invariably, one of the soldiers carried a briefcase handcuffed to his wrist. The second officer would unlock the handcuffs and pass the case to Dogg. In exchange, the contractor signed paperwork on a soldier's clipboard. Afterward, the officers would leave.

No one on the game team ever got a close look at the contents of these secret deliveries, but they could tell it was mostly paper printouts, covered with charts, graphs and equations.

Owen once asked Dogg about the deliveries and Dogg answered him earnestly, "Please don't take this the wrong way, because I really don't mean it to be a knock on you. Even if I showed you all the documents, you still wouldn't understand it."

CHAPTER TWENTY-FIVE

THE FUN FACTORY

Game programming had fallen dangerously behind schedule and Owen searched for the cause. Sorting through the activity logs, he realized that Mitch wasn't the problem. The young programmer had made excellent progress. The problem lay with Owen's best programmer, Cole.

The Brit continued to write solid code, working hard every day and deep into the night but his productivity had plunged. Owen could tell that Cole remained unhappy about the new security protocols and wanted to work from home.

Rather than upset his programmer further, Owen decided to ignore the issue for a while. He believed that Cole would eventually come out of his slump. In the meantime, the lead programmer had no choice but to take up the slack and assigned himself many of Cole's tasks.

But not everything about the game was doom and gloom. Although Miles still wouldn't speak to him, Owen thought the game's musical score was the greatest thing he'd ever heard.

Jenn was also highly productive. Her script was long and grew longer each day. By late June, it had surpassed 200 pages and featured the historical figures Sigmund Freud, Carl Jung and Alois Alzheimer.

One day, looking for a quote, Jenn turned to her shelf of "serious books." She selected a stream-of-consciousness classic. Opening it, she discovered that, while the dust jacket's title read "Ulysses," the book inside was a steamy, bodice-ripping romance called, "Lady Innocence and the Laird's Passion." Her suspicions aroused, Jenn grabbed her copy of "The Fountainhead." Someone had replaced its contents with, "Captive Heiress – Wicked Rogue."

Knowing she'd been pranked, Jenn bellowed, "Vivian!"

She heard giggles from the art room.

Viv's practical joke was just the first of a series. Many involved enormous rubber snakes and spiders. Most targeted Jenn.

The evening of Viv's romance novel prank, Viv stayed over at Owen's apartment. Left exhausted by work, the pair simply collapsed on his bed. Dropping into a sound sleep, Owen remained blissfully unaware that, back at Coliseum Arts, a brilliant mastermind had set his evil plan in motion.

CHAPTER TWENTY-SIX

ALL OUT WAR

The next evening, Mitch sensed suspicious activity. Looking up, he watched Ryan and his testers leave the office as a group. While the idea of testers socializing wasn't unusual, the timing of the outing meant that they would miss the free, company-provided dinner. That was unprecedented.

When the testers returned at eight, they meandered in, slowly and casually. Something rustled as Ryan brushed past Mitch's desk. The programmer turned and saw that the test lead had concealed a large box beneath his coat. Glancing at the other testers, he noticed that each secreted a box—either in an unmarked shopping bag or, in some cases, under a stretched-out T-shirt.

Mitch pointed out the suspicious behavior to the other programmers. All reached the same conclusion. Jenn also understood the situation but appeared disinterested.

Scouting the enemy stronghold, Mitch walked back to the test pit. Peeking in, he saw nothing awry. There were no mysterious packages in sight.

Ryan gave Mitch a surprised, innocent look.

"Good day respected colleague. How can I help you?" asked Ryan.

"Actually, I thought I might help y'all," answered Mitch. "I just dropped by to see if there were any bugs that needed fixing."

"Well, I'll ask around. You know we're always here for you," said Ryan sweetly.

"I know that," said Mitch, smiling as hard as he could. "Y'all are just the *best*."

Ryan closed the conversation with, "Aren't you the sweet one. Goodbye you dear, dear man."

Mitch returned to the programmers and reported, "Oh, it's going *down*."

"Quick! While there's still time," said Owen. Standing, he led Cole and Mitch from the building.

The following morning the programmers and artists were in early, but not earlier than the testers. The coders heard whispers, giggles and a rattle of plastic emanating from the artist's area.

"Steady on, boys," warned Cole. "Give no bloody quarter."

"Right," said Mitch, who had arrived at work dressed in Army fatigues dyed four shades too bright.

"Ready," answered Owen.

"NOW!!!!!" screamed Ryan.

Two testers wearing eye-protecting sunglasses jumped through the doorframe from the art room. Each held a Nerf Master Blaster.

Polyester resin balls peppered Mitch and Owen's workstations, leaving them no choice but to dive under their desks. Cole returned fire with his foam-sphere firing Ballzooka.

"Ha ha! Come get some, ya wankers!" Cole crowed.

A light green ball shot across the room, beaning the first tester on his forehead.

Ryan returned fire and his rubber-tipped foam dart stuck to the right lens of Cole's reading glasses. Cole's brave sacrifice hadn't been in vain. He'd bought Mitch and Owen precious time.

Emerging from beneath their desks, the pair wielded the ultimate in foam defense technology—the Arrowstorm. Made of heavy blue plastic, the Arrowstorm just felt good in the hands.

The duo launched a counter-barrage, scoring several critical hits on the invading Quality Assurance Engineers, but they were outnumbered. More and more testers overran the programmer's space.

Dogg watched the melee with amusement from behind his protective window while Jarrod simply shut his office door.

The artists joined the battle, firing their dart-flinging crossbows and chain-fed plastic machine pistols. Green and yellow balls ricocheted off lamps. Carelessly aimed darts left marks on monitor screens. Chaos reigned.

Then Miles shocked the room by firing the largest, loudest Nerf gun anyone had ever seen—the gigantic Ultimator. Its enormous "Boom!" froze the combatants, momentarily. Then everyone had a laugh at the Ultimator's wondrous impracticality.

The levity was short-lived. A commanding voice cut through the air.

"All right rookies! Now it's *my* turn!" Jenn growled, standing atop her desk.

She held an oversized, wooden rubber-band gun with a hand crank attached to its side. Owen figured the thing must've held at least 100 rounds of its stretchy ammunition.

A cry went up, "Everyone look out!"

But it was far too late.

Jenn sneered and she turned the crank. Rubber bands filled the air as she swung her toy machine gun back and forth, strafing the room's occupants. The programmer's area was so crowded with combatants that none of Jenn's targets had room to dodge. There were screams of mock terror. Jenn cackled with maniacal laughter, launching salvo after salvo.

When her attacks finally ceased, Jenn's co-workers lay in heaps on the floor, covered with rubber bands. Gently setting down her weapon, Jenn seated herself and returned to writing.

No one could dispute that Jenn Adler was the victor in the Great Battle of Coliseum Arts.

Smiling and laughing, the team members rose. Mitch poked his head into Jarrod's office.

"That was amazing," said Mitch. "Hey, Jarrod. Can we go for a walk? There's something I'd like to talk about."

"Absolutely we can go for a walk," Jarrod answered breezily. "Can you go right now? I've got a call in an hour."

Mitch said he could, so they strolled to the park. Each took a seat at one of the vacant picnic tables.

"OK, Mitch. How can I help?" asked Jarrod.

"I told you about the problems my dad's been having," Mitch began.

"Yes, you did," Jarrod said.

"It's gotten worse," admitted Mitch, "There was a big storm. A tree fell. The long and short of it is he needs to repair the roof, but he doesn't have the money to hire any workers."

Jarrod was sympathetic and said, "Oh, no. I'm sorry about that, Mitch."

"It's pretty tough, thank you," Mitch replied. "So what I'd like to do is fly back to Virginia for a couple of weeks and help him get the job done. Maybe it won't even take that long."

"That's really bad luck, Mitch but we're in the middle of crunch," said Jarrod, trying very hard to speak gently.

"I talked with Owen about it," replied the programmer. "He said it was OK with him but that I needed to double-check with you. Owen said that he could pick up the slack and add some of the features on my list."

"Well, of course he did," said Jarrod, exasperated. "Mitch, you can't take advantage of Owen. He thinks he's Superman. But he can't do it all. We can't burn out our lead programmer."

"Yes, I know but—" Mitch conceded, "—but Owen said it was OK. My dad needs to keep the hardware store open. Otherwise, he'll be out of business by this fall."

This didn't seem to move Jarrod, so Mitch tried bargaining. "Maybe we could push out the ship date? Or shorten the QA time to one week?"

"Are you kidding?" snapped Jarrod. "Mitch, you made a commitment to this project and this team. This isn't your first game. You knew what crunch mode would be. Why do you think you can just take off when we need you most?"

Mitch pleaded, "I don't, of course. But it's for my family."

"Your team is your family! I am your family! Owen is your family!" Jarrod yelled, then softened his tone. "You see us much more than you see your father. I can see that your dad needs your help, but we need your help too."

Mitch lowered his head to hide his face. He rubbed his eyes.

"You can't turn your back on this team," said Jarrod, reaching out and grabbing Mitch's arm. "They're working crazy hours every day. What would I tell them if I let you take two weeks off? Your dad can find someone else to help."

Mitch found it difficult to speak but choked out the words, "There is no one else."

"I know how loyal you are," said Jarrod, patting Mitch on the shoulder. "You'd never betray your team or your game. Owen wouldn't be friends with anyone who could."

Mitch didn't look up. His shoulders shook with each little sob.

"Please Mitch," Jarrod said as he stood up. "Do me a favor. Go home. Have a shower and take the rest of the afternoon off. You'll feel better. I'll see you back in the office for dinner, OK?"

Mitch nodded. The CEO walked back to the office, leaving the despondent programmer alone at the picnic table.

Later that evening, around 7 o'clock, the three Coliseum Arts software engineers labored at their desks, programming silently and intensely. A package of cigarettes and a disposable lighter lay on Mitch's desk.

Cole noticed. "I thought you quit smoking, mate?"

Jenn overheard and peered around her monitor.

"I did," Mitch responded, but didn't look away from his debug monitor. "But for some reason, I started again."

Cole looked at the pack and asked, "Marlboros?"

"Yes. And yes, they're disgusting. Y'all want to lecture me about it?" Mitch challenged.

"No, mate," said Cole, defensively. "No."

CHAPTER TWENTY-SEVEN

SHAKEN

On a particularly beautiful day toward the end of June, trauma again shook the office. Owen was programming with his usual intensity but suddenly stopped. Something felt wrong. He looked around the office and saw Mitch, Cole and Jenn working undisturbed.

Owen rose from his swivel chair and listened. He heard a muted thumping. Following the noise into the common area, he found Stevie sprawled on the floor next to his crayons and coloring pages. The child lay between the couch and coffee table, twitching uncontrollably. His unfocused eyes faced the ceiling. As Stevie convulsed, his right leg repeatedly smacked the table leg. Owen recognized the symptoms. It was an epileptic seizure.

Stevie's body looked like a marionette controlled by a madman. His skin, normally light brown, looked gray.

Because of Haley, Owen knew he couldn't stop the spasms, but he could keep Stevie from hurting himself. Owen pushed away the couch and table to create space. He knew he shouldn't restrain the thrashing boy, so instead rolled him gently on his side, supporting the child's head with his hand.

Urgently, Owen yelled for Dogg. Stevie's father ran into the room, followed immediately by Jarrod, Cole, Jenn and Viv. Locked in his soundproofed room, Miles hadn't heard the commotion.

"Stevie!" Dogg yelled when he saw his son convulsing on the floor.

The big man rushed to grab his child, but Owen motioned him back.

"Hold on, Dogg. Don't grab him. If this is what I think it is, it will stop pretty soon. Just wait," said Owen reassuringly.

Dogg knelt beside his son until the tremors ended a few seconds later. He looked to Owen. Owen nodded and helped Stevie sit up. The boy looked around. Recovering from the shock of the seizure, Stevie sniffed twice, closed his eyes and began crying. Dogg picked up his son and held him, placing Stevie's head on his shoulder.

"Why don't I drive you two to Marin General?" Owen asked.

"OK," Dogg said softly and asked Owen to grab his keys from the door lock.

Owen drove Dogg's Jeep Cherokee to the hospital emergency room. Dogg sat in the back seat with Stevie, holding him the whole way.

Owen and Dogg described the seizure to the attending doctor and she prescribed rest and fluids. The admitting nurse scheduled a follow-up appointment with a neurologist. Dogg drove back to Central San Rafael to drop Owen off back at work.

As he sat in the passenger seat, Owen noticed something strange about his right hand. His thumb and index finger were blackened. He didn't know where it could have come from, but it looked like soot. In true programmer fashion, he wiped it off on his pants.

Dogg stayed home with Stevie for the rest of the week but sent Owen an e-mail wrap-up from his trip to the neurologist. The attack had been child-onset epilepsy and the doctor believed Stevie's condition would be manageable.

When Stevie returned to the office the following Monday, the team threw him a special welcome back party, complete with cupcakes and streamers. Immediately, Stevie returned to his happy, playful self.

CHAPTER TWENTY-EIGHT

NIGHT TERRORS

Crunch mode dragged into July. Most of the team worked half of Independence Day. Rather than spend the second half celebrating, almost everyone just went home to sleep. That was Owen's plan as well, but as he prepared to leave, the lead tester approached.

"Hey, doofus. I broke your game again," bragged Ryan.

Owen yawned, "Specifics, please."

"It crashes."

"When?"

"All the time."

"What are you doing when it crashes?"

"Anything."

Ryan decided he'd had enough fun. "It crashes randomly pretty much everywhere. We've had it since yesterday's build and it's a blocker because the game won't play longer than an hour before it dies."

"Yesterday's build, huh?" Owen said, rubbing his eyes. He had written a lot of new code for that version of the game. A reproducible bug was easy to fix, but "intermittent bugs" like this were always a pain.

Owen assured Ryan he'd have a look. He played a level. Within fifteen minutes it crashed hard.

He fought with the monster all day, making changes, deleting, adding, documenting, tracing. By 11:30 at night, he still hadn't found the bug. Owen hated to give up, but he was too tired to be effective. He drove home, climbed into bed and fell asleep. Even Mindy's drumming couldn't keep him up.

Owen's exhausted conscious mind had given up for the night, but his subconscious would not admit defeat.

At 3 a.m., Owen's lizard brain woke him to present its solution. The bug was caused by an *Off By One* error. It was a small mistake, but it snowballed over time, eventually becoming catastrophic.

Owen jumped out of bed. Should he try going back to sleep or drive to Coliseum Arts and fix the bug? He assessed his physical condition: wide-awake, full of adrenaline, impatient and twitchy. The diagnosis led to a prescription. He would fix his game.

Finding his jeans in the darkness, he struggled to pull them on. Owen hopped a little, his left foot stuck in the folded pant leg. This elicited yelling and pounding from the apartment below. He grabbed a shirt from the dirty laundry pile and jammed his feet into his sneakers. There was no time for socks.

Owen drove the five blocks to the Third Street office, parked, ran to the building, unlocked the street level door, bounded up the stairs three at a time and fumbled with the key to the office door. Finally, the lock yielded and he was admitted.

Looking around for the light switch, he realized it was unnecessary. There was already plenty of light. This was strange because he had shut off the lights when he had left for the day.

Dim streetlight illuminated the common area, but a brighter glow emanated from the programmer's space. Owen's imagination engaged. Was someone trying to steal Dogg's military secrets? Was it spies? Ninja? He crept to the open doorframe separating the common room from the programmer area. He leaned around and looked in.

There was the usual green glow from Dogg's computer monitor. It reflected off his back wall and out into the developer space. But there was another light. It was much more intense and it came from Cole's desk. Owen turned to the right and started in surprise.

In Cole's chair sat a young woman with tidy blonde hair, pulled back into a ponytail. The woman had delicate features and wore a crisp, blue blouse under the gray jacket that matched her business skirt. Her fingers rested on Cole's keyboard. She seemed unsurprised by Owen's arrival. He supposed he had been as stealthy as a moose. She turned and smiled.

"Hello," she said.

Owen thought her accent sounded vaguely eastern European, maybe Czech. This seemed to corroborate his 'spy' theory.

"Who are you?" he asked, tentatively.

The young lady stood up and extended her right hand

professionally.

"I am Irma. It is a pleasure to meet you. And you are?"

Reflexively, he shook her hand. "I'm Owen. Why are you here?"

Although only five-two, Irma's confidence and professionalism made her seem taller.

"I work here," said Irma.

"No, you don't. I'm one of the owners and I've never even seen you before," said Owen in his "do you think I'm stupid?" voice.

"Yes, I do work here," Irma replied without flinching, "I have worked here for over two years. I was hired as a game programmer by my manager, Cole Gruff."

Irma smiled again, happy that she'd finally cleared up any confusion.

"Your what?" Owen asked, incredulously.

"My manager, Cole Gruff."

"Your manager?"

"Yes. My manager. He provides me with my programming assignments and my computer equipment. Usually, I work from my home, but he's been having me come into the office this summer. OK?"

Her question was clearly designed to end the conversation so she could return to her programming. Owen's pernicious bug had been driven completely from his head. His mind raced to make sense of this new and confusing puzzle.

"Who pays you?" Owen asked.

"Mr. Gruff pays me, in cash. It's not much, but this way I don't pay taxes. It's a good job and the schedule is really flexible. It covers my expenses. I'm just doing it while I build the technology for the Internet company I'm starting."

"Does Cole *ever* program?"

"Oh, no," laughed Irma. "He doesn't know how to program. I show him basic stuff sometimes. I explain some things, but he has no idea."

"What was your name?"

"Irma. Irma Fournier."

She was French. Not Czech. Just one more thing to make Owen feel stupid.

"Can I get back to work now?" she asked, "Mr. Gruff says I need to leave the office by seven."

Owen failed to respond. He was baffled, wondering what Cole actually did while he was "working from home."

Impatient with the intruder, Irma sat down and began typing on

Cole's computer.

For years, Cole had outsourced his programming work and no one in the office had known. Owen tried to understand how he'd missed something so basic. Cole's résumé had looked outstanding. But now, Owen remembered that he hadn't called to check with any of Cole's previous employers. He suddenly regretted his policy of not giving technical tests to job applicants. He'd hated taking the tests himself and always worried they'd be insulting to potential hires.

Owen composed himself and addressed the programmer, "Irma?"

Irma responded while still typing, "Yes?"

"You need to leave now."

"I finish at seven."

"You need to leave now. Irma, you're fired."

She stood up stiffly, shocked. Angrily, she asked, "Why? Is my programming bad?"

"No," Owen answered.

"Then why? I've worked here for *two years!*"

Owen almost pleaded with Irma, "You must've known that wasn't right? That something was off?"

"All that matters is that my programming is good. My programming is good."

"Yes, it's good. But you're fired."

"No!"

Suddenly, Owen had a big headache. He just couldn't argue anymore.

"Get out," he groaned, "or I'm calling the police."

Anger burned in Irma's eyes as she picked up her handbag. She reached out for her well-organized binder of programming assignments.

"Leave that," said Owen firmly.

She set it down. Her professionalism prevented her from slamming it on the desk. She marched past Owen and out of the office, head held high.

As soon as Cole appeared at the office's front door that morning, Jarrod asked him into his office. Cole entered and Jarrod shut the door.

There was another man in the CEO's office. He wore a dark, expensive suit. Cole soon learned that this was Ignacio Gonzalez, Coliseum Arts' retained counsel. Standing beside Ignacio was a security guard.

There was a brief discussion and Jarrod's office door opened. Owen presented a furious-looking Cole with a moving box containing his private effects. Cole accepted it and left silently.

It all happened so quickly that none of the artists or testers knew Cole was gone until Jarrod made the announcement after lunch. Mr. Gonzalez attended the team meeting, ensuring that Jarrod gave no details on the reason for Cole's departure from Coliseum Arts. This didn't keep people from speculating. The following day, Jenn changed the name of the game's main villain to 'Eloc,' in Cole's honor.

CHAPTER TWENTY-NINE

THE HOME STRETCH

The loss of Cole, or rather, Irma, from the *Apoplexy II* development team was a huge blow. There was only one game programmer left on the team. No amount of begging had any effect on Dogg, as his contract clearly stated that his whole responsibility was to Dogg's Super Awesome Secret Project 4, not *Apoplexy II*. Ignacio Gonzalez made it clear that bringing Irma back was impossible. If they did, Cole might claim she had worked for Coliseum legally and that he had been her official manager.

Left with no other choice, Owen turned to the only other programmer in the office—Jenn. She shook her head.

"I signed on at Coliseum Arts as a game writer and a designer, not as a programmer," she said, leaning forward and staring hard into Owen's eyes.

"Will sticking to your guns make you feel better if there's no game?" asked Owen. "And besides, it *is* game design. It's level layout and game scripting. It's still your design, you'd just be implementing it instead of giving it to Cole—er—Irma."

Jenn leaned back, glancing around the office as she thought.

"I'll need a raise," she said.

"I'll talk to Jarrod," Owen replied. He was over a barrel.

"On the plus side, this way I'll know my story won't get screwed up," said Jenn.

Satisfied, she nodded to Owen and he thanked her. Waving the lead programmer away, Jenn set about moving Cole's development computer to her workspace.

In the early days of her career, Jenn had been a solid Cobol programmer. But she had no training in the *Apoplexy II* scripting language and certainly didn't know how to use Mitch's tools. The project would lose weeks bringing her up to speed.

Owen knew there was only one way to finish the game on time—full crunch. The team would work 24 hours a day, every day, until the end of the project. When Owen made the announcement, no one complained. They'd been working hard, but somehow, immediately found another gear. These were game veterans, intense and determined.

With no plans to leave the building for at least two months, the teammates brought in their medicines, toiletries and personal effects. They slept little and when they did, it was on an office couch or beneath a desk.

To feed his team, Owen bought a card table and set it up as a snack station in a broom closet. He stocked it with Red Vines, instant ramen, Diet Coke, bottles of iced tea, Goldfish crackers, peanuts and some truly awful candies from Japan and Europe.

In addition to junk food, the company provided lunch and dinner each day. This usually meant pizza.

Although he worked no overtime himself, Dogg helped himself to the free food.

The developers showered infrequently and with the summer heat overpowering the building's old air conditioner, the office developed a funk of body odor, stale crusts and microwaved popcorn. The team's lack of sleep, poor nutrition and hygiene took a toll on all their nerves. Angry outbursts between co-workers became daily occurrences.

Whenever a team member looked down in the mouth, Stevie noticed. He loved making drawings to cheer up the downhearted developers. Many of the creatures in Stevie's doodles were recognizable as characters from *Apoplexy II*, but regardless of tentacles, open sores, or compound fractures, each monster had a big, happy, friendly face. Soon, almost every wall and window sported Steven Dobbs' original artwork.

Only Dogg and Stevie would get out to see the 1994 summer movie blockbusters "Forrest Gump," "True Lies" and "The Mask." The game developers that hadn't already seen *The Lion King* in June would have to wait until fall.

At any given moment, four or five Coliseum Arts employees had colds and the sounds of sneezes and hacking coughs echoed through the workplace. But no one ever took a sick day. There wasn't time to be sick.

Illness hit Viv harder than most. Throughout the summer, she couldn't quite kick her cold. Her constitution wasn't as strong as her teammates' and she lacked the passion and zeal for the game that energized her colleagues.

One evening, Jarrod ordered Italian food from the restaurant at Third and Lincoln. As the team gathered in the common room, Viv took a single bite of the garlic bread and vomited on Ryan's legs.

She tried apologizing, but Ryan said with a smile, "No, no. This is great. Do you know how expensive it is to *buy* acid-washed jeans?"

Miles quickly ran to grab a ginger ale with which to settle Viv's stomach. Then he asked Owen for his apartment keys.

"She lives all the way over in Corte Madera," said Miles, "and you just live down the street. Let me drop her off there so she can rest."

Owen handed over his keys.

The next day, Stevie gave Viv a drawing. Lovingly rendered in crayon, the picture showed Stevie and Viv holding hands and smiling. This was too much for Viv. Her emotional dam burst. She hugged the boy hard and cried. Stevie didn't understand and he cried, too.

Jenn leaned over to Owen and suggested they change the name of the game's protagonist from Brock Masters to Stevie Masters. He agreed. One global search-and-replace later, it was done. Stevie was officially a hero.

CHAPTER THIRTY

THE COURIER

Due to the twilight of the artificially darkened office, July and August felt like one, never-ending day. But as awful as it was, crunch mode was working. The game progressed rapidly. It looked great.

The project's only major compromise was the loss of much of Jenn's grand storyline. Miles didn't have time to cast and record the voices for each character in Jenn's 225-page script. Even if he could, there was no programmer or artist time left to create the hours of in-engine animation. Jenn was furious but knew she had no one to blame but Cole. Cautiously, Miles approached her with a creative solution.

"After the game ships," Miles suggested, "we could still tell your story. What if we record your script and mix it onto a separate CD, like an audiobook?"

Owen and Jarrod held their breaths.

"Miles, that's good," she said. "That's *really* good. It's the kind of thing we'd have done at DaytaComm during its heyday. I never would've thought we'd do something like it here."

By mid-August, the game had reached the Beta milestone: all features, all assets, some bugs. As the length of the to-do lists shrank, so did the stress. Accordingly, Mitch's cigarettes and lighter no longer cluttered his desk.

Suddenly, it was common to see Viv, Miles and Owen joking together again. They'd all been through the same hell and survived. Together they'd achieved something great.

The team discussed dedicating *Apoplexy II* to Maxine but due to the violent and twisted nature of the game, they decided that it wouldn't be appropriate. Instead, Owen added a message at the end of the credits. It read:

"We miss you, Maxine. You are our darling. Love, your team."

By month's end, the major bugs had been exterminated. On September 5, Owen sent *Apoplexy II* to Coliseum Art's CD-ROM burner and produced a gold release candidate for testing.

After creating the game discs, Owen deleted the game files from the hard drive of the burn machine. This time, Owen took no chances.

He entered Jarrod's office and announced his plan. "I want to go to Finland."

"And I want to go to Aruba," said Jarrod, not looking up.

Owen just stared at his friend.

There was a pause before Jarrod replied, "OK, I'll bite. Why do you want to go to Finland?"

"Here's my thinking. See if you agree. We think that our last game got leaked by the bonded courier we hired to carry the gold discs to the manufacturer."

"Right."

"So, why risk that again? I could be the courier."

Jarrod deadpanned, "And you'd stay a few extra days in Europe on vacation..."

"Why not?" asked Owen, "I haven't had a vacation in two years."

"And would Viv go with you?"

Owen laid out his scheme, "Well, she could. You wouldn't have to pay for her travel and we could share a hotel room. It would still cost you less than the courier service."

Jarrod smiled. "Why not? Go ahead and plan it."

"Really? You're not kidding?"

"Nope. Have a good time. You deserve it."

Owen practically bounced as he entered the artist area. Viv was playing solitaire on her computer while Mitch was chatting up a cute art technician. Owen knew poor Mitch didn't have a chance. After months of crunch, Mitch had deep bags under his eyes and looked god-awful. He suffered from a bad cough. Even his colorful outfits had become dingy and wrinkled.

With no preamble, Owen asked Viv, "Do you want to go with me to Finland?"

She looked surprised and so did Mitch.

"Why Finland?" she asked.

"Jarrod says I can take the gold release CDs to the disc

manufacturing plant in Helsinki. I thought you could come along and we could make it a vacation."

Viv looked up at Owen, "I can't."

"Don't worry about the cost. It's my treat," Owen explained.

"It's not that," she gave him a half-smile. "I'm just too tired. This game's taken it all out of me. I've got this cold I need to get over. I just want to go lie down in my apartment and sleep for a month."

Unintentionally, Owen reacted with a pout.

Quickly Viv added, "Maybe when you get back we can get a bed and breakfast out at Point Reyes or something."

Owen's fast-moving brain quickly processed a counter-argument, but he saw desperation in Viv's eyes.

Kissing her gently, he said "All right. When I get back."

Owen hadn't expected a rush job like *Apoplexy II* to sail through QA, but it did. For two weeks, the testers crunched and found nothing major. Ryan frowned the whole time.

Owen taunted him, "As long as you're unhappy, I'm happy."

"OK. We'll see," replied Ryan, arching his eyebrows ominously, but two weeks later, test had still come up empty.

Owen decided he should celebrate his victory. While the testers were away at lunch, he made a sign out of printer paper, snuck into the pit and with a bit of scotch tape from Mitch's desk, stuck it to Ryan's monitor.

The sign read, "Game Over. You lose."

Strutting back to his workstation, he noticed he'd somehow gotten soot on his fingers again. He shook his head and wiped it off. Someone really needed to clean this place.

When it became clear that *Apoplexy II* would ship on time, Owen finalized his itinerary. He planned to leave Friday afternoon.

The morning of the trip, Owen stopped off at the grocery store to pick up extra batteries for his yellow Walkman tape player.

Dragging his beat-up, blue-gray suitcase to the office, he hauled it up the stairs, dropped it at his desk and went straight back to the test pit. He checked out the gold release discs.

"I'm giving you two," said Ryan, smirking, "because I know you're going to lose at least one."

Ryan and Owen walked toward Jarrod's office. As they passed Miles' room, Owen saw the door was propped open. The composer was inside, wearing his headphones, smiling and playing his synthesizer. Owen paused and knocked on the doorframe. Miles took off his headphones and smiled at Owen.

"What're you doing?" Owen asked.

"Remember that personal project from a few months back? I stopped working on it for a while, but I'm finishing it up now. What's up?" replied Miles.

"Oh, I just wanted to thank you. The score you wrote for this?" Owen held up one of the game discs. "It really makes the game."

"Thanks, man," Miles held out his hand.

Owen gladly shook it but was surprised when Miles pulled him in for a hug.

Just five minutes later Jarrod, Owen and Ryan all signed off on the final build. It was official. *Apoplexy II* was done.

The plan was for Viv to pick up Owen at noon and drive him to SFO for his five o'clock flight. A little after noon she called Owen's desk. She was sorry but felt too awful to drive him into the city.

Needing a ride, Owen glanced around the office and saw Dogg's face through his office window. The green glow from Dogg's monitor made him look a bit like a huge, hairy space alien.

Owen knocked on Dogg's door and it opened. "I know it's a lot to ask, but Viv isn't feeling well. Do you think you could drive me to SFO?"

Dogg stepped out, closed his office doors and took his keys from the lock.

"Let's go," he said.

They grabbed Owen's suitcase and Stevie, jumped into the Jeep and headed south across the Golden Gate. Stevie chattered through much of the trip, but the conversation lulled as they hit traffic on Park Presidio Boulevard.

"I probably should've gone over to Richmond and then back over the Bay Bridge," thought Dogg out loud.

"It's fine. We'll make it in plenty of time," reassured Owen, "When's your wife coming back from Vermont?"

"A month ago," said Dogg, laughing a little. "But she was only back for a week. Monique's mom isn't..." Dogg paused and glanced in the rearview mirror at Stevie, "Well, it won't be long, so Monique is going to stay there a while. You do what you have to for your family."

"Yes, you do," agreed Owen.

"Still," mused Dogg. "I've been thinking about what Jenn said to me. You remember? At my welcome lunch?"

"I remember. She asked if you felt bad working for the military."

"That's right. I can't stop thinking about it. Maybe it's... maybe it's because Stevie got sick," said the big man, choking up. "You know, you always start a project with these grand plans. You get them all mapped out in your head, so you're absolutely sure about everything."

"Right," said Owen.

Dogg continued, "But did you ever stop and think that if your initial assumptions are wrong—even by a little, just the smallest possible amount—the error will grow and grow until it finally all comes crashing down? Do you see what I mean?"

"I understand the logic," Owen assured. "But I'm having a hard time coming up with any real-world examples. So, no."

"I'm probably just not expressing it right," said Dogg. "Maybe someday I'll be able to explain it better."

From then on, they drove in silence until it was time to say goodbye at the International Terminal. Stevie jumped out of the back seat, hugged Owen and happily took his place in the front seat. Owen waved goodbye as they drove away.

For the first time in as long as he could remember, Owen was on his own. He imagined himself as a romantic hero, a lone agent on a dangerous mission to deliver important data to a contact in Europe. He walked into the terminal, thinking, "Let the adventure begin!"

CHAPTER THIRTY-ONE
BY PLANE TO HELSINKI

September 18, 1994
Amsterdam, The Netherlands

Owen landed in the Netherlands and was scheduled to stay the night in the city before flying to Helsinki the next day. At SFO, he had exchanged 100 dollars for Dutch guilders and 400 U.S. for Finnish markkas. Before taking a taxi from Schiphol Airport to his hotel, he crammed the money and his passport into his new anti-theft travel wallet, which he stealthily wore around his neck and under his shirt.

He had tried to fit at least one of the *Apoplexy II* gold discs inside the wallet, but the inflexible protective CD cases made it impossible, so he left one disc in his suitcase and kept the other in the oversized front pocket of his heavy green jacket.

The taxi dropped him near his hotel. As he walked to his lodging, he saw a man approach. Owen's paranoia ran high. Was he after the game?

The strange man drew nearer, keeping his head and eyes down. His voice was low and deep. Owen couldn't understand the words, so he assumed the man spoke in Dutch. He gripped the handle of his suitcase tightly. It wasn't until minutes later that Owen's brain deciphered the sounds. The man had been speaking English.

"Hah-sheesh," the man had chanted, musically, "Co-caeeen. Hah-sheesh. Co-caeeen."

Owen sounded it out. He'd been offered drugs! It pleased him immensely. He'd been in Europe for less than an hour and already he had a colorful travel story to tell the team back in California.

His hotel sat at the corner of a picturesque square in the canal-filled city center. Not wishing to waste a moment of his limited tourist time, Owen checked in, hid the game discs under the mattress and left to explore his environs.

The tall, narrow, multi-story homes of Amsterdam were as lovely as his guidebook advertised. It was as if someone had taken the best houses of San Francisco, squished in their sides a bit and then moved them onto flat islands.

Initially, the novelty of Owen's situation felt intoxicating. The day held no milestones, no due dates and no discernable responsibilities. He was free to go anywhere and do anything he chose.

But the longer he wandered, the more ill at ease Owen became. Usually, work kept his days highly structured. This gave him defined targets and goals. But what were the goals of sightseeing? What was the desired outcome? Perhaps he should create a list of important local sites he should visit. Instead, Owen wandered the canals, passing by beautiful boats and bridges and ignoring the men relieving themselves into the canal water.

He couldn't help but feel that had Viv come, she'd have led him to find the city's soul and not just the sleazy veneer of its tourist center. Owen was pretty certain he wasn't getting an authentic Dutch experience.

He felt like a Hollander judging America by walking the Las Vegas strip. This was the land of tulips and diamonds, the country that produced the genius of Vermeer and Van Gogh, the exotic intrigue of Mata Hari and the optimism and bravery of Anne Frank. Owen saw none of it.

"I know less about Finland than I do about Holland," he thought, "I'm really going to need a guide."

Owen flew to Helsinki the following day. Viv had made him a mix-tape for the trip. On the cassette's label, she'd drawn her trademark cartoon rat, hugging a heart.

Popping the tape into his Walkman he listened to the first song. It was Billy Joel's uncharacteristically psychedelic, 'Scandinavian Skies." Owen listened to it repeatedly while he looked down from his window seat on views of Denmark, Sweden and finally Finland.

The flight felt surprisingly quick and after a short taxi ride, Owen and his trusty suitcase were installed in a third-floor room at the Hilton Helsinki Strand. He immediately pulled back the room's curtains and was pleased to find a harbor view.

Clicking open the latches of his suitcase, he looked for the gold discs.

"Oh God," he thought, flinging his clothes onto the bed "Did I leave them in Amsterdam?"

One of his shirts fell to the floor. There was the faint sound, the clack of a plastic CD case landing on thin carpet. Owen remembered. He'd wrapped the discs in his clothes to hide them from potential CD-ROM thieves. It seemed a little silly now, but he felt a little proud. He'd brought the discs safely to Finland.

Risking the exorbitant hotel fees, Owen made two calls from his in-room phone. He first called *Kopio*, the disc manufacturer, to remind them that he'd soon arrive with *Apoplexy II*.

Then he took out his wallet and removed a tattered business card. It read, "Astrid Hahl, *'Pelit Magazine'*" followed by her phone number and email address.

Owen dialed and let the phone ring 10 times. He gave up and lowered the receiver. He was an inch away from hanging up when he heard a woman's voice say, "Tässä on Astrid Hahl hei." He jerked the handset up, accidentally letting it slip from his hand. It bounced on the floor. Then Owen struggled for a moment with the tangled phone cable before successfully returning it to his ear.

"Hei?"

"Hello, Astrid. Yes," fumbled Owen, "This is Owen Nickerson from Coliseum Arts."

Astrid switched to English without missing a beat. "Hello, Owen."

Owen paused a moment, waiting to see if Astrid would say more. She didn't. It was quiet on the other end. There wasn't even any office noise.

"Yes, I'm actually here in Helsinki," he said.

"Really?" she asked.

"Yes, I'm dropping off our game CDs to the disc duplicator today. I thought that afterward, we might get coffee since I'm in town."

"Instead, why don't I drive you to the factory and then we can get coffee?" suggested Astrid.

"I don't want to mess up your day," said Owen, putting up an intentionally weak argument.

"Is there a specific time you need to be there?"

"No. Whenever," he replied.

"Your hotel?"

"Helsinki Strand."

"OK. Be downstairs in 10 minutes and I will pick you up."

Five minutes later, Owen entered the porte-cochere. To his surprise, he found Astrid waiting in her car, a tiny blue Opel Astra. He opened the passenger door and ducked in, wondering why all European cars were so damned small.

"Hello," he said to Astrid. As before, the contrast between her pale blue eyes and jet-black hair stunned him.

"Hei," she said, "You're sitting on the map to Kopio."

He had noticed. Planting his feet firmly on the floor while pressing his shoulders against the seatback, he shifted his hips forward, enabling him to free the Helsinki city map.

"Thank you for taking me," said Owen after a few minutes of driving.

"Not a problem," she said, heading east towards the city of Espoo.

"How is your article coming?"

"The software-cracking article? Good," replied Astrid. "I'm still working on it. Right now, actually."

"Oh?"

"Yes," she said casually. "I saw Flexx last night."

"Really? No way. OK... and..." Owen prompted.

"I watched him download your new game, *Apoplexy II*."

"He did what?!" asked Owen, accidentally crushing the map in his hands.

CHAPTER THIRTY-TWO

AN INSIDE JOB

"I watched Flexx download your new, unreleased game," said Astrid, then she corrected herself. "Actually he didn't download it. Someone uploaded it to his computer."

This technical detail seemed minor, but it made a huge difference to Owen. It switched his emotional state from surprise to anger.

"Who uploaded it? Who gave it to him?"

She continued, "Flexx said he had a contact inside Coliseum Arts. Around midday here, Flexx set up a server. Someone connected and sent over the game."

"Are you sure it was the full game and not just the demo? Sometimes Jarrod leaves a demo version for people to download from our marketing computer."

Owen tried to convince himself he hadn't been betrayed by a member of his own team.

"It was the full game," she confirmed. "Flexx verified it."

"Did he say who sent it?"

"Just 'someone from inside Coliseum Arts'," Astrid replied.

Owen's motions became twitchy. He felt trapped in the little car. Had he been anywhere else there would have been swearing and the punching of inanimate objects. His physical reactions restrained, Owen worked to derive the leaker's identity.

Dogg had access to the release version of *Apoplexy II*, but he arrived at the company long after Flexx got his hands on *Peacemaker*. He also had top-secret clearance from the U.S. government, which had to count for something. Mitch and Miles didn't have the permissions to access the game. Any version Cole might have would be months old, buggy and incomplete. Ryan did control the access to all the test discs, so it was possible he could've sent the game to Flexx. Despite this, Owen couldn't bring himself to suspect Ryan. He'd been with the company too long and just didn't seem the type.

Owen's best guess was Jenn. While not disliked, she didn't seem to be close to anyone at the company and, as one of the programmers, she had access to the full game. She had also joined the company immediately before Flexx got his hands on *Peacemaker*. The question then was, "Why?" Did Flexx offer her money? Jenn didn't seem to need it. In December she'd rented a big, beautiful home in Mill Valley.

During the remainder of the drive, Owen sat, silently searching for a solution to the puzzle. It ate at his mind like a bug in his code.

Owen and Astrid arrived at the disc-duplicating factory, where Owen signed over the gold release discs. The factory manager offered them a walking tour of the facility. It would have been rude to decline, so they accepted. They saw molten aluminum injectors, robot arms, clean rooms and workers in white contamination-proof "bunny suits."

Ordinarily, such a display of technology would've been as exciting to Owen as a great science fiction movie. But although his body was present during the walk, his mind was entirely absent. He needed to do something about the theft of his game, but couldn't even come up with a plan. He wanted to talk to Jarrod, but the 10-hour time difference between Helsinki and San Rafael meant that his friend would sleep for several hours yet. As they walked the factory, Owen's stress built until, finally, he had to tell his hosts that he felt unwell and needed to return to the hotel.

In true Finnish style, the manager hid his disappointment and thanked Owen for his visit and his business.

During the drive back to Helsinki, Owen asked Astrid if there were any Internet cafes nearby. Very pleased, Astrid replied, "Our first just opened downtown, very near your hotel."

"Great, I can send Jarrod an email after dinner."

Astrid suggested a restaurant with traditional Finnish cuisine and Owen agreed. He was relieved to receive the invitation. He'd been so quiet and taciturn the whole afternoon that he was afraid he had alienated Astrid. In fact, she hadn't noticed.

Over a dinner of fish, meatballs, cheese and marinated reindeer, Astrid began asking questions. Or was she making statements?

"Your games are violent. Why?" Astrid's pale eyes flashed at him from under her jet bangs.

"Are you asking as a reporter?"

"Yes, always as a reporter," answered Astrid.

"You cover games. You know that most games have at least some violence," Owen replied, not feeling threatened.

"Many games are violent, yes," replied Astrid. "But yours are…very much so."

"It's all in service to the story of the world. Nothing is gratuitous. We didn't add anything just because we thought of some cool, new way to kill a non-player character. Each NPC has a history. The locations and weapons belong in the game universe," said Owen, aware of how good this answer might sound in a magazine article. "At Coliseum Arts, we are storytellers, just not traditional, linear ones."

He continued, "A movie director or novelist wants to control everything about how an audience experiences a story. They're like dictators, in charge of the pacing, the camera position, everything. In good interactive stories, the game designer collaborates with the player. We can set up the universe, its rules and its goals. But the player doesn't *have* to do what we ask."

"Do we let them kill innocents in the game? Sure. But that's a choice they make. Is Stevie Masters evil? Some will play him that way, undoubtedly. Some won't. If I don't give players the freedom to make their own choices, I'm not playing to the strength of the interactive medium."

Owen paused, allowing Astrid the opportunity to speak, which she took.

"We will act under the assumption that you are an artist…" she said.

"OK. I do," Owen sneaked in between clauses.

"…and most artists have a message, even if the message is that they refuse to have a message. What is the message in your art? What is its point?"

"If I give it a message, I take away the player's ability to create meaning," he said. Owen thought this concise sentence summarized his position very well.

Astrid responded flatly, "You create the sets and props, but the player is the director?"

"Yes, exactly like that!" Owen was happy that she understood.

"I see," she said without emotion, "the player brings the deeper meaning. They are artists."

"Yes!" Owen responded with excitement.

"So your work, the work of the game designer, is similar to that of the man who makes the canvases for painters?" Astrid asked.

"No!" Owen contradicted. "Game designers make artistic choices, too."

"I see. So it's more like you're providing pictures to a collagist," she concluded.

"It's a bit like that, yes" Owen felt she was getting the gist, but coming at it from an odd angle.

She continued to work through her idea, "And the pictures you're supplying to your artists are of mass murder, wounded human bodies and torture. It's from this that you ask them to make art. Why not give them nicer images to choose from?"

"What? Build a game around people helping each other? That sounds gripping," replied Owen sarcastically.

"Let me give you a few ideas for free. By using the same kind of aiming and shooting mechanic, couldn't you let your players create paintings, dig tunnels, carve sculptures or grow flower gardens? You don't think you could build such a game and make it fun?"

"Maybe, but it'd be much more difficult to program," Owen said lamely. He felt a twinge of frustration, but Astrid remained placid.

"So these games are too hard for you to make?" she asked. This stung his alpha-programmer ego.

"Of course it's not too hard! It's just not what I'm interested in," he growled, staring down at his half-eaten salmon. Owen was getting sick of fish.

"You are interested in the killing, then? That is your artistic message?"

"I'm interested in giving people who feel powerless the sensation of being strong," said Owen intensely.

"It occurs to me that many of the world's greatest calamities are caused by weak men who pick up weapons to make themselves feel strong," replied Astrid impassively.

"If your article in *Pelit* is going to be anti-violence in games, I think you're going to have plenty of your readers writing in angry letters to the editor," said Owen, hoping to end the conversation.

"I don't just write for games magazines," she replied. "*Pelit* gave me the business cards for the Computer Game Developers Conference. I also do freelance stories for other magazines and newspapers. Mostly, I do criminal reporting."

This reminded Owen that a criminal had stolen his game.

"Can I ask again about Flexx? Is there anything else you can tell me about how he got my game?"

"I've told you all I know," she said.

"Then could you ask him for more information? Just a few questions? For me?"

Astrid squinted her pale eyes, contemplating the request.

"What could it hurt?" Owen pleaded. "Either he tells you something or he doesn't."

Astrid made up her mind and answered, "I will call him. Perhaps I will have more information for you tomorrow."

CHAPTER THIRTY-THREE

FLEXX

September 20, 1994
Helsinki, Finland

Astrid dropped Owen at his hotel and he went straight to bed. Groggy from jetlag, he failed to inform Jarrod that Flexx had cracked yet another Coliseum Arts game.

He also forgot to close his hotel room's curtains and at 6 a.m. it filled with the bright, diffuse light of Finland's late-summer sun. There would be no getting back to sleep.

As long as he was up, Owen decided to breakfast at the hotel's buffet. Wearing the previous day's outfit, he descended to the first-floor restaurant. Most of the food was not to his American taste. There were many offerings for Nordic and English travelers, including cold fish options, black pudding, stewed tomatoes, muesli and yogurt. He avoided these. Instead, he filled his plate with pork sausage and breakfast potatoes.

Having no one with whom to talk, Owen finished breakfast quickly and was back in his room less than half an hour later. He closed the curtains and turned on the television just to have some background noise while he showered and dressed.

For several hours he lay on top of the bed, fully clothed and rapidly changing channels with the remote control. He stopped on a European sports channel to watch what initially looked like baseball. It took him some time to realize that it wasn't baseball, but a strange Finnish variant called Pesäpallo.

In Pesäpallo, the pitcher stands next to the batter, throwing the ball straight up in the air, attempting to land it on an oversized home plate.

The batter tries to hit the ball into the field of play and when successful, runs the bases, but in a zigzag pattern, first left, then right, left again and finally back to home.

Supremely confused by this "alternate reality" pastime, Owen left the TV set on but stared at the ceiling and zoned out. For how long, he couldn't say.

The room phone's aggressive electronic ring shocked him out of his trance. He grabbed the handset and pulled it to his ear.

"Hello, Owen," said Astrid. "I have some good news. Well, it might be good news, I don't know. It's up to you"

This confused Owen nearly as much as Pesäpallo.

"I spoke with Flexx and he wants to meet you," she said.

"Great. Can I call him now?"

"He said he wants to meet in person. If he doesn't receive an answer within 10 minutes, Flexx will withdraw his offer."

Owen was concerned, "What do you think I should do?"

"That's up to you," replied Astrid, "and how much you want to know who stole your game. My own opinion... he's just a computer hacker. He's not dangerous."

"OK. Tell him I'll come."

They hung up and Owen paced the room. Fifteen minutes later, Astrid called back. She had her instructions and was on her way to pick him up. Soon the blue Opel Astra pulled up in front of the Helsinki Strand. Owen slid inside.

Immediately, he asked, "Do you think we should tell the police?"

Without glancing at Owen, Astrid pulled out into traffic. She asked, "Why the police?"

"If the police arrested Flexx, they could force him into revealing who leaked the game," he answered.

"I'm a journalist. I can't give up my sources," she said earnestly. "I also think the police have bigger crimes to solve than 'The Case of the Stolen Videogame.' You understand?"

"Where are we going?" he asked.

"Laajasalo," replied Astrid. "It's an island, not very far away. We're going to the Kruunuvuorenranta villas."

"That's a mouthful. Is it nice?"

"It was once. Germans bought the area before World War I. The villas are old mansions. After World War II they became headquarters for Soviet and Finnish communists. Now they're abandoned."

They passed over three bridges to reach Laajasalo. A few minutes later, they turned west onto a side road. Astrid swung her car around in a U-turn then pulled to the roadside. Owen looked around. Nothing. To the left of the car was a barren, rock-covered construction site, to the right a steep embankment of rock and dirt.

"Here we are. I hope you're ready for a hike," said Astrid.

"I don't see any villas," said Owen.

"They are up the hill. Come on," Astrid responded, climbing the slope.

Astrid moved efficiently and quickly up the embankment but Owen had a more difficult time. His greater weight displaced more dirt, causing small rockslides that carried him back downhill. And while Owen was naturally athletic, his sedentary programmer lifestyle had left him somewhat out of shape. He reached the top of the ridge panting and ready for a rest. Astrid gave him a minute to enjoy the view of Helsinki Harbor and the ships passing by. Then she disappeared into the woods. Owen hurried to catch up.

The forest was dense, its trees tall. After just a few steps Owen and Astrid found that the thick canopy of branches blocked most of the harsh, Finnish sunlight. Owen shivered. He'd only worn jeans and a T-shirt. Astrid was better prepared, wearing low-heeled boots, slacks and a gray V-neck sweater over her long-sleeved, white blouse.

A carpet of leaves covered the uneven ground and a soft green moss grew on all sides of each tree. Soft, bushy green plants brushed their feet and ankles. The ground cover provided so little traction that both hikers stumbled more than once. They heard the sound of the wind and the crunch of the needles beneath their feet.

Once there had been walking trails here, even streets. But that had been 40-years before. Of the walkways, nature had left no trace. Astrid took the lead. They did little speaking, focusing instead on maintaining their balance in the uneven terrain.

After ten minutes of hiking, Owen started to wonder if they'd come to the right place. They'd found nothing. He decided to risk some conversation, "How long have the villas been here?"

"Some since 1914. Some since the early '50s," Astrid said, stopping. She took a deep breath and then straightened up. "Here's one."

Astrid made a sweeping gesture with her right hand and then, out of breath, bent over, placing both hands on her knees. Owen looked ahead at the decaying edifice that had popped up out of nowhere. He supposed it must have been grand at one time. Now it looked like a haunted house stomped by a giant.

As underwhelming as the first villa was, the excitement of the discovery gave Owen a rush of energy. He hurried forward to explore the long-abandoned house.

The villa had once been a huge mansion, with two stories and an attic. At one time it could have been the home of a Nazi officer or Russian kommissar. Long ago, the exterior paint had peeled away, leaving the gray and decaying wood unprotected from the damp forest environment. Eventually, the water had penetrated the roof.

When the winters came, the water froze and expanded, cracking the house at its seams. Year after year the ice shoved the beams farther apart, inviting more water and creating more ice. During the warm months, mold ate at the floors and walls. A violent windstorm had torn a heavy bough from a tree and brought it crashing down on the roof's center. The impact had splintered the rotting timbers, almost cutting the house in half.

Owen approached the entrance, gingerly placing his foot on the stair of the front porch. The plank creaked ominously as he trusted it with his weight.

"This isn't the one," Astrid called.

Carefully lifting his foot back off the stair, Owen followed her around the back of the house and up the hill behind. They passed many more villas. Some were so decayed they barely looked like human artifacts. Owen imagined they'd make good homes for trolls.

Other villas appeared more livable, but still missed windowpanes and crucial internal support beams. Local graffiti artists had been at work, painting intricate murals of animals, people and stylized text. One house rested on its side rather than on its foundation but aside from this flaw, looked perfectly intact.

Owen and Astrid climbed higher, eventually reaching a small clearing. Here a rock and concrete stairway of 20 or 30 steps led to an enormous and relatively sound villa. Some of its decorative architecture still wore bright blue and yellow paint. It was three stories high with a gabled roof.

"This is it," Astrid announced.

The pair hurried up the concrete stairs to a wrap-around deck and double-door entrance to the house. The left-hand door couldn't be opened. The right could not be closed. They passed through and entered a sunlit great room.

The visitors paused, turning to take in the view through a long row of large windows. Forty years earlier they could have gazed out to the water and seen the cruise ships arriving at Helsinki's south harbor from the Gulf of Finland. Now massive trees blocked the vista.

Looking back into the house, they found it cluttered with dirt, leaves and old, broken vodka bottles. Mold crept up the house's walls, staining large areas of the ancient wallpaper black.

They left the great room, walking deeper into the house. Passing through an empty doorframe, they entered an inner room, with walls of dark, expensive hardwoods. This room's main feature was the huge formal staircase leading up to the second floor. From the balcony at its top, one could view every corner of the room below. It all smelled dank and musty.

Astrid gestured that Owen should lead the way.

"After you," she smiled.

"Thanks?" said Owen, wondering for the first time if he might be walking into a trap.

He climbed the stairs with Astrid not far behind. They reached the second floor and found the entrance to the master suite. The door was missing and they walked straight in. Heavy, rotting curtains still hung in front of the windows on a back wall that faced the overgrown mountain behind. This was the house's darkest room.

Owen heard a noise behind him. His heart raced as he spun around. It was only the sound of water dripping from a discolored patch of ceiling onto the rotten floorboards below.

"Hello!" said a friendly voice and Owen and Astrid jumped. There was a large figure standing in the darkness on the opposite side of the room.

"Hello, Flexx," replied Astrid quietly.

Flexx was taller than Owen by a couple of inches and at least 50 pounds heavier. His hair appeared dark brown, though it was hard to tell in the limited light. He wore a too-tight khaki T-shirt that accentuated the "table muscle" he had accumulated around the waist. Flexx tucked his camouflage army pants into his black, military boots and a sheath on his belt held a commando-style combat knife. He appeared to be in his early 30s, but the hairs of his beard and mustache were wispy and soft. Behind him lay a gray rucksack.

Flexx rushed forward and Owen instinctively took a step back. But it was no attack. Flexx only sought to shake Astrid's hand.

"So nice to see you again," Flexx grinned as he greeted the reporter. "I had no idea we'd be meeting again so soon!"

Flexx spoke a mile a minute but his English was excellent. His accent differed from Astrid's.

"Russian, maybe. He's not a Finn," thought Owen.

Then Flexx shook Owen's hand.

"And you're Owen Nickerson! I am such a huge fan of your games. I played the *Hell* out of *Apoplexy*. I mean I played the holy Hell out of it! I can't believe you guys came all the way out here. I mean obviously, I couldn't meet you at my place but it is such a pleasure. Hell yeah, it is!"

The hacker really emphasized each "Hell".

Flexx walked back to his pack and knelt. "I've got some granola bars in my bag here if you want them," he said, pulling out two green packages.

Neither Owen nor Astrid spoke. They just held out their hands and Flexx handed each a bar. In seconds the snacks were eaten. The food made Owen feel much better. He got up the energy to speak, but what came out was somewhat unimpressive.

"Thanks."

"Yes, well. Nice to meet you. Let's all sit," said the hacker. He dropped cross-legged to the dirty floor. Astrid and Owen followed suit.

Flexx continued, "So, what would you like to talk about?"

Owen furrowed his brow and looked sideways at Astrid. She glanced at him, reading his thoughts.

Astrid spoke loudly and clearly, "As I mentioned on our call today, Owen was interested in learning about how you cracked his latest game."

"Oh, what? *Apoplexy II*?" Flexx said, looking as if he'd been asked to kick a puppy. "I can't talk about that. That wouldn't be right. You understand."

"You told Astrid that you got it from someone inside Coliseum Arts?" said Owen, feeling a little braver.

"That was off the record," said Flexx.

"No, it wasn't, Flexx," said Astrid in a pleasantly feminine voice. "Remember at the start I told you everything was on the record?"

Flexx looked sheepish, "Yeah, yeah, yeah. OK, Astrid. You got me."

He turned to Owen, "Isn't she amazing? Those eyes. Am I right?"

In his heart, Owen knew he was right.

"Astrid. My darling. You know I would do anything for you and yes, that was on the record, but..." he paused for emphasis, "...but that's it. I can't give you anything more. Owen Nickerson? Can I ask

in his belt. He pivoted into a target shooter's stance, arm outstretched and gun sights aimed at Owen.

Owen recognized its model because it was one of the weapons that appeared in *Apoplexy II*. A Colt military pistol, the M1911 .45 semi-automatic. But the game's version of the gun looked normal.

Even in the darkened room, Owen could see that Flexx's .45 was over-the-top. The pistol was bright, gleaming silver and covered in gold inlaid etchings. The etchings were ornate but Owen couldn't make them out in detail. Confidently, Flexx held the gun by its shining mother-of-pearl handle, his index finger wrapped around the trigger.

"You will sign the discs now," said Flexx, unsmiling. "For the first one, make it say 'To Alvar, From Owen Nickerson.'"

The cracker kept the gun aimed at Owen, who slowly moved to the rucksack to sign the discs.

"Make the second one for me and you make it a real autograph. No jokes. No 'Screw you, Flexx. Love Owen.' You think I won't shoot you? I have no problem shooting you," Flexx said.

Upon completing the assignment, Owen backed away.

"Thank you!" sang Flexx, jamming the gun back into his pants. He zipped up and shouldered his rucksack, then strode from the room with only a glance backward. Owen heard Flexx walking and then running out of the mansion.

Astrid caught her breath, "*Paskiainen*! I'm sorry, Owen. If I'd known how psychotic he was, I'd never have brought you here."

"We'll talk about it later," Owen growled. He left the room and peered over the balcony. Flexx was gone. Astrid and Owen hurried from the decayed house and back down toward the Opel. As Astrid drove back to downtown Helsinki, both she and Owen continually swiveled their heads, looking for fresh signs of danger.

When Astrid dropped Owen at his hotel, she said, "You must let me make this up to you, please. Let me show you around Helsinki tomorrow. You leave the next day, yes?"

Owen rubbed his throbbing temples. He didn't want to think or have a discussion. He just wanted to get to his hotel room. Accepting the invitation, he turned quickly and headed for the hotel elevator.

"Sorry, Jarrod, but I'm expensing this," thought Owen, as he ordered a multi-dish, $60 room service meal. He ate the food without tasting it.

At eight o'clock, the sun went down. Owen was tired, so he showered, climbed into bed and rubbing his eyes, turned out the light. Ten hours later, he was still awake.

CHAPTER THIRTY-FOUR

HOW TO SWEAR IN FINNISH

September 21, 1994
Helsinki, Finland

The sun was up at 6:15. Owen's eyes cracked open and he sighed. He committed himself to leave the previous day's craziness behind and enjoy a normal, touristy day in Helsinki. He dressed in his 'nicer clothes' – which meant wearing a shirt with buttons and a collar—and shuffled down for his travel breakfast of sausage and potatoes.

Picking up a complimentary English language newspaper, he sat down to wait in an overstuffed chair. Still tired, he rested his eyes.

"Wake up," Owen heard Astrid say. "Owen, wake up."

She gently shook his shoulder.

"Was I asleep? Oh, I feel so much better," said Owen aloud. "What time is it?"

"It's about eleven," she said. "Do you still want to go for a walk?"

"Absolutely," replied Owen, wiping his mouth with his jacket sleeve.

They left the hotel and walked along the waterfront for a time then wandered through the streets toward the Helsinki Market Square. As they strolled, the pair happened upon Helsinki's new Internet café. Owen went in and paid for network access with a few Finnish markka bills. Dashing off an email to Jarrod, he detailed all he'd learned about the leak of their new game. While the information was limited, incomplete and probably unhelpful, sending the message helped Owen feel that he had someone with whom he could share his troubles.

Owen looked at Astrid and noticed her worried expression.

"Do you want to talk about yesterday?" he asked.

"Some," Astrid answered, "but not really. I'm Finnish."

"I understand," Owen smiled, "but for the sake of conversation, can we pretend you're American?"

"Oh, my Lord, no," she deadpanned. "Well, maybe we could."

Astrid cleared her throat and adopted a terrible, faux-American accent, incorporating bits of Texan, New Yorker and SoCal surfer. She said, "Well, I reckon we'd go on down ta thuh monstah truck rallee. Woo-ee! Yo! Hulk Hogan for president!"

Owen appraised her impression, "Very nice. I'm convinced. So, Miss America, shall we talk?"

"Yes?"

"What happened yesterday?"

"Yesterday. We went for a walk in a dark forest where we found a witch's house and inside there was an evil troll," she said.

She tried making a scary monster face, but to Owen, it just looked cute. Then Astrid was serious again, "I didn't know that would happen. He just seemed like a programmer."

Owen knew what she meant. "Harmless?" he said.

"Yes, harmless," she agreed. "To me, he was just a big fool who probably lived in his mother's basement and liked to play videogames."

"Stereotypes!" Owen faux yelled. "The language of hate!"

"Sorry, Owen," Astrid continued. "I didn't mean to imply that you're harmless."

"I'd like to think I'm harmless, but I'm probably not," Owen said, thinking of his burned-out team back in San Rafael.

"I made a mistake. Flexx isn't like you at all," Astrid interrupted. "He doesn't create anything. He just steals. And if he had stolen anything else, such as cars, furs, jewels, copper wire, or bricks even, I never would have taken you to him. But he stole with a computer, you know. But he's a real criminal and I treated him like he was a creampuff."

Owen said, "I don't get it either. He gives the software away. Why? He doesn't get anything out of it."

"Of course he does," Astrid reached out and grabbed Owen by the arm. He stopped and looked down at her hand.

Astrid continued, "Flexx gets a lot out of stealing games. Don't you see? He gets the credit that you and your team deserve, without expending any effort. When someone launches his version of the game, what's the first thing they'll see? 'Cracked by Flexx.' Thousands of people on bulletin boards around the world will thank Flexx for his great work. They'll treat him like a hero. He's just a lazy leech. But on the Internet, he's a rock star. And I'd be surprised if software cracking isn't the only crime he commits."

"He's an oversized version of the script codez kiddies," Owen said.

Astrid turned. She had a sour look on her face. She asked, "Is that supposed to be an insult?"

Owen nodded. He'd heard Mitch use it a few times about wannabe hackers who wanted respect but had no actual ability.

"Oh, no. I'm sorry but that's pathetic," she exclaimed. "I'm going to have to teach you to swear."

"You're going to teach me to swear?"

"Damn right, because that was so terrible," Astrid said seriously. "OK. Say after me. *Hevonpaska!*"

Enthusiastically, Owen repeated the swear word, "What does it..."

"Shut up. Next bad word. *Perkele!*"

"*Perkele!*"

Owen said this a bit too loud and a group of nearby Finnish schoolchildren turned, looking shocked.

"Hevonpaska," Astrid muttered under her breath. She told Owen, "You're doing great. *Paskiainen!*"

"*Paskiainen!* What does that one mean?" he asked, making sure the kids had moved on.

"That one means 'bastard'," answered the reporter. "That's a good one. Remember it. Can you use it in a sentence?"

Owen thought a moment and came up with an appropriate phrase, "Flexx is a Paskiainen!"

"Perfect," said Astrid. "Now you won't embarrass me."

They walked on, past several large buildings, topped with green copper roofs.

"Do you like videogames?" asked Owen.

"A little," she said. "Sometimes I play them for my job."

"Have you played any of my games?"

She paused a moment before replying.

"Yes. I don't like them," she said. "Sometimes the art is good."

"Is it the violence you don't like?"

Astrid spoke openly, "Yes. I do not think violence is fun. For some, perhaps, it is fun, but I don't find it so. I've taken many self-defense courses. They were for protection only, not for sport."

They crossed the Senate Square in front of Helsinki Cathedral, a huge white building with Romanesque columns and a large central copper dome surround by four smaller domes, each adorned with golden stars.

"You've covered murders?" Owen asked.

"Yes, of course."

"Well, what's different between game violence and when you describe a murder?"

Astrid looked down at her feet and composed her answer. "Intent, I think. A murder story exposes an existing ugliness. It doesn't create a new one."

For once, Owen didn't have a pat counter-argument.

By now they'd entered Market Square by the water's edge. Vendors sold crab, fresh fish, reindeer hides, hand-carved wooden cups and toys, including dolls of Sámi children, each in brightly colored clothing.

The market sold all manner of fried food. Out of respect to Astrid, Owen ordered a mixture of Helsinki specialties along with a few more familiar items. He devoured the fresh onion rings but mostly just poked at the fish dishes.

They walked, ate and spoke pleasantly for most of the afternoon, leaving Owen feeling concerned that the outing felt like a date. Was this cheating on Viv? He eased his minimal guilt by comparing the excursion to exploring Las Vegas with Jarrod. The only real difference between the two was that, in this case, Jarrod was a beautiful girl from Finland.

Eventually leaving the square, they explored the towering Eastern Orthodox Uspenski Cathedral, with its gold-capped spires, red stonework and impressive, oxidized domes.

For a few hours, they forgot the awful experience of the previous day and enjoyed the afternoon, eventually returning to the hotel. Astrid kissed him on the cheek and said goodbye.

The next day Owen's flight would take him to Copenhagen, where he would spend three nights, followed by three nights in London and then a plane home. He turned up the heat full blast, requested a wake-up call and climbed into bed. As he fell asleep, he felt deeply grateful that he was safe.

CHAPTER THIRTY-FIVE

FREE RIDE

September 22, 1994
Helsinki, Finland

In the morning, the phone awakened Owen, but it wasn't the hotel's front desk. It was Astrid.

"I want to give you a ride to the airport," she said.

Owen gave token resistance, replying that she needn't go out of her way, but she insisted.

This time there was no blue Opel Astra. In its place was a long, black stretch limousine. The tinted back window was rolled down halfway, revealing Astrid's face. She waved to Owen and the window closed. A hotel bellman stepped forward to help with Owen's bag, but the limo's chauffeur jumped out of the driver's seat and waved him away. The driver opened the car's rear door and ushered the American into the back seat.

"Astrid, this is too much," said Owen, grinning as he slid into the car.

The door shut. He looked at Astrid. She was not smiling. Owen turned his head, looking towards the front of the car. Two long bench seats ran parallel to the limousine's sides, ending at the roll-up partition that separated passenger from driver. A duo of large men sat opposite each other on the benches, both aimed black pistols at Owen's heart. He recognized the guns as Glock Gen 1 Model 20s, a type he'd used in his first *Apoplexy* game. One of the gunmen put a finger to his lips and said, "Shhhhh."

Soon they were moving, although to where Owen couldn't tell. There was no sightseeing through the car's blackened windows. They drove for 45 minutes.

For the life of him, Owen couldn't figure out why they'd been kidnapped. He had no money, no valuable game discs, no important information.

When the car door opened, the glare of the overcast day blinded its occupants. A meaty hand reached in and pulled Owen out by his jacket. Astrid followed and the kidnappers walked close behind. Before his eyes adjusted, Owen heard seagulls, smelled the ocean and felt wooden boards beneath his feet.

He squinted to take in the whole scene. The three, armed men pushed Astrid and Owen down a long, abandoned pier, the end of which had crumbled into the sea.

Docked at the last undamaged portion of the pier bobbed a fishing boat, perhaps 60 feet long. A bearded crew of five manned the vessel. One of these set out a gangplank and helped Owen, Astrid and the two gunmen aboard. Owen looked back and watched the chauffeur walk back down the pier toward the limo.

As the fishing boat pulled away from the mooring, the kidnappers forced Astrid and Owen below deck, placing them under guard in the galley. The prisoners sat on a curved bench that wrapped around a grimy, partially delaminated table.

The sea was heavy and the boat moved at top speed, which caused the vessel to rise and fall violently. Over and over, waves lifted the ship high in the air only to drop it, crashing, into a watery depression on the far side. Owen and Astrid took turns vomiting into the galley's garbage can.

They traveled in enforced silence. The boat trip took the whole day and well into the night. That was when the large waves finally subsided.

The vessel reduced speed and the kidnappers brought the captives up on deck. To the port side they saw lights from a coastal city miles away. To the starboard was nothing but ocean. Looking ahead they saw a huge white yacht, glowing in the darkness.

The luxury craft dwarfed the fishing vessel. Owen guessed that the yacht's length was at least 300 feet. It had five decks, not counting the elevated bridge and lookout's walk. All lights were on, including dive lights. These shone down from the rear of the craft, turning the black water around the boat to a luminous light blue. At the front of the yacht sat a helicopter.

The fishing boat pulled alongside the larger ship and tied up. Large, inflatable orange balls hung from the side of the smaller vessel, preventing it from scraping its neighbor's hull.

The kidnappers hustled Owen and Astrid up a ladder and aboard the yacht. The prisoners glanced into the ship's living quarters. They were large and comfortable, full of plush furniture and gold accents. However, the pair would have no tour of the lavish ship. The thugs ushered their captives up two flights of steps and across to the sleek, black helicopter. Climbing aboard, they were ordered to the eighth and last row of seats. The two kidnappers sat across from them, guns out.

At the front of the copter, two pilots threw a few switches and started the engines. They lifted off and zoomed into the night sky. Owen barely had time to look down at the yacht and fishing boat before they disappeared from view.

"We must be in a hurry," said Owen, the first words he'd spoken to Astrid since their kidnapping.

"They broke into my apartment this morning and forced me to call," she said quickly. "I don't know what they want."

The flight would barely last 25 minutes. Soon they were flying over a large city with brightly lit, golden domes.

"St. Petersburg," said Astrid, stiffening a little. "We're landing in Russia."

They overshot the city center and landed at a dark airstrip, which was surrounded by chain-link fence and woods. Watching through the side window, Owen and Astrid had a good view of the Russian policeman who approached from his checkpoint at the heliport's security gate. One of the captors exited the craft.

He and the officer spoke briefly, then smiled and shook hands. The policeman motioned a midnight blue Rolls-Royce town car through the gate then walked back to his station.

As the car pulled alongside the helicopter, the gunmen escorted Owen and Astrid into its rear passenger seats. The larger kidnapper slid in as well, jamming the end of his gun into Astrid's side so she'd give him more room. The second kidnapper sat up front with the chauffeur.

Owen was not a connoisseur of luxury automobiles, but this one impressed him. The inside was full of dark hardwoods, gold-plated fixtures and blue leather seats. It was an exceptionally long sedan, but it accelerated smoothly and seemed to make no noise at all.

They pulled out onto an unlit country road. The driver hit a switch on the console and light bars, mounted above the front and rear windows began to flash red, white and blue. Owen wondered if this was a police car. He'd never had heard of a police Rolls-Royce, but he realized he knew next to nothing about Eastern Europe.

In any case, the flashers were overkill because there weren't any other drivers on the road. Less than ten minutes later they turned onto a narrow street bordered by tall green hedges. At a break in the hedges, the Rolls came to a security gate made of steel panels and wrought iron. It slid open with a click from the town car's remote control unit.

The car rolled up a winding driveway that traversed a lush, private garden, passing several large topiary animals, ornamental trees and manicured lawns. At a cobblestone turnabout, the kidnappers stopped, opened the car doors and gestured with their guns. This was the end of the line.

Owen slid out first, looked up and gasped. Astrid exited the car and stamped her sleeping foot. Then she noticed Owen's expression. Following his gaze, she raised her eyes and gaped. They stood before the most gigantic, ornate house either had ever seen.

From where they stood, the building appeared to have four stories, but it seemed likely more would be discernible were they to view the building from a distance. Hundreds of ornate, sculptures adorned the façade. These appeared to be painted gold, but might actually have been covered in gold leaf. Owen quickly counted the windows in one row of the house's front. He multiplied this by the number of stories, tallying 80 windows.

"I think the Tsar must live here," Astrid whispered.

Their keepers prodded them forward, through open entry doors and into a spectacular, marble-floored room. It was the design of the architect to draw visitors' eyes up to the vibrantly painted ceiling, where angels flew among gauzy clouds, surrounded by a border of gleaming gold. The abducted pair gazed in amazement, oblivious to the approaching figure until it was too late.

"Hello, asshole," sneered Flexx, throwing a fist into Owen's eye.

CHAPTER THIRTY-SIX

MIKHAIL

The hacker's sucker punch knocked Owen to the floor. Flexx moved forward to kick his downed opponent, but the two kidnappers intervened, pushing the man back. Flexx skulked away, surveying the room as if trying to find a way around Owen's bodyguards.

"What the hell is wrong with you?" yelled Astrid at the sullen criminal.

"His crap game is what's wrong," Flexx spat in an accusatory tone at Owen before throwing himself down into a chair that resembled King Henry VIII's throne. With his good eye, Owen noticed Flexx's rucksack on the floor beside the hacker.

From a long, wide hallway came the sound of footsteps. These announced the approach of Leonid Morozov and his partner, Dr. Ilizarov. Owen sized them up.

Ilizarov wore a camelhair coat over his dark blue shirt and pants. In his late 50s, the balding doctor wore spectacles and a thin, brown mustache.

Morozov was shorter and a few years younger. He was solidly built, like a barrel packed with muscle. His ruddy face stood out against his full head of snow-white hair and bushy eyebrows.

The men stopped as they entered the foyer, appraising Owen and Astrid. The shorter man looked at Flexx and asked him something in Russian. Flexx's short answer didn't satisfy and the man stepped forward, yelling threateningly.

Flexx pointed directly at Owen. "Yego!"

"You are the game designer?" asked Ilizarov, addressing Owen in Russian.

Astrid affirmed Owen's occupation. She asked if Ilizarov spoke

English.

"Of course," he replied, using Owen's native tongue. "I am Dr. Ilizarov."

"I'm Owen. Please. Can you tell us why we are here?"

"Yes, let's get right to that. Among other things, I am the Morozov family physician. Yesterday, my patient's uncle, Alvar, received your game as a gift," said Ilizarov. "He let Leonid's son, Mikhail, play it. But you see, Mikhail is a photosensitive epileptic. When he played the game, it triggered a seizure."

Owen rubbed his sore eye. He was aware that studies from the early 80s proved that certain videogames flashed light in patterns and rhythms that would trigger seizures in certain epileptics.

"And *how* do you know the game triggered the seizure?" said Owen, defensively.

Dr. Ilizarov glared at Owen, "Watch yourself, boy. The first seizure was small. A bodyguard saw Mikhail in the computer chair and gave him aid. But a couple of hours later, Mikhail went back and played again."

Owen scoffed, "If he's epileptic, he should've known to stop."

The thickly built man addressed Astrid in Russian, "You will tell your stupid friend to shut up and listen. I am Mikhail's father, Leonid Morozov."

"Owen," said Astrid, not looking away from Leonid. "Don't argue. Shut up and listen."

The doctor looked at Owen to see if he would interrupt again. When the young man did not, Ilizarov continued.

"Mikhail is a fit man. You know? Tough! He thought he would be all right the second time. He wanted to play the game, so he did. Come with me."

Following Ilizarov, they walked what felt like a quarter of a mile, down a hallway to the house's north wing. The doctor pushed open one of the hall's many 12-foot-high double doors. They entered an enormous bedroom, occupied by three medical attendants and a gigantic bodyguard. The technicians bent over a convulsing man on a canopied bed.

It was Mikhail. One of the attendants struggled to hold an IV drip in his arm. Every muscle in Mikhail's body contracted spasmodically. Suffering contorted his formerly perfect face. Drool rolled from his mouth through clenched teeth and he emitted a string of unpleasant grunting noises. The entire scene was horrific. Ilizarov pushed the visitors back out of the room.

"You don't understand," said Owen to the doctor. "If it really is the game that's causing the seizures, then all he has to do is stop playing."

"No, *you* don't understand," growled the agitated doctor. "He stopped playing the game 30 hours ago! The longest recorded epileptic seizure on record was 33 minutes. Mikhail has seized for more than a day!"

"But why did you bring us here?" said Owen, really trying to understand.

"It is your game," said Ilizarov with fury in his eyes. "I want you to tell me what it does and I want you to tell me right now."

"It could've been *any* game, not just *Apoplexy II*! Clearly, there's something broken in his brain," Owen said.

Ilizarov slapped his face. Raising his voice, the doctor spat at Owen, saying "No! No other game does this! Ever! Nothing in the world has ever done this! Now you tell me. What did your game do to Mikhail?"

Owen raised his voice back, "It doesn't do anything! It's just a…"

The programmer didn't get to finish his thought because a gun butt struck him on the side of the face. He fell to the marble. Leonid had turned loose the two goons who had kidnapped Owen and Astrid in Finland.

Leonid said in Russian, "Hurt him badly, but don't cripple him. Keep him conscious."

A boot caught Owen in the stomach. Then a fist pounded his face. In just a few seconds, the henchmen had left Owen sprawled on the marble, bleeding from the mouth and nose. Leonid bent down on one knee over the young man.

Leonid spoke, "That is my son in there and I hold you completely responsible. Now you tell me what your game does or I will kill both of you and no one will *ever* find your bodies!"

"OK," said Owen, gasping for breath. He struggled to get up and the bodyguards lifted him to his feet. "Show me the game. Maybe I can —have a look."

The thugs shoved him down the hall and into a spectacular office with high ceilings and a mammoth wooden desk. On the desk sat a big computer monitor. The attached computer rested in the generous leg space near the center of the desk.

Owen sat down, blood pouring off his chin. Leonid walked over and held out his handkerchief. The game designer flinched, bracing for a punch. Realizing the gesture wasn't an attack, he took the cloth and stanched the flow.

"Pussy," called Flexx. He stood against the wall, away from the rest of the group.

Owen could sense Flexx's unease. After all, Flexx had made a present of the game to Mikhail's uncle Alvar. How would such a gift be repaid?

Owen turned the silver security key in the computer tower to the 'unlock' position and pressed the power button. There was a heavy clunk and the computer's cooling fan spun up. He watched the text from the BIOS check flicker across the monitor.

He saw it was a 486/66 with plenty of memory and a built-in, quad-speed CD-ROM. Owen found this particularly impressive. He ejected the CD-ROM cartridge. Removing the disc, he found it had his autograph on it. He jammed the cartridge back into the computer.

Up popped the DOS prompt. Owen checked the autoexec.bat and config.sys. Both files were normal. Back at the command line, he typed:

C:\ColArts\Apop2.exe

This launched the game. Owen quickly cycled through the many menu screens. He checked the graphics and sound settings. Everything was set to best quality, which made sense for a game running on such a high-end multimedia machine. He left the settings screens and began the first level.

Owen felt ridiculous. He'd been kidnapped to play a computer game. *Apoplexy II* seemed fine, although he expected slightly better performance from a 66-megahertz machine. Owen played poorly and "died" quickly.

His head throbbed. Probably the result of having it kicked in.

Exiting the game he looked through the files on the CD. Again, it all looked good. He was about to give up when he noticed something wrong. There were two extra files in the root directory that should not have been there. He froze when he read the first filename.

DSASP4.dll

He tried not to show any reaction, but Owen's heart filled with suspicion and fear. He remembered. The filename stood for: "Dogg's Super Awesome Secret Project 4."

CHAPTER THIRTY-SEVEN
THE INTERROGATIONS

September 23, 1994
San Rafael, CA

Jarrod read Owen's email 14 hours after it had been sent, thanks to the 10-hour time difference coupled with the Coliseum Arts post-release hangover. No team member felt the need to show up at work first thing in the morning - not after racking up hundreds of hours of overtime.

Only Dogg continued his workmanlike schedule. He was in by nine.

The team's lackadaisical attitude had spread to Jarrod. That morning, he parked in the alley behind Coliseum Arts around ten-fifteen then walked down B Street to Muffin Mania where he grabbed coffee and a huge blueberry scone. Walking to the park, he sat on a bench and warmed his cold nose in the sun.

He could feel it was going to be a good day. Carrying his coffee cup back to the office, Jarrod cautiously stepped over Stevie, who lay on the floor with his coloring pages.

The CEO plopped down at the marketing computer and flipped it on. It was very slow compared to the newer machines in the office. Jarrod sipped his coffee while it booted.

The e-mail message at the top of his list was from Owen. The header read *"Apoplexy II Cracked."* All drowsiness gone, Jarrod opened the message and read its contents—twice.

He wanted to swear but remembered the artistically inclined six-year-old on the floor.

"What-the-fudge?!"

The businessman jumped up, leaped over the boy and ran to his office. There he closed the door and made a call. Mitch sat at his desk, playing Wolfenstein3D. The tools programmer couldn't make out any of the conversation's details, but Jarrod was definitely yelling at someone. Twenty minutes later the office door swung out again. Jarrod stormed to the test pit. He found Ryan alone, swapping out audio cards as part of ongoing driver compatibility testing. Ryan stood up as Jarrod entered.

"What can I do for you, boss?" asked the test lead.

"Are you missing any game discs?"

"No?"

"Are you sure?" Jarrod asked urgently.

"Yes," said Ryan with assurance.

"How about two days ago? Maybe three?"

Ryan stared directly into Jarrod's eyes.

"I've never lost control of any game discs during development, ever. Certainly not after code lock," Ryan said in a serious voice while maintaining his goofy thin smile.

"Maybe an older version?"

"I personally ruin all the old versions," said Ryan. He held up a house-key, the favored weapon of disc destroyers. "Why do you ask?"

"Someone leaked *Apoplexy II* two days ago. It was someone from inside the office!" Jarrod blurted.

"Dang, you caught me," said Ryan calmly. The words dazed Jarrod, who was searching for something to say.

Ryan continued, "I hate the human race so much, I wanted them all to play this crappy, crappy game. That's why I leaked it. Because it's so bad. It's the punishment the people deserve. They must suffer."

Ryan was as serious as an undertaker. He deadpanned so perfectly that the CEO missed the sarcasm. Jarrod stood silently, jaw open.

"C'mon! Why would I leak the game?" said Ryan. "It's not nearly good enough to leak. What do you think it is? *X-Com*?"

Jarrod turned and left the test pit, kicking himself. He realized Ryan didn't have anything to do with the leak and was far too capable to let someone steal a disc, even for a few minutes.

The CEO looked around the art room. A pixel artist was working on some color-reduced backgrounds. Nearby an art-tech chatted on the phone.

Viv hadn't come in yet. Since the game shipped, she'd only been in the office for a few hours, here and there. Jarrod felt stupid even considering Viv.

But thinking of her gave Jarrod a different idea. What about Miles? Before Owen and Viv had become a couple, Miles' crush on the young artist had been obvious. And since the Developers Conference, there had been definite tension between Miles and Owen. Perhaps Miles had wanted to hurt Owen by denying him royalties.

Lost in thought, Jarrod stared blankly into the artist's room, remaining motionless for at least a minute. He snapped out of it and poked his head into Miles' darkened office. Empty.

Jarrod entered the programmer room where he finally found a reasonable target. Regaining a little confidence, he swaggered to Mitch's desk.

"Someone leaked *Apoplexy II*," said Jarrod, coolly. Mitch didn't respond. He simply kept blasting Nazis. "Do you have something to say about that, Mitch?" Again, Mitch kept playing his game.

Jarrod screamed, "Mitch! Did you leak the game?"

Mitch finally noticed Jarrod. The programmer removed his headphones, allowing muffled Wolf3D game noises to fill the room.

"Sorry. What?" said Mitch, pausing his game and switching off the sound. Then the programmer gave a soft cough. Mitch was still physically recovering from the effects of crunch mode.

Jarrod was again on the back foot. He sighed and said, "*Apoplexy II* got leaked. Do you know anything about it?"

Mitch gave him a look of utter disgust. "Goddam it, Jarrod! How dare you?! I don't even have access to the build directory. Remember? You and Owen didn't trust me! Remember? After like a year and a half of devoting my life to this place, you didn't trust me! I didn't 'need to know!' Remember that?!"

Mitch threw his headphones at his monitor and stormed out, fearlessly muttering the word, "asshole" as he passed by his employer.

Jarrod looked to the floor, breathing heavily. He waited until his heart and respiration slowed then looked around the room. Jenn sat in the corner. Without speaking, Jenn's expression gave him very clear instructions: "Don't even ask."

Suddenly remembering Dogg, Jarrod entered the programmer's office. As he did, Dogg rose to his full height and stepped forward.

Jarrod looked up at the intimidating man, thinking, "How big is this guy? Six-nine? Six-ten? Oh, my lord."

"What?" said Dogg, moving up to loom over the hapless CEO.

Defeated, Jarrod shuffled back to his office and closed the door. Sadly looking out the small window on the back wall of the room, he gazed out into the daylight, wondering how much damage he'd just done.

He watched a small white car pull into the alley parking lot. Jarrod saw Miles step out of his Honda Civic and reach in to remove some drums. As he did, a second car pulled up. Jarrod recognized it as Viv's red 1984 Ford Mustang. She drove it hurriedly, scraping its bottom on a speed bump as she maneuvered, then parking diagonally across two spaces.

Viv flew from the car and ran to Miles. Miles saw her coming, but barely had time to set down his drums before she reached him.

Throwing her arms around Miles' neck, Viv pulled him close, resting her head on his shoulder. Slowly, Miles wrapped his arms around her. For some time, Miles and Viv remained locked together, swaying and embracing.

Jarrod's jaw dropped.

"What the Hell?"

CHAPTER THIRTY-EIGHT

DARK WARRIOR

September 23, 1994
Saint Petersburg, Russia

The implications of Owen's discovery were too much for him to process, but he did know one thing: If Dogg's code did trigger massive seizures this was neither the time nor place to acknowledge it.

Dr. Ilizarov, Leonid Morozov and his two, hairy bodyguards stared at him from across the desk. Owen's mind was racing. Buying time to think, he loudly struck the computer keys, typing random and pointless DOS commands, attempting to give the impression he was working hard. He did this for at least two minutes, having no idea what to do.

As he did, he glanced around the massive, wooden desk. Mikhail's uncle Alvar was quite the gamer, it seemed. The desktop was littered with dozens of computer discs. One immediately caught his eye and his blood turned to ice in his veins. The CD's label featured a picture of Gene Autry with a hole in the center of the cowboy's head. It was one of the demo discs Owen had given Max at the Consumer Electronics Show.

Owen was just an instant away from a full-on panic attack when an unexpected visitor diverted the Russians' attention. A diminutive, white-haired woman entered the room, her hard-soled heels clacking on the stone floor. She was wearing a long-sleeved white blouse and a beige dress skirt that ended below her knees. Her hair was shaved on the sides with the top sculpted nearly flat. The woman looked unnaturally pale. From where Owen sat, he'd have guessed her eye color was black.

Everyone turned toward Olga. She walked to Leonid and shook his hand, then Ilizarov's. Only then did she turn and nod at Flexx.

Leonid didn't bother introducing the newcomer to the captives. He just waved at Owen to continue his work.

The bodyguards watched the American closely while the remaining Russians assembled in a corner of the room to confer. Astrid took the opportunity to walk behind the desk and look at the computer monitor from over Owen's shoulder.

She whispered in his ear, "Leonid Morozov is a Russian kleptocrat."

While Owen appreciated the information, it seemed unhelpful to his predicament. But the sound of Astrid's soft voice somehow broke his brain out of vapor lock.

He suddenly remembered the second unexpected file. He checked its title. Not recognizing the word, he quietly asked Astrid, "Does 'moja3.txt' mean anything to you?"

"In Russian, Moja means 'mine'," she whispered back.

He launched *edit.com* and opened the moja3 file. It opened, filling the screen with densely packed, Latinized Russian text. Owen quietly rolled his desk chair to the side, making it easier for Astrid to see the monitor. In silence, she read rapidly. Every few seconds, she'd nonverbally indicate that Owen needed to advance to the next page.

When they'd reached the end of the file, Owen asked, "Anything about seizures?"

"No," Astrid shook her head, "It's all mining research."

"How did it wind up on this game disc?" Owen asked himself.

The room's other conversation grew louder. Owen and Astrid looked and saw the oligarch and his cohorts ending their huddle. They shook hands somberly and spoke a few more words in Russian. Astrid seemed to catch a few phrases from the exchange.

Flexx followed Olga toward the exit, flipping Owen the bird behind his employer's back. As he left the room, the software cracker nearly bumped into a nurse as she rushed in. The nurse cried out for Dr. Ilizarov and the two hurried away, leaving Owen and Astrid alone with Leonid and his two bodyguards.

The quick exit of his son's doctor left the oligarch panicked and restless. He glanced around the room, looking for something, anything to do. His eyes fell on Owen. He yelled something at Astrid and she replied in her calm, unflappable way.

"What did you tell him," asked Owen, his swollen lower lip making his 'd's sound like 'b's.

Astrid answered, "I told him you're still looking."

Unsatisfied, Leonid spoke directly to the taller bodyguard who immediately pulled out his sidearm and handed it to the tycoon. Leonid approached Owen, shouting and waving the weapon at the programmer. In what seemed like an uncharacteristic display of cowardice, Astrid stepped away from Owen and around to Leonid's side of the desk.

The red-faced man kept shouting. There was no need for translation. He was counting down to zero. Leonid's bushy eyebrows danced up and down as he counted, "Pięć! Cztery! Trzy!"

The counting ceased when a cry came from the back of the room, "Leonid!"

It didn't sound like someone trying to stop a murder – more like someone communicating a tragedy to a friend. Dr. Ilizarov approached Leonid Morozov with his arms outstretched. He shook his head slowly and spoke sadly in Russian. Morozov's face transformed from anger to uncontrollable grief.

Leonid fell forward, trying to hold himself up by grasping Ilizarov's coat. He slipped to the floor, falling to his knees, while tears rolled down his cheeks. His hands dropped to his sides and rested on the marble floor.

Astrid looked down. Her gaze sharpened.

Without warning, her left foot came down on Leonid's right hand - his gun hand. A second stomp and she made certain it was broken. Leonid's pistol clattered to the floor. Astrid scooped up the fallen weapon but the bodyguards reacted quickly.

The smaller man went for his gun while the taller, unarmed one lunged for Astrid. Firing twice, her bullets struck the closer man twice in the chest.

As he tried to clear it from his shoulder holster, the second gunman's pistol caught on his sports coat. By the time he'd dislodged it, he was looking down the barrel of Astrid's Glock. He knew she had the drop on him. With no time to aim he threw his gun hand forward and squeezed the trigger. His shot pulled well left of the target, lodging in a gilded wall.

Astrid pulled her trigger twice more. Both shots hit home, jerking the man off his feet. His skull hit the marble floor with a sharp crack.

Owen sat dumbstruck in his chair. Dr. Ilizarov didn't move. His eyes remained focused on Astrid's gun. The wounded men screamed in pain. Pressing their wounds with their hands, they twisted in agony.

Rivers of dark blood flowed from each and pooled together in an ever-growing lake of scarlet.

Leonid lay on his side, cradling his fractured hand. Pushing up with his left, he tried to regain a kneeling position. Astrid ran to him, screaming "No!" The word came out mechanically, almost as though it were part of a chant. She smashed the gun against the side of Leonid's head, cutting him and knocking him back down.

Owen saw the rage and fear on Astrid's face but found not a trace of regret. Again she bashed Leonid's head with the pistol. Astrid was taking no chances.

She yelled to Owen, "Get up!"

Still, Owen didn't move. He just stared at the wounded men. One bullet from the Glock had shattered a bodyguard's rib and now the end of the splintered bone stuck up through the skin of his chest.

Finally, Owen recovered from the shock.

"Hold on, just one second,' he called.

Owen pressed the eject button on the CD-ROM drive. It was maddening to him how long it took to disengage the disc caddy. As he waited for the physical mechanism to complete its motion, he typed: del /s c:\

With that short command, Owen destroyed all the data stored on the Morozov's computer.

Finally, the CD caddy popped out. Owen extracted the game disc and with a ballpoint pen that had been lying on the desk, scratched his autograph off its shiny surface, leaving large, clear holes in the disc's silver coating.

"OK, I'm ready," he said.

"Then run!" Astrid shouted.

Owen headed for the door. Astrid sidestepped toward the exit, keeping Dr. Ilizarov in her gun's sights.

The fugitives sprinted away from the office, down the long corridor and past the throne-like chair near the building's entrance.

Out front, the chauffeur smoked a cigarette and leaned against Leonid's midnight blue Rolls-Royce. Astrid waved the gun in his face then reached into the man's jacket, removing a chrome revolver.

Backing away from Astrid's smoking Glock, the chauffeur indicated that his keys were in the car.

Owen jumped into the front seat and started the engine. Astrid edged around to the passenger side, keeping the driver covered. At last, she slid into the passenger seat. As she slammed the car door,

Owen stomped the gas pedal and the enormous vehicle accelerated like a Ferrari sports car.

Unfortunately, it didn't handle like one. Owen found the vehicle much heavier than expected. It just didn't want to turn. He had no choice but to drive straight down the hill, over the manicured lawn toward the exit. Along the way, the Rolls mowed down a beautiful topiary elephant.

Back at the mansion, an alarm blared. Owen could see the exit gate ahead and hit the remote control to open it. Careening towards escape, he saw something he hadn't on his way in. Inside the hedgerow, next to the gate, sat a small guardhouse. The guard inside, alerted by the house alarm, ran out to block the road with his body. He held a machine gun, which he shouldered, aiming at the approaching vehicle.

Owen held course. Both he and Astrid screamed as the guard let loose two bursts of automatic fire into the Rolls-Royce's windshield. They instinctively ducked, but to their relief, the windshield didn't shatter. The guard leaped from the Rolls' path. As the car cleared the gate, Owen turned right and accelerated. Bullets pelted the trunk and rear window.

"He'll shoot the tires!" cried Astrid. The guard tried just that, but somehow the Rolls sped away, undamaged. The armor of Leonid Morozov's vehicle was top of the line.

Soon Owen and Astrid were well out of gun range.

"Where do we go?" asked Owen.

"I don't know! Just keep driving!"

They zoomed away at top speed. Owen turned on the police-flashers, thinking they might protect them from being pulled over for speeding. After an hour of aimless driving on the dark back roads of St. Petersburg, he switched off the lights and pulled to a stop behind a thick stand of trees. Owen realized how much his body ached. He touched his upper lip and felt the blood still trickling from his nose. How long had it been doing that?

Then a wave of nausea hit. In the nick of time, Owen threw open the door, leaned out and vomited blood on the grass.

"Do you need a doctor?" Astrid asked.

"No," said Owen, sitting up. "I'm good."

She patted Owen on the back. "Now. What the Hell, Owen?!"

Owen leaned forward, placing his forearms on the top of the steering wheel and his forehead at its center.

Astrid yelled, "That man died, Owen. Mikhail Morozov. The son of one of Russia's richest men died tonight and you know why, don't you!"

"I'm not sure," he said. Owen inhaled deeply, which caused him to wince in pain. "Maybe."

"Here's what I know," he began. "I don't have any details. I'm just a videogame programmer. That's all I've ever done. My business partner, Jarrod, thought we needed to make more money, so we took on a contract for the United States Army. The intelligence division, I guess. We were told they were going to run some tests and needed a modern game engine. Mine is pretty good. Carmack even said so."

"I don't care."

"Right. For the military contract, we brought in this guy, Dogg Dobbs. He's a computer graphics expert. All he asked me to do was to set up the game to look for this file he wrote. When the program found the file, it ran his code. But we never meant to ship his file with the game. We couldn't even access it. The code only lived on *his* machine."

"Yes?"

"Back at the mansion, I found Dogg's code running on Flexx's version of the game."

"I don't understand. Even if your game is running a military program, how does that hurt anybody?" Astrid asked.

Owen strained to remember a name he'd heard long ago. It took him a few seconds, but he finally got it. *"Dark Warrior!"*

"What's *Dark Warrior*?"

"An arcade game," Owen replied.

Astrid looked at him like he'd completely lost it.

"In 1981 there was this 17-year-old girl, I think she was from England. She was a big gamer. She liked the *Space Invader*-type games. You know? There was a *Space Invader* rip-off called *Dark Warrior*. But it wasn't black and white, like *Space Invaders*. *Dark Warrior* was in color. It had a ton of color and in one part of the game all the colors really flashed all over the whole screen."

He continued, "So the girl plays the game and the flashing colors give her an epileptic seizure. It was the first reported case of a videogame causing an attack."

"Did she die?" asked Astrid.

"No, but there was another kid who died from a seizure while playing *Super Mario*."

"Like Mikhail?"

"I don't think so," answered Owen. "During his fit, I think he choked on his own vomit."

"How awful!"

"Yes, but the publicity of his case made the games industry aware of the danger. Now they take steps to avoid creating those types of dangerous, flashing color patterns."

"Then how does this relate to Mikhail?"

"I call Dogg's code right before I blit the image buffer to screen memory. I actually pass Dogg a pointer to the offscreen buffer," said Owen, hoping he was being clear.

"I have no idea what you're saying right now."

"OK. Very simply. Before I draw a picture on the screen, I first give it to Dogg. He can do whatever he wants to the picture before it appears on the monitor."

"All right. That I understand."

"Dogg is an expert at computer graphics," said Owen. " Every week Army Intelligence officers bring him these huge folders of scientific data."

"Yes?"

"What if they're actually *trying* to induce epileptic fits?" Owen considered. "Dogg could be manipulating the patterns and colors on the screen to maximize the chance of a seizure. All those research papers he got from the military? Maybe they told him exactly how to flash the screen to amplify a seizure's effects—maybe make one so powerful that it could fry someone's brain."

"Did the screen flash when you played?" asked Astrid.

"I didn't see anything. But the game ran slowly on Uncle Alvar's hot-rodded game machine. Flexx said it ran slow for him, too. Whatever Dogg's code does, it's computationally intensive, like image processing. The real programming trick would be to add the 'super-seizure' flashes but make them subtle enough that you wouldn't notice them with the naked eye. That's something only someone like Dogg could do." "But why?" Owen asked himself.

Astrid had a simple answer, "Armies break things and kill people. They want to turn computer screens into weapons."

"That's a lot of effort to put into killing photo-sensitive epileptics," Owen said, skeptically.

"Who says they stopped at photo-sensitive epileptics?" she asked.

This made Owen stop and think. Studies had shown that the same flashes that caused epilepsy attacks could also disorient and nauseate non-epileptics. Flexx had complained about having a bad headache after playing *Apoplexy II.*

Owen didn't think Dogg was epileptic, but he still hung a big green filter in front of his computer screen. Maybe the code could cause super-seizures in anyone—could kill anyone. For some people, it might just take a little longer.

He looked directly into Astrid's pale blue eyes and said, "I think you might be right."

Astrid was already a step ahead, "If Flexx leaks the game on the Internet... how many people do you think would download it?"

"Tens—maybe hundreds of thousands," Owen murmured.

He considered their options. They could go to the St. Petersburg police. But they would be two foreigners without visas, driving a Russian billionaire's stolen car and raving about a killer videogame.

Astrid thought a moment. "We could find Flexx ourselves. We could steal the game back."

"Or... he could shoot us," said Owen, predicting a different outcome.

Owen wanted to run. He wanted to sneak back to Finland and just fly home. But he thought about Stevie and the kids like him. Owen thought of Haley.

If Flexx were to spread the game around the world, thousands might die in terrifying, excruciating agony. He couldn't let that happen. If it did, he knew the guilt would consume him, breaking his mind and effectively ending his young life.

Owen glanced down and noticed his own hands shaking. He gripped the steering wheel hard, trying to hold them still.

"We'll find him. We'll steal the disc if we can. Did you hear anything? Did you hear them say where he was headed?"

"Site Three," replied Astrid.

"That's all you heard? Site Three?"

"Yes. The white-haired lady said 'Site Three' before she left with Flexx."

A chagrined Owen realized that wasn't enough information. Site Three might be anywhere.

"Any idea where it is?" he asked.

Astrid answered, "I do. It was in the text file you found—the one with all the mining data."

"Yeah, what about that?" said Owen. "Why was that with the game?"

Astrid brought Owen back on track. "I don't know. Site Three is a diamond mine. It's called, 'Luster'."

"And where is the Luster Mine?"

"Near a village called Svetly. It's in Murmansk Oblast, above the Arctic Circle."

"Oh, damn," hissed Owen. "How do we get there?"

Astrid didn't know exactly, but they were agreed. They would take a chance and look for Flexx at Site Three—the Luster Mine.

Quickly, they made a plan. Owen found a highway and drove north.

"How did you learn to speak Russian?" Owen asked, making conversation.

"Ethnically, much of my family is Russian," Astrid replied, "I also speak Finnish, English – obviously - and Swedish. What languages do you speak?"

"Assembly, C, BASIC, Pascal," answered Owen.

He saw a gas station sign ahead and Owen pulled to a stop in front of a pump. Astrid glanced toward the back seat of the Rolls. She'd brought her handbag on the trip and left it in the car's back seat when she had been rushed into the mansion. Now the purse was missing.

"*Samperi!* Do you have any money?" she asked.

Owen pulled the anti-theft travel wallet from his shirt.

"These things really work, don't they?" he asked. Inside was his passport, a large number of American dollars some Dutch guilders and Finnish markka. "But I don't have any rubles."

"No problem," said Astrid, as she grabbed his money and exited the car. It was quite late now. As the car door opened Owen was blasted by the frigid, 36-degree wind. Astrid slammed the door and ran to the cashier station, where she made a purchase through the small opening in the bulletproof window. When she jumped back in the car, she had a map of Northwestern Russia.

"Pop the trunk and pump the gas," she ordered.

Owen pulled several knobs inside the cab until he felt a satisfying 'thunk' from the rear of the car. He pushed open the driver's side door but the strong wind blowing through the station's carport kept slamming it shut. Finally extricating himself from the vehicle, Owen grabbed the handle of the rusty pump. He wished he had some gloves. A gust of wind blew through his light windbreaker and he trembled in the cold.

Sufficiently warmed, Astrid got back out of the town car and went back to check the trunk. She looked inside then yelled for Owen.

Owen ran to the back of the car where Astrid stared into the open trunk. Her purse lay inside, on a large plastic tarpaulin. The edges of the tarp were folded up along the walls of the compartment, forming a waterproof barrier designed to protect the trunk's upholstery from any spills. To the left side of the trunk were two sets of workmen's full-body coveralls, gloves and shoe covers. On the right were two long-handled shovels. In the very center of the trunk was a big bag of what looked like cement. On the sack was a single, Cyrillic word.

Astrid translated it for Owen. "Lime."

"They were never letting us out of there alive," said Owen.

He shivered and pulled one of the heavy coveralls from the trunk, putting it on over his clothes. The denim garment had been waterproofed. Once Owen had his arms through the sleeves, he immediately felt warmer. Astrid copied her companion, but needed to roll up her cuffs. Three Astrids could have fit into one of the coveralls.

Owen zipped up and slammed the trunk shut. The two clambered into the Rolls and they continued their getaway. Not really knowing where he was heading, Owen plowed north, trusting Astrid to read the Russian map. She determined it was a little less than a thousand miles from St. Petersburg to the tiny hamlet of Svetly. In three hours they'd covered less than a sixth of that.

"If Morozov reports the shootings, I hope the police will think we've headed for one of the nearer border crossings with Finland," said Astrid.

They drove up European route E105, heading northeast. There were no side roads to take and they felt like sitting ducks driving on the major highway around Lake Ladoga. E105 would have been an obvious route for anyone fleeing to Finland. A fugitive would first head north, then go west at the A-121 junction, toward several potential border crossings.

Terrified, they drove for three more hours until they passed the A-121 junction. Rather than turning west, they continued north past the city of Matrosy. Owen pulled to the side of the road, where they got out and switched seats.

"We should be good now," said Astrid as she started the car. "Only a pair of idiots would try driving to the Arctic Circle."

CHAPTER THIRTY-NINE

TOURISTS IN MURMANSK

Astrid and Owen motored through hundreds of miles of unremarkable, thinly forested land. On their car's radio, they could only find Russian stations. These weren't programmed according to musical genres and Owen found them maddening. A station would play a classical piece followed by an accordion-heavy polka, followed by some Finnish death metal, a Russian folk song and an ABBA B-side. Eventually, he gave up and drove in silence.

Owen thought about Maxine. He wondered if Alvar, Mikhail's uncle, had been her kidnapper. Her killer, maybe. But why? For a videogame?

Astrid looked at him from the corners of her eyes. She could only guess his thoughts.

Softly, Owen asked, "What can you tell me about the Morozovs?"

"The story I know begins when the Soviet Union collapsed three years ago," she began, "President Yeltsin wanted to move Russia from the centrally controlled Communist system to a western-style, free-market economy. Of course, many members of the Russian government were anti-capitalist, so he had to make the transition quick and irrevocable, leaving no way to return to the Soviet system."

"Yeltsin hired a man named Anatoly Chubais to come up with a plan. In Chubais' scheme, everyone in Russia got 10,000 rubles in vouchers. With the vouchers, everyone in former Soviet countries could purchase government property - like businesses and real estate. You understand?"

"Yes, I think so. What about the Morozovs?" Owen asked.

Astrid recounted what she knew, "As a crime reporter I've done plenty of research on the Russian Mafia. A lot of it couldn't be printed because it was hearsay, but mostly, I believe the rumors."

"When Chubais started the voucher plan, the Morozovs were just poor brothers living in St. Petersburg. I think Mikhail's uncle, Alvar Morozov, drove a truck. I'm not sure what Leonid did, but he was the smarter one, extorting people out of their vouchers. Then he started taking people's apartments by force. Alvar was the hitman. Anyone who didn't give Leonid what he wanted—bang! Dead. With a little money, the Morozov's operation grew more sophisticated. They could bribe the voucher officials directly. When the Morozovs spent a voucher, the authorities wouldn't cancel it. They could use their vouchers repeatedly."

"So, they had unlimited money," concluded Owen.

"Just so. Yes," Astrid confirmed. "And when vouchers became too inconvenient for them, they simply started printing their own money. They became so rich that Leonid set up his own bank."

"Come on, really?" Owen asked incredulously.

"Really!" she assured. "Here in Russia, it's easier to start a bank than it is to buy this Rolls-Royce. By this time they had a lot of power and influence over many government officials, who would gift whole businesses to the Morozovs in return for kickbacks. Do you want to know how they got control of the mining company? Somehow they were the only people to show up at the auction. They bought it for 25 million rubles."

"Twenty-five million? That sounds pretty good," said Owen.

"About $10,000," replied Astrid. "Since then they've stripped the companies of their resources and sold them in the west. They funneled the profits to hidden bank accounts outside of Russia and as the money leaves, the country gets poorer and poorer."

"And there's no way to return the stolen money?" asked Owen.

"There's no public record of any transactions," she replied. "It's one of the advantages of having your own bank."

Astrid switched subjects, "Your turn, Owen. How did the seizure code end up on the game disc?"

"I don't know. Let's try to figure that out," he suggested. "It wasn't on the disc I gave to the duplicator. We run a full audit on our release candidates. We'd have found any extra files. Flexx's copy of the game had to come from Dogg's computer. That means the source was either Dogg or someone with access to his computer."

"Who else had access?"

"Dogg had the only key. He's the only one with security clearance.

Maybe he had a copy somewhere," Owen suggested.

"Did Dogg ever leave his office unlocked?"

"Never," Owen shook his head. "He always closed and locked his office if he was going to be away, even for a few minutes. It would take a long time to copy a game across the Internet, maybe more than an hour. Dogg's computer doesn't even have an Internet connection, so I just don't know."

During the trip, the Rolls' poor gas mileage created unlooked-for suspense. The passengers watched in terror as the gas needle hovered at the 'empty' mark. For 45 minutes they drove this way before coasting into a gas station. Astrid purchased enough fuel to fill the tank. She also bought and filled three 10-liter gas cans, which they stashed in the trunk. The backup gas cans reassured the pair of fugitives. If they ended up stranded deep in the Russian wilderness, it wouldn't be because they ran out of gas.

Astrid and Owen alternated sleeping and driving, minimizing travel time as much as possible. As they approached the city of Murmansk, they passed through villages more frequently. When they stopped for breakfast, Astrid checked the map and realized that they'd crossed the Arctic Circle. After having driven more than 1,000 miles on the E105, the pair crossed over the Tulum River and turned west onto the P11 toward the village of Svetly.

The farther they drove, the lovelier the scenery became. The countryside was green in the late summer sun, though the outside temperature was barely 45 degrees. They passed many lakes and streams, flowering tundra and forests.

The terrain became more varied as small hills and mountains dotted the landscape. Light gray clouds rolled in from horizon to horizon. Then in a 10-second span, the clouds turned slate and the ambient light dropped as if God had turned down a dimmer switch. Rain spattered the Rolls' windshield, turning its accumulated dust to mud. Thunder rolled in the distance.

Owen was so distracted by the Arctic storm that he didn't notice the khaki-colored four-by-four parked by the side of the road until he'd raced past. He stared into the Rolls-Royce's rearview mirror and muttered softly, "Don't follow, please don't follow, please don't follow."

The four-by-four pulled out onto the road. It was following. Owen was driving 80 miles per hour, but slowed to 55. The pursuit vehicle quickly pulled behind the Rolls.

"Maybe he isn't going to…"

Red and blue police lights flashed from the four-by-four.

"Son of a…"

The siren blared and Owen considered his options. He was in an armored car. It was really tough. Maybe he could crash into the police car and disable it.

Whatever Owen was going to do, he had to do it immediately. He gripped the wheel tightly. His body tensed, ready to jam the brakes and let the cop rear-end him.

"Owen, what are you thinking?"

Astrid eyed him with great concern.

Before Owen could execute his conscious mind's terrible plan, his subconscious had a better idea. "What the heck? Let's give it a try."

Owen eased his right hand down to the wood veneer console between the luxurious bucket seats. He flicked a button, lighting up the Rolls-Royce's own flashing lights. After a few seconds, he switched them off again.

Immediately, the siren quieted and the flashing police lights went dark. The four-by-four pulled alongside the Rolls, revealing the two officers inside. They looked bored. The officer in the passenger seat turned to Owen and gave a distracted wave. Owen waved back, just jiggling the fingers of his left hand. He and Astrid watched as the police car drove away down the straight road into the dark weather ahead, framed by the bolts of lightning in the distance.

"I'm a billionaire," said Owen, pompously. "What more do I need to say?"

When the cops were out of sight, Owen pulled to the side of the road and got out. It was cold. The rain fell in big heavy drops but he didn't care. They'd been riding in the car for nearly 20 hours. His legs ached, his head burned and he was covered in stress-induced sweat.

They both welcomed the cold and together waddled around the shoulder of the road, looking like two bull-riders after a rodeo. Owen looked to the sky and released a prolonged scream of relief.

After a few minutes of feet-stomping on the gravel, they sloshed back into the Rolls. The car's heater immediately converted the rainwater in their clothes to steam.

Astrid laughed a little, "I don't understand why they didn't pull us over. There's no way we look like police."

"I don't know either. Maybe they recognized Leonid's car," Owen suggested. "Honestly, I don't care if we never find out."

Pulling out the map, Astrid approximated their location.

"We're actually very close to the Luster Mine. The pullout is just a mile from here."

CHAPTER FORTY

THE LUSTER MINE

Owen turned the dark-blue Rolls onto an old mine road running up between two rocky hills. Despite the luxury vehicle's smooth suspension, Astrid and Owen bounced up the grade. It was clear that the tundra had been attempting to reclaim the route for many years.

They bumped along for several miles until they crested a hill and stopped at an overlook. There could be no mistaking it – they had found the Luster Mine. Owen threw the Rolls into reverse and quickly backed it off the road and out of sight. Climbing out, he and Astrid crept to the overlook to take in the view of the diamond pit.

The scale of the thing was shocking. Luster was a full mile and a half across and three-quarters of a mile deep. Over time, rain and seepage had flooded the pit, leaving a deep, murky pool at its bottom.

In the 1960s, when the Luster mine was still running, it would take an earthmover over an hour to drive from the top of the mine to the bottom, making fifteen complete loops around its circumference along the way.

The corkscrew road running from top to bottom had eroded, leaving only the suggestion of its original purpose. To the northeast of the mine sat mountains of black waste rock.

Owen and Astrid also had an excellent view of the era's decaying buildings. To the far west of the site was the vehicle entrance from which a road ran along the great pit's southern rim. This led to nearly two-dozen large factory buildings set along the east edge; each colored a combination of steel gray and rust orange.

There were more modern structures as well. In the 1970s, new management had attempted to reach the diamonds with a traditional drilling operation. They dug a vertical shaft next to the pit and excavated angled tunnels beneath the gigantic hole. Like the previous strategy, this also failed to turn a profit and the great mine closed for good in 1985.

The Luster pit was in the center of a depression between hills. East of the buildings was a steep incline, upon which sat several enormous water tanks.

The only modern objects in the scene were the trucks parked at the far north end of the building complex, next to a five-story structure with corrugated steel walls. There were three pickup trucks and one larger military vehicle with a flatbed trailer.

It was late September and there would be no sunset this far above the Arctic Circle, but heavy storm clouds darkened the landscape. Thin white lines of lightning fell continually, surrounding the pit in a giant curtain of electricity. Through the gloom, Astrid and Owen spied a flicker of yellow light coming from a mining tower near the trucks.

"Do you think Flexx is in there?" asked Astrid.

"Your guess is as good as mine," Owen replied. "Get it? Good as mine?"

She ignored the pun. "How do we get in? Walk down?"

Owen surveyed the distance.

"Everything down there is so big, I think it's hard for us to judge the scale," he said. "I don't think that's walkable. Those buildings might be three miles away."

Astrid scanned the pickup trucks again. They looked tiny.

"I see what you mean," she agreed. "We'll have to drive. Will they see us?"

"Maybe not," Owen said. "The size of the place might be to our advantage. We can drive in with the headlights off and stay way to the right. Maybe we can park behind those buildings, then sneak around to the tower."

"All right, but first—" Astrid locked eyes with Owen, "—I need to show you how to use this."

She held out the revolver she'd taken from Leonid's chauffeur. It wasn't a lengthy lesson. Like most pistols, the gun was designed for ease of use. Safety off. Aim. Pull the trigger.

A few minutes later, they were back in the armored car, bouncing along the unpaved mine road. The track twisted through the undulating terrain. It was three miles to the mine complex from the overlook, but the winding car route made it feel twice as far. Lights off, they bumped down toward the huge hole in the earth.

Owen drove as close as he could to the south wall of the basin. Although the car's wheels crunched over the gravel, the posh craftsmanship of Rolls-Royce kept any outside noise at bay. Owen worried about how much noise the car might be making. He rolled down his window and was pleased to hear nothing but the screeching wind.

He looked in the rear-view mirror. Since the rain was turning the dirt to mud, he didn't need to worry about kicking up a dust trail. But because they rode within a direct sight line to the mining tower's lit window, they still felt vulnerable. Owen wasn't at all sure he'd even taken a breath during the final minutes of the drive.

When they pulled to a stop behind the southernmost building, they both exhaled. They still hadn't seen any signs of life. The thought was both comforting and disconcerting. What if Flexx wasn't here? What if they'd driven a thousand miles for nothing? Were they too late? What if Flexx had already given away a hundred thousand copies of a deadly weapon disguised as a videogame?

Parking the Rolls, they made their way around the back of the buildings and headed toward the five-story mine tower a half a mile away. Upon reaching its corrugated steel base, Owen asked, "What's the plan?"

Astrid thought a moment.

"Got anything?" Owen prodded.

"Shut up! I'm thinking," she scowled. "You can think of something, too. I won't have us pissing while we run."

Owen wasn't up on his Finnish idioms, but he guessed at what she meant.

"Why don't I peek in the window and you cover me from here?" he offered.

He expected Astrid to scoff at the idea. Instead, she said, "Yes. Go."

Pistol out, Owen walked stealthily to the window, trying to keep his tennis shoes as dry as possible. The window was several feet above ground, next to the entrance door. Owen had to climb a short flight of stairs to reach a level where he could peek in.

Through the window, he saw a large, dark mudroom filled with benches. A brightly lit control room lay beyond, its light spilling through the mudroom and out its window. He motioned to Astrid to join him at the entrance. Owen prepared to open the door but stopped cold.

He'd seen a shadow moving in the control room. Again, he peered inside. It was Flexx! The hacker sat on an office chair with rolling casters. Gripping the armrests tightly, Flexx kicked with his feet, rolling the chair around backward and circling the room at high speed as if he were a racecar at the Indianapolis Motor Speedway.

Astrid looked, too. "What an idiot," she said.

Owen pulled open the door to the mining building, letting Astrid pass inside. Following her, he shut the door firmly. Flexx must've heard the sound of the door and the wind, but had no reason to think it wasn't a comrade. He continued to circle the room. Without hesitation, Astrid walked into the control room and aimed her Glock at his back. Aware of a new occupant in the office but unaware of her identity, Flexx rolled to a stop and spun his chair 180 degrees.

"Astrid?" he blurted and bugged his eyes. When he saw Owen, Flexx looked as if he might have a heart attack.

"Why in *Hell* are you two here?" Flexx asked, absolutely stupefied.

Owen looked around for the rucksack. It wasn't visible.

"Where's the game disc?" Owen asked.

"You have got to be joking with me," said Flexx, his eyes still popping, but with a spasm of a smile appearing around his lips. "You came all the way out here to get your game?"

"That's right," said Astrid. She kept her pistol aimed at his midsection.

"You two are insane. I mean it."

Flexx leaned forward a little, testing how quickly he might launch himself out of the rolling chair. The deep cushion of the seat and low-friction casters worked against him. He leaned back again.

Owen tried reasoning, "You can't release it. It caused those seizures in Mikhail."

Flexx had less patience with Owen, "Of course I can! Idiot. Mikhail is epileptic. Epileptic assholes shouldn't play videogames."

"You don't understand. It *killed* Mikhail," said Owen, trying to get through the hacker's dense skull.

This information was new to Flexx. He paused a moment to process. Then Flexx crossed his eyes and bobbled his head, mockingly.

"Mikhail brain no work right," condescended Flexx in deliberately broken English. "No game fault Mikhail die."

"Give me the disc!" Owen commanded. He walked behind Flexx, taking out the chrome revolver. Astrid's eyes fixed on Owen.

"Or what?" sneered Flexx.

Owen placed the muzzle of the gun against the back of Flexx's skull.

The cracker arched his neck backward so he could look at Owen upside down. The gun barrel pressed dead center of Flexx's forehead but the Russian wasn't concerned.

Owen raised the gun above his head, intending to smash it down on Flexx's goofy face, but couldn't. Flexx just smiled. Owen lowered the gun to his hip. He had disappointed himself.

As Astrid kept Flexx covered with her gun, Owen scanned for Flexx's rucksack. The room was windowless, with a bare-bones control panel, a few unlit green and white buttons and a white door at the rear corner.

He cracked open the door and peeked. Beyond was a narrow metal ledge connected to a steel staircase. Stepping in, Owen discovered a huge machine room filled with giant gear wheels, engines, chains and dusty maintenance bays. At the back of the building, an enormous shaft descended into the earth.

A chain-link fence surrounded the shaft. There was a sliding gate at its center, beyond which were two industrial elevators designed to take workers deep into the earth.

"It wouldn't be back here," Owen called to Astrid.

"It must be in one of the trucks," she said. "Flexx, stand up."

"Or what?" Flexx repeated his rejoinder to Owen.

Astrid did not hesitate with her response, saying, "Or I will shoot you in the knee."

Flexx stood up immediately.

Owen gave him a "what gives?" look. Flexx hadn't complied when Owen had threatened to shoot him.

"Something about her makes me believe she'd shoot," said Flexx. "It's in the eyes."

Astrid marched Flexx through the mudroom and out the front door. Once outside, Flexx flopped down on the stairs.

"What the hell are you doing?" Astrid asked, looking down at the big man. When she and Owen looked up, they understood.

At the base of the entrance stairway, stood a party of seven people. Four were large men wearing heavy-weather work gear. The fifth and sixth men wore the winter military uniforms of the Russian army. These two carried machine guns, which they quickly aimed at Owen and Astrid. The seventh member of the group was the smallest but was obviously the outfit's leader. Owen recognized her as the white-haired woman from Leonid's palace.

"Hello," said the small woman, speaking in Russian and giving a little wave to the intruders. "How do you do? Shall we go inside? It's a little windy out here."

CHAPTER FORTY-ONE

DARK AS A DUNGEON

September 26, 1994
The Luster Mine, Murmansk Oblast
Russia

Enemies crowded the control room. The soldiers still held rifles but felt no need to brandish them. Disarmed, Owen and Astrid posed no threat. One took out a thermos and poured coffee for his comrade.

"I am Olga," said the pale, dark-eyed woman, still speaking in Russian. "Who are you? Why are you here?"

"Do you speak English?" asked Owen.

"Da," laughed Olga, then repeated her questions in the American's native tongue.

Flexx couldn't resist sharing his knowledge with the room. "They're here because I stole his computer game."

"Flexx, please," snapped Olga, shutting him down.

"He's right," said Owen. "He stole my game and I want it back."

"Really?" Olga responded sincerely. "That's a little difficult to believe. Two foreigners travel north of the Russian Arctic Circle to a mine in Murmansk Oblast to retrieve a computer game. It must be a really good game."

"*PC Gaming World* thought so," responded Owen, stiffly.

The little woman looked impressed. "Oh? Is that a magazine? Well, if *PC Gaming World* says so, then it *must* be great. You two were at Morozov's when we left."

She paused to let one of the prisoners speak up. Neither did. "I suppose we should call him."

"Good luck with that," thought Owen to himself, sure that the mine's phone lines wouldn't work following nine years disuse.

Olga pulled a small, black device from her fur-lined coat. It was a phone with the word 'NOKIA' written on the front. She pulled up a button on its top to extend a silver antenna. Punching a few buttons, she placed a call. In spite of himself, Owen was impressed. He had seen only a few cellular phones in his life. Of those, most were the boxy, foot-long versions he'd seen on the Miami Vice TV show.

He whispered to Astrid, "She's making a phone call from way out here? How is that even possible?"

"That's simple," she said. "Nokia is a Finnish company."

In Russian, Olga chatted on her phone for a couple of minutes, then hung up and collapsed the antenna. She smiled at Owen.

"Morozov is coming," announced Olga. "He sends you his regards."

"Why?" demanded Flexx.

"He didn't say," she replied. "But he flew up yesterday to tour his iron mine in Kovdor, so he's nearby. He'll be here in an hour."

"Nice guy," thought Owen. "He watches his bodyguards get shot, his son dies in agony and next day it's 'business as usual.'"

In Russian, Olga barked orders to her men. The soldiers set down their coffee cups and lifted their rifles. The workmen straightened.

"We don't have much time. This way, please," said Olga in English, opening the door to the machine room. The soldiers pointed their arms at the Finn and the American. As Owen and Astrid walked toward the door, Flexx threw himself back into his favorite rolling chair, laughing.

"Flexx," said Olga sternly in Russian. "You too."

Two of the huge workmen grabbed him, lifting the shocked hacker to his feet by the arms. Olga relieved him of his knife and gaudy pistol, placing them on the control panel.

"You can get them later," she told him reassuringly as the burly guards hustled them through the inner door and down the steel stairs into the machine room. From there, Olga led the way to the mineshaft with its large double elevators.

She pushed open the elevator's accordion-style gate and ushered the party in through the double doors. All ten of them fit easily into the space. Fifty, of them would have fit comfortably inside the enormous elevator.

Olga stepped to the front of the transport, pulled the gate shut and pressed a yellow button on the control box hanging by a rubberized cable from the car's ceiling. This set off a five-second warning alarm that was loud to the point of pain.

Olga pressed the green button and they descended into the mine.

While the elevator mechanism looked old, Owen noticed several shiny new parts, indicating recent repairs.

The lift moved slowly and Astrid, always the reporter, took the opportunity to ask questions.

She turned to Olga. "What are you doing here?"

"Research," said the scientist pleasantly.

"What research?" Astrid was persistent.

"Are you really interested?" asked Olga. "Yes? I'm actually happy to talk about it. I am using reflection seismology to discover the location of natural resources underground. Do you understand?"

"Yes, generally," said Astrid, nodding. "But why here?"

This pleased Olga. She continued, "You're smart. I like smart. Around this mine, I place numerous seismic sensors called geophones on the surface. Then I transmit seismic waves through the earth. These waves radiate outward, away from the mine. The waves strike and bounce off underground geological features, even if they are many miles away. I record the data from these seismic reflections with my geophones and from the data I build a treasure map! From my maps, I can determine the location of diamonds, oil and even pockets of natural gas. In this case, we're expecting to find diamonds."

Astrid continued her interview, "I thought the Luster mine was out of diamonds."

"Yes, the Luster is all played out. But we're not looking for anything here. We're looking for telltale geologic features nearby. But here is where we will create our seismic event. We use mines for two reasons. The first is simple. To reach the deep mineral deposits, our shockwaves must originate from far below the earth's surface."

Astrid looked at Olga with some confusion.

"What's the second reason?" asked the reporter.

Olga smiled but didn't answer.

With a metallic clang, the elevator shuddered, locking into place. They'd reached the bottom.

Olga gave the order, "Get out."

Flexx, Astrid and Owen walked ahead of the guards. From the vertical elevator shaft, the group entered a lightly-angled transverse tunnel leading directly under the great pit. Owen was surprised to find how loud it was down in the mine. Even though no digging was taking place, the great rattling hum made by ventilator pumps shook his teeth.

About eight feet off the ground, cables pinioned to the stone walls carried electrical current to the regularly-spaced lamps illuminating the 40-foot wide tunnel. The floor to the left and center of the tunnel was clear and smooth. On the right, steel rails ran the length of the passage.

No one spoke as they walked deeper and deeper into the earth. The sound of the pumps faded away and the air grew thicker and warmer. Owen glanced at Flexx, who sweated profusely. After the group walked 100 yards, Olga stopped and ordered Owen, Astrid and Flexx to keep walking. Flexx held back.

"You too, Flexx," ordered Olga, without emotion.

The hacker obeyed but muttered an obscenity.

"They're going to shoot us in the back," Owen predicted.

"No. They won't," Flexx barked hoarsely. "This deep there might be methane gas. Flash from a gun ignites the methane. Boom. Everybody dies."

The three prisoners continued to walk ahead. After a while, they heard no more footsteps from behind. They approached the end of the tunnel. It was only 40 yards away. At the tunnel's end, a sizable green object sat on a flat-topped rail cart. It looked like an old Mercury space capsule but was smaller.

"What is that?" asked Owen, hoping he hadn't already guessed the answer.

Flexx answered, "That? Yes, that. Well, that is a nuclear warhead."

At this, Owen yelled so his words echoed down the tunnel, "Why, Flexx? Why is there a nuclear warhead?"

"It's very simple, really," said Flexx. "You see...the bottom of the mine is more than 900 meters deep. That's over half a mile down and this whole area already has been heavily mined. Naturally, we believe there are few resources left to be discovered near the surface. So we want to look for resource pockets *super* deep."

Flexx paused a moment to catch his breath.

"The geophone sensors are on the surface. Seismic waves must be powerful enough to reach the mineral structures, then bounce all the way back up to the surface. Understand? An air gun certainly isn't powerful enough. And we can't pack enough dynamite or plastic explosive down here to do it. So, of course, we have to use a nuclear device. And if we're going nuclear, we also must be as deep as possible to... you know... contain the residual radiation."

"Flexx, I truly hate you," spat Astrid.

The hacker bowed dramatically.

Then the lights went out. None of them had ever known darkness so complete, so utterly disorienting. Just a second before Owen had known for certain that he faced the end of the tunnel. Now he was sure of nothing.

In the darkness, he heard a deep-throated yell, "*Chtob tebe deti v'sup srali!*"

"That's not helping, Flexx," chided Astrid.

Owen decided they needed to find their way back to the elevators. Dropping on all fours, he made an educated guess and began crawling. Completely disoriented, Flexx tripped over Owen. Astrid winced as he heard the big man's head crack on the rock floor.

"Are you OK?" she asked Owen.

"I'm fine," Owen replied, still crawling.

He cut his palm on a small, sharp rock. Reflexively, he thrust it into the pants pocket of his overalls.

A disembodied voice swore energetically in Russian, "*Chtob u tebya hui vo lbu vyros!*"

Owen's hand hit one of the rusted rail tracks. He stood up and placed his foot against the rail.

"Over here," he called. He continued vocalizing until Astrid found him in the darkness and took his hand. As quickly as possible, they started working their way back up the tunnel, Owen using the rail as a guide.

From far behind they heard Flexx's pitiful cry, "Don't leave me! You can't leave me!"

"All right!" called Owen, "This way!"

In a few moments all three were holding hands and stumbling uphill through the unlit mine shaft. As they ascended, Astrid demanded some explanations from Flexx.

"Where did *you* get a nuclear weapon?"

"*Weapons*," corrected Flexx. "We've done this twice before and we've been very successful. Olga is the geologist. She sets up the experiments. Then she gives me her data and I process it with my computers. In Siberia, we found a reservoir of natural gas. Morozov financed the operation. He'll probably make a few hundred million from that discovery."

Astrid restated her questioning, "Where did you get the nuclear weapons?"

"Olga is from City 42. It's a closed city. Do you know what that is?"

asked Flexx.

"I don't," said Owen quickly.

"All right. I will explain." Flexx continued, "The Soviet Union was afraid of nuclear attack from the United States, so they built many hidden cities. Each had crucial strategic functions: leadership continuity, weapons development, training. All sorts of things, you know? Olga told me City 42 is very, very far north. Very cold. They built it to stay warm and to withstand an American nuclear missile strike. So it was, as you Americans would say, 'DUMB.'"

"Yep. That sounds pretty stupid," said Owen.

"God, you're a fool," Flexx declared, "D.U.M.B. is a United States acronym, if you know what an acronym is. It stands for 'Deep Underground Military Base.' City 42 is inside a mountain. Its job was to build nuclear weapons. Under the mountain, they run several nuclear reactors. These keep the city heated. They also produce high-grade uranium and neptunium. Every day, each reactor produces a ball of uranium the size of a... how do you say? A softball. Every day a softball of uranium from each reactor. They have centrifuges so they can refine it. Olga says they also have a chemical processing plant under the mountain to convert the neptunium into plutonium. During the Cold War, ships brought warhead assemblies and raw materials, so they could build nuclear warheads themselves. Then they would load them on boats and submarines and send them south."

Astrid asked, "And what does City 42 do now that the Cold War is over?"

"That's a problem. City 42 was once comparatively rich, very valued during the Cold War. The government sent them the best of everything. They were very well paid," said Flexx, pausing. "But then the USSR broke apart. They are no longer paid. It's too cold to grow food and they have no one to buy their product. And so City 42, with its brilliant, educated scientists and mathematicians, starves. They starve and freeze to death by an ocean covered in ice that almost never melts. But they have a lot of warhead parts. Lots of uranium. Five softballs a day. And plutonium. They can make millions, maybe billions selling warheads."

"I guess it's lucky they just use the bombs for mining," said Owen.

"For now. But who knows what's in the future," replied the hacker grimly. "You know how it is. When your family starves, you will do anything to feed them."

They had no way to judge how much farther they had to go to reach the elevators, but they felt they were walking faster going up than they had coming down. Finally, Owen's foot ran out of rail. Still, there was no light.

"I think we're at the elevator," Owen told his companions. "Find the gate."

All three groped through the darkness. Flexx found the chain-link safety fence and followed it to the elevator gate. His news wasn't good.

"It's padlocked," Flexx reported, with a sob in his voice.

"Is there another way up?" asked Astrid.

"I didn't have time to look around. Flexx, how long do we have?" Owen suggested.

For half a minute there was just silence and blackness.

"Flexx!" Owen yelled, thinking the hacker might've gotten lost and wandered away.

"I'm right here." The voice originated only an inch from Owen's face, the breath hot on his nose.

"Damn!" Owen exclaimed reflexively.

"Calm down," said Flexx. "I'd say we have about an hour and fifteen... maybe an hour and a half before the bomb blows."

"We can't give up," he said, doubting his own words. "Feel around. See if you can find something!"

They tried, fruitlessly. Time ticked past. Their efforts in the dark were inefficient. More than once Astrid caught a poke in the eye from one of her sight-deprived partners. She chose to move away from the clumsy, noisy men and walked in blackness toward silence. Astrid prayed she wouldn't take a wrong step and plunge into a bottomless pit. Every time her foot struck rock she breathed a sigh of relief. Ahead, she heard something.

"Owen! Over here," called Astrid.

Shuffling through the darkness, he found her.

"I can hear water," she said.

To Owen, this seemed like an academic discovery, interesting, but of little practical value. Since he had no better idea to contribute, he groped ahead, finding only rock.

"I wish we had a light," he heard Astrid say.

"Oh man, I'm an idiot," groaned Owen.

"Don't say that, Owen," said Astrid, kindly. "You are just... American."

"No, I mean, I forgot I had this. Wait!" Owen reached under his coveralls and pulled a key ring from his jacket pocket. Pressing in on the sides of the CES tchotchke flashlight, he turned it on. Dimly, it lit up the wall of the cave.

"Where the *Hell* did you get that?" yelled Flexx.

The faint beam of light moved along the tunnel wall until it revealed an opening in the rock. Excitedly, all three ran to the opening only to find disappointment. Around the corner, a metal gate blocked the way. A heavy padlock held it shut.

Owen grabbed the chain-link, finding it cold and wet.

"Stand back!" ordered Astrid and the men stepped away.

The water had given her an idea. Maybe the lock was new and maybe it wasn't, but she knew what nine years in a warm and damp environment would do to steel. She let loose with a scream and kicked. The padlock survived the blow, but the rusted metal hasp holding it to the gate sheared free.

"Astrid, you're amazing!" said Owen.

"Thank her after we survive the nuclear explosion," said Flexx.

"Come on," urged Astrid. "We have to go."

The party moved forward and found an ascending steel stair.

Astrid went first. The men followed, tripping their way to the stairwell. All grabbed the handrail and started upward as quickly as possible.

It was 2624 feet straight up; nearly double the height of the Empire State Building. An elite runner might climb the Empire State in about 10 minutes. But none of the three was a runner, the stairwell wasn't lit and only Astrid was in great shape. They emerged from the stairwell 40 minutes later, pushing open a heavy steel door into the machine room. The light here was minimal, but still overpowered the dilated pupils of the three escapees. They waited for their eyesight to return to normal while catching their breath. Slinking toward the control room door, they heard no voices on the other side. Owen looked in and found it deserted.

"Let's go!" urged Flexx.

Owen closed the control room door again, blocking Flexx's exit.

"Where's the disc, Flexx?" he asked.

"What?"

"If you're coming with us, you have to give me the *Apoplexy II* disc," Owen demanded.

"OK, OK. Don't be an idiot," chided Flexx, "It's just a stupid game. It's in there."

He pointed to the control room. Owen entered first. He saw Flexx's ridiculous pistol on the panel and ran for it. Instead of grabbing for the gun, Flexx sauntered to the segment of control panel nearest the door. Reaching underneath, he pulled out his rucksack, casually handed it to Astrid and walked out to the mudroom.

Astrid looked inside the bag and nodded to Owen. The disc was inside.

They all peered out the window of the darkened mudroom. Olga and crew were standing in front of a sleek helicopter, chatting with Leonid Morozov. The red-faced oligarch spoke to the group, gesturing broadly with his left arm while keeping his splinted right hand still. The billionaire appeared simultaneously furious and victorious.

"They don't look like they're in a hurry to leave yet," whispered Astrid. "We might still have some time to make it to the car."

"Not much," responded Owen. "Look."

Morozov waved his crippled hand at the pilot who lowered the copter's entry stairs.

Astrid, Flexx and Owen crept east, away from the helicopter until they reached the edge of the mining complex. Shielded by the old buildings, they turned south.

It was a half-mile run to the car, but Flexx just didn't have it in him. By the time the other two had reached the Rolls-Royce, Flexx was pathetically jog-walking, still only halfway to the car. Owen fired up the Rolls engine and drove back to pick him up. The back door opened and Flexx literally fell across the bench seat. Owen cranked the wheel and the car swung back around.

When the Rolls emerged from behind the buildings, Astrid looked out the window to her right. Near the helicopter, some of Olga's party were pointing and gesticulating. One of the soldiers aimed his rifle at the Rolls and fired. The bullet shattered Astrid's window.

"Hell of a shot," she said reflexively.

"So much for stealth," thought Owen as he pressed the accelerator to the thickly carpeted floor. There was a second shot, but they only heard it. The bullet had missed.

Morozov pointed at the car through the helicopter's side window. He yelled in Russian, "They're headed for the mine road! We'll cut them off."

The pilot threw some switches and the rotors of the machine began to pick up momentum. Everyone was on board and seated except the two soldiers. Olga rose to give the pilot instructions, but Morozov shoved her back down and screamed to his men to get aboard.

Morozov kept yelling, shouting orders until the military men jumped in. Then the helicopter rose into the air. The tycoon ordered the soldiers to leave the boarding hatch open so that they could shoot through the opening. Sitting on the right-hand side of the copter, Morozov couldn't see the fleeing Rolls-Royce. He stood up, braced himself as best he could and popped his head out of the left-side hatch to have a look. Squinting to protect his eyes from the wind, he looked forward, along the helicopter's heading. Finally, he got a good look at his quarry.

"That's my car!" he screamed in surprise.

The Rolls had a good head start. Unless Morozov moved quickly, there was a chance the fugitives would escape the mine complex. If they made the highway, they might reach the authorities and expose his whole operation. The Russian government might look past some crimes, but they couldn't ignore the theft of its nuclear weapons.

To get his snipers the best possible shot, Leonid decided to position the helicopter directly above the exit to the mine road. To escape, the fleeing car would need to drive directly at the copter, presenting Morozov's men an easy target. While the Rolls Royce did have bulletproof glass, Leonid's military friends used armor-piercing rounds.

"Fly that way! Straight over the pit!" he ordered the pilot.

Olga sat in the second row of seats behind the boarding hatch. Hearing Morozov's command, she stood.

"No! Stop! You can't!" she cried urgently.

The red-faced man clubbed her with his left hand, breaking her nose and knocking her to the aircraft's floor. Face bloodied, Olga struggled to get up in the pitching helicopter.

"Fly across!" screamed Morozov.

The pilot pressed the control stick, tipping the rotors forward. The helicopter shot toward the Luster Mine. The helicopter's sudden lurch threw Olga back to the floor and Morozov into a passenger seat, where he still had an unobstructed view out the open hatch.

Through her fractured window, Astrid observed the pursuers. She assessed the situation for her companions. "I think they're going to beat us to the mine road."

Flexx sat up and laughed as he saw the copter fly straight over the huge hole.

"Oh! Bad idea! That's a bad idea!"

"What is a bad idea?" yelled Owen.

"Bad for them! Good for us!" clarified the Russian.

With satisfaction, Morozov watched his prey. The helicopter was at least three times faster than the car. Once he reached the other side, there would be plenty of time for his snipers to blast out the windows of the Rolls-Royce and kill the driver. With the car disabled, shooting the rest would be simple. He ordered his men to prepare their weapons.

Suddenly, something felt very wrong.

"Fly away from the pit!" Olga screamed, but it was too late.

First, the helicopter dropped 100 feet in just three seconds. Morozov, Olga and the gunmen hit the ceiling hard, then fell back. Morozov landed hard on his right hand and yowled in pain.

The pilot compensated for the downdraft, applying thrust to gain altitude, but the aircraft shot up much faster than anticipated.

As the copter bounced up and down, Flexx provided commentary from the car. He seemed amused.

"As Olga explained it to me, there are no-fly zones over these big pit mines. They are so huge that they create air vortexes. Cold air flows in over the sides, warms up at the bottom, rises up really fast then gets sucked back down again."

In a panic, the pilot gave the helicopter as much forward thrust as the engines could provide. The chopper responded by shooting ahead at great speed, approaching the far edge of the pit. Inside, all but one of the passengers breathed a sigh of relief.

"They're going to make it!" yelled Astrid.

"Wait for it," said Flexx, coldly.

A column of cold air bashed the helicopter like a hammer. The centrifugal force of the rotors kept the ship upright, but the aircraft plummeted. As it fell, the cabin began to spin uncontrollably around the rotor mast.

Flexx and Astrid watched the ship's violent free-fall until it dropped below the pit's edge and out of sight. Inside the copter, Morozov struggled to hang on.

There was fury in Olga's eyes as she roared, "You've killed us, you bastard!"

She had reached her feet and braced her arms between two of the aisle seats. Olga swung her legs forward, kicking Morozov with both feet, dislodging him from his chair and knocking him out of the helicopter's open hatch.

Having less wind resistance than the helicopter, Morozov

plummeted faster to the bottom of the pit, but still had plenty of time to contemplate his death. Below him, he saw the lake of muck-brown sludge. Above, he heard the screaming whine of the helicopter's engines as it tumbled toward the pit floor. Morozov opened his mouth to let out one final obscenity.

Flexx rolled down his window. From the pit, he heard a distant crashing of metal against stone. An explosion followed. He gave a grin, waved. "Bye-bye," and rolled up his window.

At first, transfixed by the scene in the pit, Owen blinked and realized time was running out.

The Rolls hit the mine road and headed upward. The car was fast in a straight line but Owen couldn't make great time through the winding route. It took several minutes to reach the mine overlook. From there it was a pretty straight shot downhill. He felt like he was pressing the accelerator through the floor. The mine road flattened as it approached the highway. Owen glanced in the rear-view mirror.

Owen had surfed Steamer Lane in Santa Cruz more than a few times. On one occasion an 18-foot monster wave had sneaked up on him. A wall of water picked him up and tossed him high into the air where he hovered helplessly before falling flat on his face in the deep-water trough behind the swell.

The image Owen saw in his rear-view mirror was similar, but instead of a wall of water, this wave was a six-foot-high rolling crest of earth, approaching fast. It struck the back of the Rolls-Royce, tipping its rear tires into the air at a steep angle. The vehicle would've flipped, but an instant later, the wave hit the front tires, launching the front of the car in the air.

The violent, bone-jarring vibrations of the seismic shock made Owen's head hurt so badly he thought he was dying.

The waves rolled away, leaving the car hanging unsupported in the air. For a moment, the Rolls' three occupants floated. Then the luxury car dropped, landing on all four tires. Hitting the ground hard, the car bottomed out, stalling its engine.

Several smaller ripples rolled beneath the Rolls-Royce, panicking its occupants but doing no real damage. Finally, all was still. Owen, Astrid and Flexx looked back and forth at each other in shocked silence. Screaming followed.

When they all felt a bit calmer, Owen turned forward in his seat. He reached out for the ignition key and turned it. The engine roared to life.

"Can I tell you? I *love* this car," raved Owen as he jammed the midnight blue Rolls-Royce into drive and turned west onto the highway toward Finland.

CHAPTER FORTY-TWO

THE BORDER CROSSING

They raced toward the village of Svetly, finally pulling onto a dirt road with some twenty miles still to go. Driving up the road for half a mile, Owen pulled the Rolls to a stop. They climbed out and performed their usual stretching and stomping.

"Oh, my god!" Flexx exclaimed, "That was amazing! Guns and helicopters and explosions!" He addressed Owen, "Man, you have got to make a game about this. You've got your mine level, the factory level... the car chase—am I right?"

"Right," said Owen unenthusiastically, "Astrid, would you mind bringing the rucksack over here?"

"Not at all," she replied and set it in the dirt at his feet.

First, she pulled out the *Apoplexy II* disc autographed to Flexx.

"Yep. OK, there it is. You've got the game," Flexx babbled.

Astrid grabbed a large, jagged rock from the roadside and smashed it into the game disc over and over. Not content with merely scratching the aluminum coating, she battered it until it shattered into plastic shards. Then she turned the rucksack upside down and shook out its contents. There were granola bars, cans of Jolt Cola ("All the sugar, twice the caffeine!") a windbreaker, a can of Skoal Bandits chewing tobacco and an old T-shirt. There was still something inside the sack, slightly bigger than the opening to the main pocket, that hadn't fallen out at first shake.

"You get it out. I'm tired," Astrid ordered.

She handed the bag to Owen. He shook it vigorously until Flexx's laptop landed on the ground.

"Hey! Easy with that!" cried Flexx.

"IBM Thinkpad 500? Nice," said Owen. "Astrid, can you handle

194

this, please?"

He held out Flexx's .45.

"Sure," she answered, casually taking the chrome-plated gun. She thumbed down the safety then aimed.

"What are you doing?" Flexx squealed. "Wait! Waitwaitwait!"

Astrid let loose three blasts from the Colt.

"Sukinsyn!" Flexx swore, throwing up his hands.

The Thinkpad exploded in expensive bits of black shrapnel.

"You're bastards! You know that?" yelled Flexx.

"You ready to go?" she asked Owen.

"Sure thing," he replied and the two walked to the car. Astrid kept Flexx covered with the Colt.

"I'm going to find you," Flexx threatened. "When you don't expect it...expect it!"

Owen and Astrid climbed in. She locked the doors. Flexx ran to the Rolls and pulled furiously on the door handles.

"You can't leave me here!" he yelled, banging on the driver's side window. Owen rolled it down. At this Flexx leaned forward. There was hope in his eyes.

Owen said, simply, "Good luck, Flexx."

Spinning the car around, Owen drove back to the main road. In the rear-view mirror, he saw the big man yelling and flipping them the double-bird.

Alone at last, Owen and Astrid made their plan as they approached the Finnish-Russian checkpoint at Raja Jooseppi. Three miles from the border crossing, they turned south onto a small side road.

Passing several small lakes, they stopped at a large pond, ringed with trees. There they parked the beautiful Rolls-Royce with its wheels aimed toward the water. Stepping out, Owen and Astrid removed their coveralls. Astrid balled hers up and threw them into the car. Owen prepared to follow suit but paused. Remembering the pebble from the mine, he removed it from the pocket of the discarded garment.

"What's that? Ooooh," asked Astrid excitedly, "Is it a diamond?"

"I don't know," Owen replied as he threw his coveralls into the front seat. "Maybe. I'm not an expert."

The stone was gray with flecks of white, rounded and about the size of Owen's thumbnail. He stuffed it into the front pocket of his jeans.

They'd become quite fond of the Rolls and hated to see it go. Owen set the parking brake, put the car in neutral and left the engine running. Finding a heavy rock, Owen successfully wedged it against the car's accelerator. He reached across the steering wheel and released the hand brake, then quickly pulled the shifter to 'drive.' The car door slammed shut as the Rolls rushed forward. Owen and Astrid watched as the armored vehicle splashed into the water.

"That's done," declared Owen.

But it wasn't. Although heavy, this was a precision-made luxury car with perfectly fitted seams and gaskets. In horror, they watched the gigantic luxury car bob like a cork in a bathtub. Owen felt like an idiot. Why hadn't he wedged open the car door?

A floating Rolls-Royce was certain to be noticed by anyone passing by. If the Russian authorities caught them crossing the border and found the car, they'd be arrested and detained. They might even be charged with espionage. Owen paced the shore. He looked for rocks to throw at the car as if that would help in some way. He could feel a panic attack building.

Astrid just stared bleakly at the car as the Rolls-Royce floated and spun to the center of the lake. Was their trusty, motorized friend mocking them? Was it challenging Owen to swim out and try to sink it? He sat at the water's edge and pulled off his sneakers. He looked at the frigid water and prepared to wade in. But then he squinted at the car. Was the waterline higher on the fenders than before?

"I *think* it's sinking," said Astrid.

Owen wanted to believe it. There was car noise from the nearby road. He prayed the drivers wouldn't see the unsinkable Rolls-Royce. The pair watched the door handles. Initially, they had been three inches above the water. Now it looked like two. Then one.

"It is sinking!" Owen called out.

"Quiet!" Astrid hissed back.

It took two interminable minutes for the water to reach the shattered passenger-side window. Things escalated quickly after that. Soon after, the beloved Rolls was gone.

Astrid held Flexx's silver Colt .45 1911 Automatic with its custom gold inlay. Drawing her arm back, she prepared to fling the pistol into the water.

"Hang on," said Owen. Astrid looked at him, concerned. They couldn't be found with a gun at the border. He held out his hand and she placed it in his palm.

Owen hadn't had a chance to fully appreciate the gun. The pistol's shining surface showed no smudges or scuffs, leading him to believe that it really was coated in silver and not chrome. Etched in gold on the pistol's sides were the characters from the videogame *Mortal Kombat*. On one side, Owen recognized the ninja named Scorpion, his mask lowered to reveal a skeletal face. Scorpion blew a deadly fireball at the dazed and helpless four-armed Goro. On the opposite side, Shaolin monk Liu Kang delivered a deadly uppercut to Hollywood bad-boy Johnny Cage. Along the top of the gun's slide were two words, engraved in gold. They read, 'Flawless Victory'.

Almost unconsciously, Owen muttered, "That's wicked cool!" then hurled the gun into the deep waters of the arctic lake.

"You know what, Astrid?" asked Owen.

"What?"

Owen replied, "I've changed my mind. Killing isn't fun."

Astrid nodded, saying, "I'm glad to hear you say so."

Owen and Astrid began their hike toward Russia's western border with Finland. They moved as quickly as they could, but the cold and the terrors of the day left them clay-footed and out-of-sorts. They cursed the never-ending Arctic sunshine that had them feeling conspicuous.

As they walked, Astrid proposed a cover story in case they were questioned. They were tourists who'd taken the bus up from Helsinki. After three days, they'd arrived that afternoon in the town of Ivalo. They'd wanted to see the border so they hitchhiked to Raja Jooseppi.

Their driver had stolen their bags, taking off when they got out to stretch their legs near the checkpoint. They'd wandered into the woods and gotten lost.

Owen questioned whether the story made sense. Astrid assured him it would be quite likely the Finnish border patrol would believe a story about an American behaving like an idiot.

"I've still got a black eye," Owen pointed out. "How will we explain that?"

Her answer was, "I punched you."

They hiked through two hours of pure paranoia. When they finally reached the border, Owen found it disappointing. He'd expected a Finnish version of "Checkpoint Charlie" with searchlights, gun towers and barbed wire. What he found was two wooden poles, one red and the other blue.

They walked west into Finland. About 100 feet past the border, they heard an angry voice from a loudspeaker. Not 20 feet away was a Finnish Border Patrol's Land Rover. The immigration officers unholstered their pistols.

Soon Owen and Astrid were safely escorted to a Finnish border detention facility. Border Patrol officers interviewed them separately. Owen told them the story about getting lost in the woods.

"Sorry," said Owen, grinning sheepishly.

When the official rolled his eyes at his American idiocy, Owen knew everything would be all right.

Astrid rejoined Owen in the waiting area.

"I blamed it all on you," she said.

"As well you should," he answered, sincerely.

The patrolmen took pity on the unprepared tourists, offering them some soup and a lift to an inn in Ivalo, about 40 minutes away. The innkeeper led them to one of the few available cabins. Once inside the rustic shack, they pulled the heavy curtains closed, took turns showering and went to sleep, each in one of the room's twin beds.

Because the sun never set, they awoke not knowing the time of day. Cleaning up as best they could, they stepped from their little bungalow into the bright sun. Had they been ordinary tourists, they'd have sought out a reindeer farm or looked for one of the several tourist traps claiming to be Santa Claus' home. Instead, they bought a breakfast of blodpalt, a dumpling made of reindeer blood and flour. Neither cared for blodpalt but both found it filling.

They bought tickets for the drafty, rattling, 4-hour bus ride to the city of Rovaniemi, climbed aboard and headed south. From there, it was an easy two-hour flight back to Helsinki.

Astrid invited Owen to stay the night at her small apartment. She cooked dinner and let him use her CompuServe account to send Viv and Jarrod emails. Astrid scanned the previous day's Helsinki Times and found a small report on the minor earthquake detected in Murmansk.

"If only I knew an ace reporter that could tell the world our story," laughed Owen.

"Should I sell it to the *New York Times* or *Pelit*?" asked Astrid, slyly.

Early the next morning, Astrid walked Owen to his departure gate at the Helsinki airport. They spoke to each other softly and formally, but as the attendants called for Owen to board, they embraced. Astrid wrapped her arms around his neck and pulled on him so hard he couldn't breathe. He didn't push away. Owen just held his breath until she let go a minute later.

Astrid's tears left a wet mark on his T-shirt. She backed away, Finnish reserve restored.

Owen boarded the plane for home.

CHAPTER FORTY-THREE

BACK AT THE RANCH

September 28, 1994
San Francisco, CA

Just 11 days after his departure, Owen's plane touched down in San Francisco.

Before leaving for the airport in Helsinki, he had recovered his old, bluish-gray bag from the Helsinki Strand Hotel. He sat by the baggage carousel at SFO, anxious for it to arrive. Forty-five minutes later, when it crashed down onto the conveyor belt, Owen had a forlorn look. Neither Jarrod nor Viv had arrived to meet him. He supposed that they hadn't checked their emails.

Owen sighed and bought a ticket on the Marin Airporter bus to San Rafael. Despite his best efforts, he had found it impossible to sleep during the flight back. He thought he might get some rest on the ride home. He shuffled his way to the back of the bus, slipping into a comfortable velour bucket seat.

"Nice," he thought, letting his head lean to the side and rest on the window.

The hydraulic door hissed shut and the bus lurched and shuddered as it pulled into traffic. The jarring motion caused Owen's head to bounce away from and then smack into the window glass. It was OK, he thought. Pretty soon they'd be on the freeway. It'd smooth out and he'd get some sleep.

"Welcome aboard," said a loud voice, crackling with distortion from the bus's PA system. "I'm Ethan and I'll be your driver for this evening."

Owen kept his eyes closed and breathed deeply. He was sure that

Ethan would finish his greeting and then he'd be able to get the rest he needed.

"A few things you might not know about San Francisco," Ethan continued. "The 'fortune cookie' was actually invented here in the late 1800s by a Japanese businessman." There was a short burst of static and the PA went quiet. Owen smiled and relaxed.

The static came back, followed by a click. Owen tensed.

"It's Ethan, your captain today. So happy to have you aboard. Levi Straus created his famous blue jeans here in San Francisco. He died at age 73." Hsssss-Click.

Owen wanted to slug good old Cap'n Ethan but wondered if the other riders might actually be enjoying their guided tour. With insights like, "Since 1901 it has been illegal to bury bodies in San Francisco," he wasn't sure how that could be possible. On and on he went, mile after mile. At most, there were five minutes in between Ethan's useless Bay Area factoids.

Hsssss-Click. "Captain Ethan. North America's first major bubonic plague epidemic began here in San Francisco in the year 1900." Hsssss-Click.

Hsssss-Click. "San Fran passed a law in 1867 making it illegal for ugly people to be seen in public." Hsssss-Click.

After they crossed the Golden Gate Bridge, Ethan revealed his encyclopedic knowledge of all things Marin County. Owen wasn't even sure if all of the "facts" were true. All he knew for sure was that Cap'n Ethan wouldn't let him sleep, so he gave up.

After an hour and a half in bad traffic, Owen stumbled off the bus, grabbed his heavy bag and dragged it to a payphone. Twenty minutes later, a green and white taxi arrived to carry him to his apartment. He lugged his suitcase up the two flights of stairs to his door. It took him several minutes of rummaging through his suitcase to find his keys.

Home at last, Owen kicked off his shoes, threw down his travel wallet and lay face down on his bed. "Thank god," he thought.

That's when the drumming began.

Lying immobile in the darkness, Owen appraised his neighbor's percussive performance, "Neil Peart, eh? Impressive."

Owen slept until four the next afternoon, wasting a golden California day. His circadian rhythms were bonkers, disrupted by living a week ten time zones away, traveling to a land where the sun never set and experiencing the stress of trying to escape a nuclear explosion.

Only hunger forced him from bed. Deciding to eat at the sports bar near work, he walked several blocks. Before reaching the restaurant, an idea occurred to Owen. He changed course and climbed the stairs to the Coliseum Arts office.

"Hello!" he called. All was dark, except for the sunlight illuminating the common room. Receiving no answer, he walked back through the programmer's area, then the art space and finally poked his head into the test pit. There was Ryan, leaning back in his chair and staring at Owen.

"Hey, asshole!" said Ryan, smiling, "You done with your company paid vacation? Wow! You lose a fight or were you always that ugly?"

"Hi Ryan," Owen grinned back. "I'm really glad to see you, too. Want to get dinner?"

They walked to the bar and took a seat at one of its wooden tables. All the food they ordered was fried to United States perfection. Owen ate happily. As he wolfed his second order of fries, he asked Ryan what went on at Coliseum Arts in his absence.

Ryan folded his arms and leaned on the table, "Well...Jarrod accused everyone in the office of leaking the game. *That* was fun. Miles is using company equipment for his pet project instead of working on the *Apoplexy II* story CD, so Jenn's pissed. Dogg says he's almost done with his project and is getting ready to leave, so maybe I'll get his office. Stevie's a little monster, which makes me so proud. I feel like I'm really making a difference with that child. Vivian's not coming to the office at all. And when Mitch does come in, he bites everyone's head off. He's freaking out about something."

"Is he smoking again?"

"Was he ever? No, he's not smoking. Which is good, because he smells bad enough. In programmer school, do they teach you guys to not bathe?"

"First day," said Owen, "just like they teach us to mark all tester gameplay suggestions: 'CLOSED.'"

"Oh, *sure*. Ignore the lead tester. It won't be my fault when the reviews say, 'Game Too Short. My dog finished it in 10 minutes.' Oh, I forgot to mention. Carmack called. He says your engine sucks."

"Harsh words, Bug Man," said Owen, shaking his head.

They spent the evening trash-talking and enjoying each other's company. Owen didn't know why, but he avoided discussing the details of his momentous trip. Something just told him he should keep it to himself for a while.

Ryan didn't drink, but he watched Owen sample beers until 11, then ferried his lead programmer home.

Owen tiptoed around his apartment as he prepared for bed, but stubbed his toe on the bathroom doorjamb. He gave a little cry.

"Quiet up there!" screamed Mindy from the apartment below.

Teeth brushed, Owen went to sleep. Well, his forebrain went to sleep. His problem-solving subconscious was working hard on a problem. At 3 a.m. it had figured it out. Owen sat upright, in shock.

"Oh, no!" he said aloud.

By 3:45 a.m. he was in the office, making coffee and eating powdered doughnuts from a pack. He did some investigating and tried one or two experiments with the office supplies. He was satisfied with the results.

At 5 a.m. he dialed directory assistance for help and received a couple of east coast phone numbers. Copying them down, he hung up and dialed. There was no answer, but when he dialed five minutes later his party picked up. The call was short.

When it was over, Owen looked crushed. He felt his eyes well up and his nose begin to run. He made a second call and the tears came a little faster. He needed to distract himself, so he started his computer, hoping a game might take his mind off the discovery. But by the time the machine was ready to go, Owen was face down on his desk, crying hard.

Ryan was in the office at nine. He found Owen perfectly composed.

"We're going to have a wrap party today," announced the programmer.

"Will it suck as much as the last one?"

"More!" said Owen, proudly. He sent emails marked "Urgent" to the team. Mitch and Jarrod replied immediately. They'd be there. Owen caught Miles when he came into the office and called Viv at home. Viv seemed nervous.

"Will there be time for us to talk after the party?" she asked. He assured her he would make time.

"OK," she said, sadly.

The lunch party was at the Chevy's restaurant in Greenbrae. Afraid the team was still burned-out, Owen feared they'd skip the get-together. He was surprised and pleased when almost everyone arrived. Even Dogg and Stevie were there. Miles and Viv arrived together. Only the red-haired art tech skipped because she had a pre-scheduled sailing lesson in Tiburon. They all seemed to enjoy the Mexican food. It beat sure more pizza. Or blodpalt.

Mitch seemed uncomfortable at the start of the meal but slowly loosened up. He lied and told the waiter that it was Jarrod's birthday. This meant the boss had to eat the cold, sweaty birthday flan, listen to the wait staff's terrible singing and wear a big, goofy sombrero.

Before the party broke up, Owen stood up and smacked his plastic water cup with a butter knife until he had the room's attention. Owen made his announcement.

"I know the last thing you want to do right now is be in the office, but I have one final surprise for everyone. It's very important, so let's all please meet in the common room in 20 minutes? Thank you!"

Owen rushed to the office to greet the team as they entered. He stood at the front of the room while the rest gathered around. A large sheet cake sat on the coffee table in the center of the room.

"Before we get to the cake…" Owen began.

Because all eyes were on Owen, no one noticed Ignacio Garcia, Esq. slip in the office door.

Mitch rolled his eyes, thinking Owen was going to give another long "you're all amazing" speech.

Owen continued, "…I want you to know that you're all amazing. You really are. But I have something important to tell you. I'm sure you all remember that this summer, we informed you that a hacker named Flexx had stolen our game *Peacemaker* and put it up for download, free on the Internet, cratering its sales."

The low-level office-party murmur stopped. All was dead silent.

With regret in his voice, Owen asked, "Well, I know who did it. Does the individual who actually leaked *Peacemaker* want to come forward and admit what they've done?"

There was no response, just a lot of glances around the room.

"Come on now. If you leaked *Peacemaker*, now is the time to come forward. No one here leaked the game?" asked Owen, incredulously. "That's what we're saying here? None of you leaked the game? No one leaked *Peacemaker*."

"Stop playing, Owen," said Jarrod. "This is mean. If you know the leaker, just tell me and I'll call our counsel."

"I'm here," said Ignacio Gonzalez, attorney at law from the back of the room.

"What?" asked Jarrod, glancing over, "Oh, well…good. Whoever it is, we'll be filing a legal action against—"

"No, we won't," said Owen forcefully.

Jarrod shook with anger, "What is the matter with you? Who leaked *Peacemaker*?'"

Owen closed his eyes. He took a deep breath, attempting to clear himself of all the emotions that were making it hard to speak.

"I just told you, Jarrod. No one leaked *Peacemaker*," said Owen.

"What are you talking about? You've seen the sales figures." Jarrod felt this statement of fact would resonate with Owen.

"Yes, I've seen them." There was venom in Owen's tone. "But the truth is, sales are great. Better than *Apoplexy's* were, actually."

Jarrod looked at Owen as though he'd gone insane, "No, they're not. You can call the fulfillment center yourself and ask."

"I did call Georgia," Owen responded. "They gave me the same numbers they gave you. They're low."

"There you go!" shouted Jarrod. "Where are you getting the idea that the game wasn't leaked?"

Owen faced his partner, saying, "I got it from the horse's mouth, Jarrod. My friend Astrid interviewed Flexx in December. He didn't mention stealing it. Trust me. I've met that asshole. If he'd stolen it, he would've bragged about it."

"Then in the spring, I got an email from Flexx," Owen continued, "He talked about *Apoplexy*, but not *Peacemaker*. And when I met him in Finland, he wanted me to sign a disc he'd cracked. Do you know which game he wanted signed? Let me tell you, it wasn't *Peacemaker*."

"Well, it sounds to me like you've had a lot of contact with this Flexx guy, Owen," sneered Jarrod. "How much did he pay you to leak your own game?"

Owen laughed a little.

"It took me a while to figure it out, but you know my motto, 'You need all the data,'" said Owen. "After we made the last *Peacemaker* build, you took a trip—a solo vacation, which was weird in itself—to the Bahamas. You came back without a tan. What were you doing while you were in Nassau, Jarrod?"

The CEO scowled.

"And you made sure we added a check-box to our order forms, where people could indicate whether or not they had Internet access. 'Marketing research purposes,' you said," Owen scoffed.

"So what?" asked Jarrod.

"This morning I called the mail forwarding service. You know, the one you told us would allow us to expand if our shipping company couldn't fulfill demand?" Owen asked, smiling.

Jarrod choked a little.

"Well, my friend, they walked me through the instructions you gave them. When an order arrived, they opened it and looked at the marketing survey. If it said they didn't have an Internet connection, they forwarded the order to Georgia. But if they *did* have Internet access, they sent the order to the Coliseum Arts office in *Nassau, Bahamas*. Funny thing is, when I spoke with our counsel, Mr. Gonzalez didn't know anything about any office in the Bahamas."

Menacingly, Owen approached Jarrod. He said, "I figure that you set up a one-person office on Nassau. All that person did was deposit checks in a Bahamian bank and mail purchasers information on how to download *Peacemaker* over the Internet. It was perfect. Everybody gets their game, so no one complains about not getting their disc. Meanwhile, you get half the money in a bank account that only you know exists. Then you explain the missing profits by telling everyone that *Peacemaker* isn't selling because Flexx cracked it."

"You can't believe that. Owen. Please," Jarrod implored.

Owen felt them again, the tears welling from the corners of his eyes. "We were partners! Partners! I trusted you."

"Well, maybe you shouldn't be so trusting, Owen." Jarrod had the look of poker player hiding a derringer under the table. "You trusted Cole. You trust Miles. You even trust Viv!"

"You son of a bitch!" scowled Miles.

"Oh, yeah. Miles and Viv! Viv and Miles!" Jarrod took off the sombrero and threw it to the floor. "You weren't gone two days before I saw them making out in the parking lot."

Viv cried, "No!"

Jarrod lashed out again "I saw it from my window when you thought no one was watching. I'd say everyone in here is screwing someone over. How do you like that, Owen? Your girlfriend is a slut!"

Miles shot off the couch and threw a punch at Jarrod's face, but Owen caught the musician and pulled him back. Owen held him tightly, not giving Miles any space to twist free.

He whispered in Miles' ear, "Please. It's all right. Just let him go."

A moment later, Miles stopped struggling and Owen released him.

Miles turned to Owen, "Viv was telling me she's sick. She needs surgery, Owen. That's why I was with her in the parking lot. She'd just found out. That's why I was holding her."

Owen looked at Vivian. She covered her face and cried into her palms.

"Everyone thinks you're such a genius, Owen," Jarrod sneered. "But the truth is, I could've made this place a success with anybody. I don't need you or any of the damaged souls you employ to make my widgets. You're all just a line-item on my business plan."

"That's enough," said Ignacio Gonzalez, Esq. as he handed Jarrod a manila envelope. "Mr. Jarrod Young, this is a legal notification that all your access to Coliseum Arts and its resources is suspended, pending investigation. All information in our possession about any alleged embezzlement by you to any and all unknown accounts will be transferred to the FBI for review. Please leave the premises without removing any items or I will be required to summon the police."

Jarrod had no more words. He looked at the shocked faces of his former employees, staring at him with hate or disgust. Testers, artists, programmers. The CEO edged toward the exit.

Ryan met him at the door. "You forgot your hat!" he said cheerfully, pressing the sombrero into Jarrod's chest. Unthinking, Jarrod grabbed it and escaped down the stairs.

Ryan turned to the room and grinned, "Wow, Owen. Hell of a party!" He picked up the plastic knife. "Who wants cake?"

CHAPTER FORTY-FOUR

THE AFTER-PARTY

September 30, 1994
San Rafael, CA

After Jarrod's exit, most of the Coliseum Arts team quickly fled the office. Vivian was just wrecked by the whole scene. She asked Owen for his keys, took his car and drove to his apartment to sleep.

Owen asked Mitch to wait behind after everyone else had left.

"What's up?" asked Mitch, with a hopeful smile. In the dimly lit office, his day-glow orange outfit looked like a convict's work suit.

"Mitch, I know you leaked *Apoplexy II*," said Owen.

At this, Mitch teared up. He was caught.

"Why, Mitch?" asked Owen. "What happened?"

Mitch took a deep breath and tried to explain.

"I'm sorry, Owen. Over the summer, Flexx sent a message to my personal e-mail. He knew my dad needed money. I don't know how. I guess he'd hacked me. Flexx said he wanted to impress some friend by giving him a copy of *Apoplexy II* before we released it to the public. He offered me $10,000 for the game. But Flexx promised that he would only make one copy—the one for his friend. I didn't see any harm in it, Owen. It was just supposed to be one copy. I had to do it—for my dad. Oh god, I'm just so sorry… "

Mitch broke down.

As he waited for his friend to recover, Owen thought about his part in the story—the part Mitch had kindly left out.

Finally, Owen said, "Mitch. I don't think it's your fault. I think it's my fault. Mine and Jarrod's. *I* am sorry. We worked you to death. And when you said you needed our help, we did nothing. All I could think about was finishing my stupid game. I let *you* down, Mitch, not the other way around. It's my fault the game leaked. It wasn't yours."

They embraced.

"I'm going to pay y'all back," said Mitch quickly. "With the money, we got the hardware store back on track. I think we can start making payments in January. I'm pretty sure."

"We can talk about that later. OK, Mitch? Why don't you just go home?"

"OK," said the tools programmer. He stood and walked towards the door, but upon reaching it turned back.

"How did you know? That I leaked it?" Mitch asked quietly.

"Do you really want to know?"

"Yeah."

Owen visualized the logic tree in his head and read it aloud.

"Let's see," he began. "You had no reason to leak *Peacemaker,* so I didn't suspect you at first. But when I realized *Peacemaker* was never stolen, it was clear that you had the best reason to sell the game. Your dad needed the money."

"Lastly, there were your cigarettes. You said you were smoking again, but you weren't. I never saw you smoking and when you smoke, you stink. You didn't stink," answered Owen.

Mitch laughed a little and said, "Y'all figured it out because I wasn't smoking? I don't get it."

"Oh, there was so much more," Owen explained. "The day Dogg and I took Stevie to the hospital, we both got soot on our hands. At the time I just thought it was one of those weird things that happen and you can't explain them. But then I found more soot on the tape dispenser at your desk."

"You didn't have access to the game files. The only people with access were Ryan, Jenn, Dogg and I. You couldn't get to Ryan's copies because, well, he's Ryan. Jenn and I always log out of the network when we leave."

"Your best chance of getting the game was from Dogg's computer. He trusted his door lock, so he never logged out of the network. You just needed a copy of his office key. Dogg always left his keys hanging in the lock when he was programming. So, when everyone ran out of the room to help Stevie, you used the lighter to blacken the door key."

Mitch was beside himself, "Honestly, I didn't know Stevie was having a seizure. I didn't know what was going on. I just saw that y'all had left the room. If I'd known I would've helped, I swear!"

Owen was on a roll. He kept talking, "You blackened Dogg's key with the flame from your cigarette lighter, got some scotch tape and stuck it to the scorched key. When you removed the key it left a silhouette on the adhesive. From that, you just cut a new key from the outline on the tape. But in the process, you got soot on the tape dispenser."

"The way you put things together Owen...it amazes me," said Mitch.

"Do you have the key you made?" asked Owen.

Mitch nodded sheepishly and walked over to his desk. Pulling open the top-right file drawer, he reached in, pulling out a key he'd taped to the underside of the desktop. He handed it to Owen.

"It's just some cheap sheet metal," Mitch offered. "I used to cut keys all the time at my dad's hardware store."

Owen carried it to Dogg's office and with just a little jiggling unlocked the door. "Useful," he concluded.

"Yes, it was," Mitch agreed, "Dogg left himself logged in and I copied his version of the game to the disc burner. I made a disc and put it in the marketing machine. Then I uploaded it to Flexx."

Mitch shook his head, saying, "Owen, I know I'm fired, but I wonder if y'all can't just tell everyone that I quit."

"You did what you thought you had to do for your family," Owen replied. "You're not fired and I won't tell anyone. I didn't say this at the meeting, but you're the reason I caught Jarrod embezzling."

"Me?" asked Mitch, surprised. "How was that?"

"You suggested that Jarrod might be lowballing *Peacemaker's* sales figures to keep the company from paying employee bonuses. That's why I analyzed Jarrod's shareware system to see if it could siphon off sales revenue. It could and he did. Pretty well, too."

"Damn good, Owen," Mitch chuckled, again wiping a tear from the corner of his eye.

"There is one mystery I didn't solve," Owen admitted, "The cracked copy of the game had an extra file in Russian. Where did that come from?"

Mitch furrowed his brow, then his expression changed to a look of recognition.

"Oh yeah, the Russian file," he said. "I did that. Flexx is sloppy. He didn't change the default settings on his file transfer server. When I logged in as 'visitor' I had full read access to his files. I clicked around and downloaded one, probably to the game directory. I thought Flexx might have something interesting, but the file was in Russian, so I didn't grab any more. When I pushed the game to Flexx, I must have sent back his own file along with the *Apoplexy II*."

Talking about the theft seemed to make Mitch feel bad again. "Owen, again I need you to know that I'm..."

"Just stop," Owen interrupted. "In the end, the game didn't even leak. Spend your energy thinking about what we're going to make next."

"How did you stop Flexx from leaking the game, Owen?" asked Mitch.

Owen smiled and said, "I just used my stellar interpersonal skills."

Mitch smiled back, waved goodbye and left.

Owen walked to his car and sighed. He sure missed the Rolls-Royce.

The sun was setting. He *loved* that the sun set here. He found Miles leaning against his Honda.

Miles said, "Here's what you need to know, Owen. Viv has a heart defect. The doctors say she needs surgery to fix it. Viv wanted to tell you herself, but it's out now, so...there it is. I know you are her boyfriend, but she's *my* best friend. We're going to get her through this together. But you've got to know. Viv and I are going to keep coordinating our Halloween costumes, because, dude, yours just suck. 'Free Willy'? What the hell was that?"

They laughed a little, hugged and the composer drove away.

CHAPTER FORTY-FIVE

HEARTS AND MINDS

Owen headed down D Street and up to his apartment. The kitchen light was on, but everything else was dark. He tried to sneak in quietly but instead kicked a table leg.

"Owen, is that you?" Viv called.

He quickly went to the back bedroom, where Vivian sat up in the bed, bathed in moonlight.

"Yes, it's me."

He sat down beside her, took her hands and kissed them. "I'm sorry I made you work so much this summer."

Viv shook her head. "It's not like crunch mode gave me a bad heart."

"But it was our first five months together and I wasted them making a stupid game."

She nodded her head, "Yes, *we* did."

Owen looking into her eyes, said, "And that's the thing I don't understand. You always thought the game was stupid. Why did you work so crazy hard when you didn't care about it?"

Viv touched his face, "Because you cared about it, you idiot. I love you. Now climb into bed. I need some sleep because in the morning I'm going to bore you with a ton of medical stuff."

She turned on her side and he slid into bed beside her. Owen pulled the comforter up above her shoulder and they fell asleep. To Owen's surprise, they slept until morning.

The next day they decided to drive up to Petaluma. On the way, they talked about Viv's upcoming surgery. She explained, surgeons had told her that even though the procedure had serious risk, waiting would be riskier.

They parked downtown and walked the boardwalk along the Petaluma River until they reached Viv's favorite sandwich shop. They ate at a table by the water, enjoying the sunshine and fresh air. Owen recounted his adventures with Astrid: the visit with Flexx, Dogg's code and the deadly seizure, the kidnapping, shootings, police, the Luster mine, nuclear shockwaves and the border crossing.

Owen finished his story and awaited Viv's response. He expected something demonstrative, with lots of 'wow's and 'amazing's. Instead, she was quiet. Not silent, just quiet. It was clear to Owen that Viv wasn't at her vivacious best.

After lunch, they wandered through the old town, strolling up Petaluma Boulevard, past the Mystic Theater and McNear's Restaurant. At the old bank building, they turned left and walked up Kentucky Street past the vividly painted Victorian homes.

Viv turned to Owen, "Dogg has finished his project. He's going to give his code to the Army."

"I know," he replied.

"We've got to stop him. We can't have a part in killing people. We just make stupid games," said Viv emotionally.

Owen sighed, "I've been thinking about it a lot, but I don't know what to do. Dogg's got backups of backups. He's got that huge air-conditioned RAID array in his office. I guess I could go in there with an axe or something."

Viv shook her head, "You'd go to prison. *Federal* prison. And besides, Dogg probably has the code stored off-site, too. Maybe we could talk to him about it. Try to convince him not to turn it over to the military. He'd be directly responsible for murdering people, or assassinating them or whatever the army calls it these days. Do you really think he's OK being a part of that?"

"Not sure," said Owen, "I think so. He's an, 'ends justify the means' kind of guy. In his mind, he's just making a good living for his family. That's all he cares about."

"Well, we've got to think of something," she said, taking Owen's hand.

Viv suddenly felt tired and sat down on a low stone wall. Owen brought the car around and they headed back to San Rafael, stopping for dinner out at a new Italian restaurant on Third Street. Upon returning to Owen's apartment, Viv went straight to bed. Owen stayed up late, thinking up crazy but ineffective strategies to stop Dogg from turning his deadly algorithm over to the government.

The Army Intelligence officers would arrive on Thursday to collect Dogg's code and equipment. This left Owen and Viv only a few more days to devise a plan.

They spent much of Monday at Viv's medical appointments. By Tuesday evening, they seemed no closer to a solution for the Dogg situation. Owen went to bed accepting his fate. In the morning, he'd have to physically destroy Dogg's computers and would probably end up back at San Quentin. This time for real.

At three in the morning, Owen's subconscious came through. He woke Viv and went over the plan.

On Wednesday, Dogg and Stevie arrived early, as usual. Stevie sat on the common room floor to draw while Dogg walked to his office. To Dogg's surprise, he found Owen already working.

He greeted Dogg, "Morning!"

Dogg returned the welcome.

"Hey, are you going to pack up your stuff today?" Owen asked.

"Yeah, this afternoon. I was going to pick up some moving boxes at lunch," answered Dogg.

"Since you guys will be leaving us, Viv and I wondered if we could take Stevie to Double Rainbow for ice cream. We could go while you're out getting your boxes," Owen suggested.

Dogg smiled, "Yeah. That'd be really nice, thanks. Stevie would like that."

They worked until noon. Then Dogg left the building to run his errand. When he returned at one, he noticed the plastic spoons and ice cream take-out bowls in the common room's trash can.

Something else in the room caught his eye, and Dogg's expression turned to one of deep concern and confusion. Lying face down on the coffee table was the enormous, green-tinted filter screen for his monitor. Owen walked in.

"What's that doing there?" Dogg asked.

Owen explained, "Well, we knew you were moving out and you left your office door open. I remembered carrying that monster up here, so I knew how heavy it was. Mitch and I decided to do you a favor and carry it out here. Man, it was a bear getting it through your office door."

"My office door was open?"

"Sure. I guess you forgot to lock it."

It took Dogg a few seconds to assess the situation. Suddenly he had a dreadful thought. He looked around the common room. Not seeing what he hoped to see, he demanded, "Where's Stevie?"

"Stevie?" said Owen, casually. "He's in your office. I think he's playing the game."

Without hesitation, Dogg ran for his office, shoving Owen out of the way and into a wall. Through the office window, Dogg couldn't see Stevie's head because the enormous monitor blocked the view, but he saw his son's hand on the computer mouse.

As he rounded the corner into his office, Dogg screamed, "No! Stevie!" His hands shot out and grabbed the boy, yanking him from the computer chair. Dogg spun Stevie's face toward the wall, then crumpled to his knees. He held his son tightly, shielding him from the screen.

The shouting and unexpected violence of the action was too much for the six-year-old and Stevie began to cry. Dogg's eyes were closed. He was afraid to open them though not from fear for himself. He feared what he'd see on the monitor. He feared what he might have done to his son.

"What did I do, Daddy?" Stevie cried, grabbing his father around the neck. "Daddy, what did I do?"

Dogg glanced up at the screen then quickly looked away. It took a moment for his mind to analyze what he'd only momentarily seen. It wasn't *Apoplexy II*. Opening his eyes more boldly this time, Dogg took a good look at the monitor. He didn't recognize the program immediately. Still holding Stevie over his shoulder, Dogg stood up and moved to get a closer look. He read the text in the upper left-hand corner. "DPAINT"

It was the pixel editor the artists used to draw game graphics. There was a misshapen figure scribbled in the center of the screen. It looked like a monster and it would've been unrecognizable were it not for the clumsily written word scrawled at the top of the screen. It said, "DOGG." Stevie had just been drawing on the computer. He was going to be all right. At this realization, Dogg hugged his sobbing son.

The big man cried, too.

Softly, in between sniffles Stevie still asked, "What did I do, Dad?"

"Shhhh," said Dogg, trying to soothe his boy. "You didn't do anything wrong, Stevie. You are perfect. It was me. I made a mistake. I'm sorry, Stevie. I made a mistake."

Dogg held his child, slowly rocking him back and forth. He turned toward the door. There he saw Owen and Viv watching. Somehow, they knew. He scanned their faces for anger but saw only fear, pleading and hope. Breathing in deeply, Dogg tried to set Stevie down on his feet. It took two attempts before the boy's legs supported him.

Standing up again, Dogg spoke shakily to the young couple. "Could you...would you take Stevie to the park for a couple of hours. I...I have a few things I need to take care of before tomorrow. Could you do that for me? Please?"

They nodded to Dogg and took Stevie down to the playground. By three o'clock, Stevie was worn out and Owen carried him back to the office. After gently placing the child on the common room's couch, Viv and Owen walked into the programmers' area. Dogg met them.

"I have some bad news," said Dogg with no hint of irony, "I lost it."

"You lost it?" Viv asked.

"Yeah, I lost it. All my work for the past five months," Dogg deadpanned. "The computer crashed and corrupted my whole development system. Then I think there was a chain reaction or something because whatever it was, it spread to my RAID array, so that's all gone, too. That caused a magnetic pulse that degaussed my backup tapes. Wow. I'm really sorry, Owen because I don't think the Army is going to pay out my contract now. That's too bad because I know you need the money and all. But you know, shit happens. There's no way of getting any of it back. So...sorry."

Owen tried to keep a straight face, but it was hard. "That's OK, Dogg. I...I know you did your best. I wouldn't worry too much about the money. We've recently saved some money that would've gone to executive pay so, I think we'll be all right."

"Yes. Well, have a nice night. Stevie and I are going to pick up my wife at the airport. It'll be nice for the family to all be together again. Bye."

Dogg lifted his son from the couch and carried him out to the jeep.

"Well?!"

Owen and Viv winced as Jenn's voice boomed from the corner of the programmer's room. "What the *Hell* was that?" she demanded.

CHAPTER FORTY-SIX

THE NEW MANAGEMENT

October 6, 1994
Moscow, Russia

Flexx sat under a multicolored afghan on Ludmilla's couch. Miserable and sick, he sneezed into his handkerchief so violently and so often that the skin around his nostrils had become red and chapped. He had his sister running the radiator full blast. Despite sweating buckets from the heat, Flexx still had the chills.

It had taken him two exhausting days and nights to reach Moscow. He'd hitchhiked a ride to Murmansk with a trucker, then grabbed what sleep he could at the rail depot before the rattling, freezing, daylong train ride back to St. Petersburg. From there, he took another train four and a half hours to Moscow. Then there was the long walk through the cold to his sister's. Finally arriving at Ludmilla's apartment, he'd collapsed, very ill.

He'd been in his sister's care for a week and wasn't sure he would ever recover from the horrible trip. Flexx was equally unsure he'd ever escape Ludmilla. She smothered her newly dependent brother with the fierce love of a mother bear.

Flexx could hear his sister bumping around in the kitchen.

"Luda?" he called.

She peeked her head around the corner at her patient.

"Yes, Fyodor?"

"Do you think..." asked Flexx, sheepishly, "Do you think you could make me some soup?"

Ludmilla felt so happy she almost burst.

"Of course, my Fedya," she answered.

Before she could return to the kitchen, the telephone rang.

"Hello," she said, into the receiver. "Oh, yes. Yes, he's here. Fyodor, the phone is for you."

"That's Goddamned weird," Flexx mumbled to himself.

Since the mine disaster, he'd spoken with no one. Dragging an afghan with him, he shuffled over to take the handset from Ludmilla.

"Hello?" Flexx coughed. A man replied. It was Dr. Ilizarov.

The big man shivered—this time from fear. He tried to bluster his way through the conversation.

"Oh, yes. Hello, doctor," he said. "It's good to hear from you."

"So, you're not in Murmansk?" asked Ilizarov, pointedly.

"No, no," answered Flexx. "Obviously not. I got really sick on the way up, so Olga sent me back to my sister's."

"Then you don't know that she and Leonid are dead?"

"Dead!" Flexx exclaimed a bit too dramatically. "Oh. No. That's just awful. Was it some sort of horrible accident?"

There was a pause before Ilizarov resumed, "Yes. An accident."

Flexx sneezed but quickly returned the handset to his ear.

"I know you're lying, Flexx," said Ilizarov. "But with the death of my friend Leonid, I now control the syndicate. Listen carefully. You are going to do two things for me. First, I need that flight control software from Phrenetiq. I have several groups of 'freedom fighters' that will pay handsomely to upgrade their Stinger missiles."

"OK," acknowledged Flexx, robotically. "Yes. Absolutely."

Ilizarov continued, "Second: For better or worse, I have inherited the Nevada Project. With Olga dead and gone, I will require your help at Site 4 in Nevada. You will do these things for me or I will kill both you and your sister Ludmilla. Do you understand, Flexx?"

"Are you still on the phone, Fyodor?" called Ludmilla from the kitchen.

"Yes!" Flexx called out, simultaneously answering both his sister and the doctor.

"Fine," said Ilizarov. "Mister Flexx, you will soon be a very wealthy man. I look forward to seeing you in my St. Petersburg office early next week. Goodbye."

CHAPTER FORTY-SEVEN

THE ROAD TO RECOVERY

October 6, 1994
San Rafael, CA

On Thursday the Army Intelligence officers arrived at Coliseum Arts to take possession of Dogg's work. They squeezed into his office, which was still cluttered with boxes and equipment. Dogg shut the door and lowered the window blinds. Owen left his desk and brought Viv in so she could also listen. They heard enough to know that Dogg had told one whopper of a lie.

Addressing his clients, Dogg said, "I understand you're upset. I am, too. I just want to make sure you understand what we're up against."

From their vantage point in the programmer's area, the eavesdroppers heard some indistinct mumbling.

Dogg continued spinning his yarn. "Oh, yes sir. Yes sir. It was a worm. Created by a technological genius. It infected my computer and spread through the entire system. Everything was lost."

"Mumble… mumble… mumble."

"Oh, yes. This guy is a master. He's the best I've ever seen. If he could do this, he could break into NORAD and steal the launch codes. I'm serious. He may be the greatest threat to American intelligence since the Rosenbergs."

"Mumble… mumble."

Without warning, Dogg's door flew open. Owen and Viv quickly looked away and tried to act nonchalant. The military men just ignored them and stalked past.

"Lieutenant Baird!" the more senior officer addressed his subordinate as they stormed out. "We need all hands on deck. I want the CIA. Get all our resources focused on the identification and rendition of the terrorist known as Flexx!"

Dogg swaggered a bit as he followed the intelligence officers, smiling and waving goodbye to his friends.

Later in the day, a team of soldiers arrived and removed the remainder of the government's property, leaving Dogg's office empty.

Soon after, Owen noticed Ryan carrying a crate of personal effects out of the test pit. To Owen, it looked like Ryan was making good on his threat to appropriate Dogg's abandoned office.

He watched Ryan walk past Miles and toward Dogg's area. But the test lead made an unexpected turn into Jarrod's office. Owen peeked in as Ryan set his box down on the CEO's desk. Ryan grabbed Jarrod's framed diploma from the Haas School of Business and tossed it into the garbage can.

"Hey, Ryan," asked Owen, curiously. "Whatcha doing?"

"The company needs a CEO, right?"

Owen answered slowly, "Right."

"And it's clear that you suck at choosing CEOs, right?"

"Uh... right," Owen admitted.

"And I'm clearly the most competent person at Coliseum Arts."

This time, Ryan didn't wait for confirmation. He just declared, "I'm the new CEO."

Ryan arranged his effects on the desk.

Owen's instinct was to resist, but he honestly couldn't think of a good argument against the posting. He turned away, confused but not entirely unhappy.

"Hey, Owen!" called the new CEO.

The programmer turned. "Yes?"

"Get the Hell back to work. What am I paying you for, anyway?"

Owen laughed and Ryan slammed his office door.

Late in October, Viv received her heart operation. The surgery went well, but she was confined to her hospital bed for a week after. Viv seemed most disappointed by the fact that she'd be stuck in a recovery ward on Halloween. When the holiday arrived, Owen brought Miles to the hospital. The musician arrived in a doctor's costume and raised Viv's spirits by prescribing her candy from a medical bag.

After her discharge, Owen spent most of his time with Vivian. While helping her recovery was certainly high on Owen's list of priorities, his main goal was to finally be a good boyfriend. As soon as she felt well enough, he took Viv on day trips and out for fancy dinners.

"Change sure comes fast these days," said Owen.

"Yes. Fast and getting faster,' Viv replied, "Speaking of changes… I've been thinking. I need to make some changes."

A blip appeared on Owen's "she's breaking up with you" radar. "Oh?"

"I want to do something else for a living. Something besides art," she said.

Simultaneously, Owen was relieved and concerned.

"But why?" he asked, "You're the best artist I've ever met."

"Maybe. But I just sort of fell into the game business. I don't really care about it. I mean, it's really stupid, Owen."

"Yeah, yeah," laughed Owen.

"But does it matter if you're great at something and it doesn't make you happy?" she asked, seriously. "You only get one life, you know?"

"What would you do, if not art?"

"I don't know exactly, but I'll tell you one time I really got excited," Viv bounced a little as she spoke, amped up by just the thought. "You're going to think this is really weird, but I got super-jazzed when Mr. Gonzalez hit Jarrod with the legal papers. He had all this power and confidence. It was so sexy. Being a lawyer looks totally badass."

Viv's eyes shone with an intensity that left Owen a little intimidated.

"You're into Gonzalez now?" asked Owen. "Dang! I did not see that coming."

Viv punched him in the shoulder and Owen laughed.

"No, I get it," he said, "You want to be a lawyer. Wow!"

"I can still do art when I feel like it," she continued, but the statement was little more than an afterthought.

"That… that sounds great," said Owen supportively, "Why don't we look at law schools when you're all healed up?"

In late November, Jenn unexpectedly asked Owen to breakfast. Because she wasn't known as the most social of people, Owen knew something was up. He drove down to Tiburon to meet her at Sam's Anchor Café. After parking by the blue and white Tiburon Playhouse, Owen crossed the street to Sam's, passing straight through its antique bar.

He joined Jenn at her waterfront table outside, and the two enjoyed a perfect view of "The City." Sam's wooden deck overlooked a marina filled with small sailboats, with the bay, Alcatraz and Angel Island visible beyond. They could see a panorama stretching from San Francisco's Presidio to Coit Tower.

Jenn ordered crab cakes, fries and mimosas for them both – her treat.

Their food had arrived when a splash in the water below caught their attention. Standing up to get a good look, they discovered an otter playing beneath the pier. Taking advantage of this distraction, aggressive seabirds descended on the table, making off with most of the fries. With flailing arms, the pair drove away the flying bandits.

Laughing, Jenn was done beating around the bush. "Owen, I'm quitting."

Owen spit out some of his mimosa.

"Quitting? Why?" he stammered, wiping his mouth with his sleeve. "The audio storybook turned out great."

"It did. But I'm quitting for the same reason I came to Coliseum Arts."

"What reason is that?" asked Owen, truly surprised.

"You," Jenn answered.

"Thanks?" Owen was irked. "You're going to have to explain that one to me."

Jenn smirked, saying, "Didn't you ever wonder why I came to a company that made shooter games? You know that's not who I am."

"I guess I thought you needed a job," he replied.

"I can get a job," she said a little arrogantly. "That's not a problem. I took this job because of you."

"But you just said you hated the games I made."

"I do," she agreed, "I hate them. But when we spoke that first time, I heard something in your voice. You had passion. You had desire! You wanted to do something great! We did that with *Apoplexy II*. It's a shooter and shooters suck, but this one had depth and feeling and intelligence. I knew that with our next game we'd do something really fantastic."

"But if we've just done this great thing, why quit now?"

Jenn spoke earnestly, "Because I sense you've changed. When I arrived last year, I could tell that you would do *anything* to make a great game."

"And now? "

"You're different, Owen. You know it's true. I've seen how you are with Viv, with Miles, with Mitch," Jenn explained. "Your priorities have changed. For you, it's no longer all about the game."

He couldn't deny it.

"And that's why I'm quitting," said Jenn. "You can't make great art without sacrifice. People need to expend their whole selves to change the world. Most people don't understand games. They look at what we do and think it's like a pinball machine. They don't respect us. They don't respect our art. Most don't even *see* it as art. But when *we* don't see it as art, then we're done. We become hucksters on the midway, scrounging for quarters."

"I can't trample over people anymore, Jenn. It's not worth it." Owen answered. "Games are an art form that just doesn't last. Today you have a hit game. Great. Six months later, it's an old game. People move on and buy a newer one. Three years later your game is a dinosaur and so are you. Just to try and keep up, you'll be crunching over and over again. It will kill you."

"Then I guess I'm going to die for my art," answered Jenn, finally.

"Good luck with that," Owen laughed. "So much for me talking you into staying. Do you mind telling me where you're going?"

"Second Stage Films," she answered, taking a bite from her Benedict, "It's a 'Siliwood' company that's going to merge linear and nonlinear storytelling. We're going to completely redefine the paradigms of the interactive dialectic."

"I'm sure you will, Jenn," assured Owen. "Whatever that means."

CHAPTER FORTY-EIGHT

YOU CAN'T MISS

April 4, 1995
Black Sea Coast

The two-man Stinger Missile team could see the government jetliner approaching, but they didn't hurry. They still had time to prepare. The "Missile Chief" wore khaki and green military camouflage. The second man, designated "Crew," dressed in a pastel nylon jacket and blue jeans. Both sported black, balaclava masks.

Though Chief no longer held any official government standing, he still had friends at the ministries. Through them, he'd received the plane's passenger list. The jet carried diplomats, military advisors and business envoys – a vanguard of dangerous agents from the encroaching west.

"Here come the victorious Cold Warriors," Chief said to his partner, smiling grimly. "They say they come to rescue us with their capitalism. But these are vultures, come to pick clean the bones of the Soviet Union."

This would be Chief's second attempt at shooting down a plane of western barbarians. He had tried before, launching a Stinger at a departing airliner. His missile had been an ancient leftover from the Soviet-Afghan War; good enough to hit slow, low-flying, Russian helicopters, but not planes deploying anti-missile technology.

That first time, Chief fired as the plane took off, but the jet pilots had caught sight of the rocket and immediately released their decoy flares. Badly overloaded by the flares' heat signatures, the missile badly undershot the target.

Realizing that he had wasted his militia's precious resources on a

Off By One

dozen outmoded weapons of war, he shelved the project, wondering how he would ever accomplish his mission.

Months later, Chief discovered a glimmer of hope for his obsolete rockets. Agents of a Russian arms dealer named Ilizarov had advertised an upgrade for out-of-date Stinger Missiles. With the promised enhancements, a Stinger could finally differentiate a plane from its anti-missile flares.

That October, Chief and his militia leadership traveled to Russia for Ilizarov's live-fire demonstration. Rubles and software were quickly exchanged and soon every missile in the militia's arsenal received the deadly, new computer logic.

As Crew prepared his state-of-the-art weapon, Chief congratulated himself. "Soon, the western powers will understand that we will not be overrun."

Crew hefted the Stinger-RMP up to his shoulder and opened the sighting mechanism. Chief helped him adjust it, balancing the long, narrow tube so that the pistol grip was at just the right angle.

In keeping with his training, Chief moved to Crew's left side and, with his left hand, held out a cylindrical Battery Cooling Unit. Crew took the BCU and jammed it into a hole at the bottom of the missile launcher.

With one hand under the launcher and the other holding the pistol grip, Crew threw several switches with his fingers and thumbs. The weapon emitted an irregular clicking noise.

Chief pointed at the incoming jetliner, helping his partner sight the target. The frequency of the clicking noises increased until it became a low, unbroken tone. Crew adjusted his aim. The pitch became high. *Target Lock!* Chief gave the instruction to fire and Crew pulled the trigger.

The Stinger missile exploded without leaving the launcher, blowing the two men to bits in a ball of fire.

* * *

When Captain Donahue noticed the cloud of white smoke that had appeared suddenly on the ground ahead of the plane, his hands flinched on the flight controls. Straining his eyes, he searched the sky but saw no telltale stream of rising missile exhaust.

Donahue relaxed, assured that his passengers and crew were in no danger. He sighed heavily, muttering, "I need new orders. I *hate* flying

225

into this sunofabitch country!"

CHAPTER FORTY-NINE
THE GRAND EVENT

For all the trouble it had caused Owen and the team, *Apoplexy II* was only a modest seller. Just as it hit the market, id Software released *Doom II*. With id's game dominating the 3D shooter buzz, *Apoplexy II* fizzled, providing just a few months of solid sales. What saved Coliseum Arts were *Peacemaker's* profits, repatriated by Jarrod as part of his plea bargain with the U.S. Justice Department. The former CEO would spend only six months in a minimum-security prison.

The money meant that tiny Coliseum Arts could stay in business for a while, even without a new product on the shelves.

In February of 2005, Owen proposed to Viv. It was a foggy evening at Point Reyes. They stood atop a hill, overlooking a gray Pacific Ocean. He knelt and placed the ring on her finger. Viv screamed the word, "Yes!"

In defiance of her October surgery, she tackled her fiancée, knocking him down and covering his face with kisses. Eventually rising, Owen dusted himself off while Viv looked at the engagement band on her hand. The diamond in the setting was enormous. She knew that Owen made a good living writing software, but the stone must have been at least three carats.

"Owen! How in the world did you…?" Viv paused, then asked. "Is this diamond from the mine?"

He nodded.

In joy, she again jumped on Owen, wrapping her arms around his neck and her legs around his waist. She kept kissing him as he carried her all the way back to the car.

Romantic proposal accepted, Owen drove her to a nearby Western saloon where Vivian's friends surprised her with an engagement party.

Afterward, she told Owen that she'd had the best day of her life.

Driving home along the dark forest road, Owen caught a glimpse of Viv from the corner of his eye. He instantly recognized her "hungry mink" look. Desperately, he searched for a secluded pullout where he could stop the car before his fiancée pounced. He found one with mere seconds to spare.

Viv didn't want to wait for spring, so they set a wedding date for later in the month. They'd have a quiet civil service at the Marin County Civic Center and hold the reception at a mammoth three-story Queen Anne style mansion near Central San Rafael. There was no time to waste, so they abandoned fancy wedding invitations in favor of phone calls, note cards and emails.

One of Owen's phone calls was to Astrid. Since their Russian adventure, he'd kept in touch, but now he had something big to share. In her Finnish way, she was thrilled to hear from him.

"You're engaged? That's good, Owen. Congratulations."

He thanked her. When no additional questions or statements came from the other end of the phone, Owen asked a conversational question.

"I liked your last article," he said.

"The one about software cracking? If I'm honest with myself, it was a little bit dry. But the story I did on Russian nuclear weapons trafficking is a big hit."

"I read it," Owen said, wryly. "But I noticed you left some important people out of the article."

"Why Owen?" she scolded, "You know I never divulge my sources."

"Is anything coming of it?" asked Owen.

Suddenly, Astrid was excited.

"Oh, yes. The Russian government is investigating. They take this kind of thing very seriously, but I doubt we'll ever get any details."

"What about your other story?" he asked. "The one about... epilepsy and videogames."

"Yes, well we should talk about that sometime. Not now, though, all right?" she asked, seriously.

"Well, OK. But I do have one more thing to ask you," he said.

"Yes?"

"The wedding is next week and I'd really love for you to come."

"You want me to fly to California? Thank you, Owen but I'm afraid I can't afford it. *Pelit* paid for my California trip last year."

"Don't worry about that. I'll pay for the whole thing, put you up in a hotel, everything. I just really want you to come. I need you to come."

"All right," agreed Astrid. "When I have it, I'll send you my flight schedule. I have to go now. Goodbye."

Astrid arrived at SFO two days before the wedding. Owen toyed with the idea of putting her on the Airporter so she could get a cultural tour from Captain Ethan, but decided that it would be too cruel. Owen and Miles met Astrid at the gate, collected her baggage and hauled it to the pick-up area where Viv waited with the car.

They all went to dinner on Nob Hill at one of San Francisco's most popular restaurants. Tiki sculptures welcomed visitors to the Tonga Room, a wonderful nightmare of heavily themed 1940s South Pacific cultural appropriation. A darkened ceiling and bright accent lights gave visitors the illusion of outdoor dining while they supped beneath palm-thatched roofs. The dining tables surrounded the large rectangular pool of water occupying much of the restaurant's floor space.

Owen felt something different in Astrid that evening. He didn't know whether it was exhaustion from the trip, the whimsical theme of the restaurant, or just too many mai-tais, but Astrid was definitely more relaxed than he'd seen her before. When a faux Polynesian boat floated an orchestra to the center of the pool and played during a man-made rainstorm, Astrid nearly laughed herself out of her chair. Owen found it most out of character.

He noticed that the Finn remained buoyant throughout the weekend, particularly when near Miles. Only at Viv's bridal shower the next day at the Coliseum Arts offices did Astrid return to her introverted ways.

Viv and Owen were married at the Civic Center on Saturday afternoon. Afterward, a limousine picked up the couple and whisked them away to the reception, where family and friends waited. The evening began without a hitch, though one of the game testers defied the facility's ban on dogs, bringing her young golden retriever as her "plus 1." Stevie fell in love with the puppy, giving the pooch all his attention and most of his hors d'oeuvres.

Halfway through the celebration, it was time for the toast. Miles called everyone into the opulent music room. There was a substantial brass section, stand-up bass, electric guitar and pianist. Mindy played drums.

When the room quieted Miles spoke, "First I want to thank the bride for letting me be her person of honor at the ceremony today. As such, I know it's my job to give tonight's toast. But I'm not going to. Instead, I'm going to give the bride and groom my wedding gift. It's something I've been working on for a little over a year and I'm dedicating it to this wedding. I hope you like it. It's called, 'Vivian.'"

Miles spun in place, bringing the ensemble to attention. The song began and within five bars of the music, Vivian was crying. The piece was in four movements. The first part featured funky syncopation and heavy bass beats. This flowed into something gentle and smooth, with a romantic tone. From this height, the tune descended into sadness, but this did not last. The bright tones of the horns rose above the piano, musically moving from struggle to rebellion and at last to triumph.

As the final chord concluded, the reception erupted in cheers and applause. Admirers surrounded Miles, including one in particular. Owen watched, bemused, as Astrid rushed in to grab the composer's arm and congratulate him on his artistic achievement.

Viv was the star of the event, deservedly receiving the lion's share of the attention. So by the end of the evening, Owen found himself on his own while large groups waited to take pictures with the bride. Taking advantage of the break, Owen found Astrid and invited her out to the porch.

"Are you having a good time?" he asked.

"Oh, it's wonderful. Thank you. You two are a beautiful couple."

"I'd like to ask you something," said Owen, becoming very serious.

Astrid replied with an overly serious face and voice, "What do you need to know, Owen?"

"All right, all right," Owen brightened up. "Look, I'm suddenly in need of a writer."

"Work on one of *your* games?" she asked.

Owen sensed her meaning.

"This time I want it to be different," he said. "This time I want to *add* some beauty to the world. I need your ideas."

Astrid looked surprised. Pleased and surprised.

Owen decided to sweeten the pot.

"Also, do keep in mind," he said. "Miles lives *here*."

She replied, "I will think about it."

Taking advantage of the open-air setting, Owen took out a celebratory cigar.

"Ugh," said Astrid with disgust. "With that, I return to the party."

When she had gone, Owen pulled out a disposable lighter and

attempted to light the stogie.

"Hey asshole," said a familiar and unwelcome voice. "I'd save that for later if I were you."

The groom looked up slowly, hoping he was wrong. He wasn't. It was Flexx. And Flexx wasn't alone.

CHAPTER FIFTY

DEATHMATCH

March 4, 1994
San Rafael, CA

The four gunmen all wore long, black jackets and ranged in height from six-foot-three to six-foot-five. Owen didn't get a good look at their faces, as he was transfixed by the machine pistol pointed at his sternum.

Owen asked, "Flexx, what do you want?"

In a distressed tone, Flexx answered, "I need you to get your best programmers and bring them out here. Do it quietly. If you don't, I truly believe that comrade Alvar here will order his men to shoot everyone at your party. Don't ask questions. Just do it."

"Alvar?" Owen blurted out. He looked up.

Seeing the hitman's features, Owen's jaw went slack; his arms limp.

"Oh my god," murmured Owen, astonished.

"Hi, gamer-asshole Owen Nickerson," sneered Alvar. "Good to see you again."

There was no forgetting the man's thin, wide mouth, ponytail and the ragged scar along the base of his jaw. Alvar the gangster was the Russian man he'd met at CES, over a year before. The man who had taken Maxine.

"You better run," Alvar threatened.

Owen glared and walked back inside the mansion. As he searched desperately for Dogg and Mitch, he was certain everyone at the party would notice his trembling hands. At six-foot-eight, Dogg was easy to spot. Owen approached and the huge programmer bent down so the groom could whisper in his ear.

Dogg looked over at his wife, making sure she was watching Stevie, then nodded and followed Owen. Mitch had worn a bright-red tuxedo to the party and was quickly found.

The trio's erratic movement through the crowd caught Astrid's attention. She noted Owen's hard expression. It wasn't the look of a man on his wedding day.

Mitch and Dogg followed Owen to the porch, where they discovered several men holding semi-automatic weapons.

"What the hell, Owen?" Dogg asked.

"All I know," said Owen, "is that if we don't do what they ask, they say they'll shoot up the party."

Dogg nodded slowly, "What do you want us to do?"

Flexx spoke, "Right now, we're going to casually walk to our car."

The three programmers followed the instructions, heading down the long trail of brick steps to a large, black sport-utility vehicle. Flexx walked behind, followed by Alvar and two of his three strongmen.

At the car door, Owen looked back and saw the fourth henchman still standing outside the mansion.

"What's he doing?" demanded Owen.

No one answered.

The car had three rows of seats. Flexx climbed into the rear seats along with one of the gunmen. From this position, the armed man had a good angle to shoot anyone attempting an escape. Owen and Mitch sat in the center row along with Alvar.

The killers seemed very concerned about Dogg. Even for the gunmen, his huge size posed a threat. They placed him in the front passenger seat. Owen gave the third gunman directions and they drove to Coliseum Arts. When they arrived at the offices, the three hostages sat at the adjacent desks in the programmer's room.

The gunmen and Flexx stood back a few feet. Alvar stood in the center, covering the hostages with his machine pistol.

Owen addressed his compatriots, "Mitch, Dogg...this is Flexx. I've mentioned him before."

The programmers were shocked but remained silent.

"Boot your computer and I'll tell you what's happening," said the hacker. Owen pressed the green-blue button on his machine. There was the sound of a cooling fan and a monitor snapping on.

"A year and a half ago," Flexx began, "I was contacted by a hacker named Phrenetiq who offered to sell me a Stinger missile system upgrade. You know, making them more accurate, that kind of shit. So, I figure that's pretty badass, right? I put together a deal with this other guy to buy it and we buy it. We test it. It works really good. So this guy I work with sells it to a bunch of these other guys. You know? Freedom fighters. They upgrade all their missiles. I make some money. Everybody is happy, right?"

Flexx continued, "But no. You know what happens then? Like, last month… the Stingers start blowing up on launch. A few people die. It's all fucked up, yeah? Now all of a sudden, everybody's mad. The customers put the software on all their missiles and now they can't fire them without killing themselves. Ilizarov found this out like, yesterday, while I was in Nevada for some work."

"And now you're here," Owen interrupted. "Why are you here?"

"So, Ilizarov's pretty pissed at me, right, which is totally unfair. But I'm the guy that got him the Stinger upgrade, you know?" Flexx explained. "And the guys we sold it to are some pretty serious guys. So, Ilizarov tells me I've got to get this bug fixed tonight, otherwise, these gentlemen here are going to kill me *and* you."

Owen's computer had booted. Flexx inserted a disc into the floppy drive.

"Dogg," said Owen. "I think this is kind of your thing."

"Who knows?" Dogg answered. "I'll take a look. It'd be pretty lucky if this turned out to be Dogg's Super Awesome Secret Project 2."

Dogg and Mitch rolled their chairs toward Owen to get a look at the screen. The lead programmer copied the file and ran it through a decompiling program, transforming the machine code into something human-readable.

Dogg talked as he analyzed the text, "Yes. Uh-huh. Of course, nothing in this has any names. If I didn't know what this program was supposed to do, I'd have no idea what it was. All right. Here we go."

He pointed at the screen.

"Right here… these are probably digital outputs. This is the steering function. See, how it takes the difference in the angles between the missile's vector and the targets? It adjusts for each angle then adds another 10 percent. That's so the rocket leads the target, instead of trying to catch it from behind."

The big man kept digging through the code.

"Here's some shit that—I don't know what it does. Yadayadayada. If this returns zero then—OK. Now *this* is interesting. If this function fails, it drops out of the flight loop and switches on this digital output. Then the program just ends."

"Why would it do that?" Owen asked.

"It's probably when a missile can't find its target anymore. It shuts itself off. That would prevent it from flying around and accidentally blowing up the wrong things," said Dogg, completing his analysis.

"But why turn on the digital output before ending the program?" Mitch asked.

"Self-destruct switch?" mused Owen.

"Probably," Dogg concurred.

"OK. Hold on," said Owen, narrowing his eyes.

He scrolled up two pages.

"Right there. That line there *also* hits the self-destruct switch," Owen whispered.

Dogg and Mitch studied the logic carefully.

Again Dogg narrated his thoughts but, like Owen, lowered his volume so only his friends could hear.

"It takes 'date stamp two' and subtracts 'date stamp one.' That provides the number of days between the dates. If the result is greater than 60, the missile blows itself up."

"It waits two months after the software update," said Owen under his breath. "After that, the missile explodes on launch."

"This was intentional," Mitch whispered. "The patch is a booby trap."

"We can't help them fix this," Owen said quietly, "We'd be responsible for every person the Stingers kill. We need to—"

"How's it going, American dickheads?" yelled Flexx, shoving his face in between Dogg's and Owen's.

The Americans started with surprise.

"We can't hear you back there. Did you find something?" the hacker asked.

"Well for one, your breath stinks," sneered Dogg.

"You and I. We have a lot riding on this, am I right?" asked Flexx. "Now, just you forget about me. I know you think I'm an asshole. But if you don't fix this, they will kill my sister, Luda. So make your changes. Walk me through them so I can verify. Then we will leave and you three can go back to your party."

The three programmers spun their swivel chairs around to face the kidnappers.

"I don't think we can," said Owen.

"Don't be an asshole," whined Flexx. "You don't know these men!"

Owen's declaration caused an immediate reaction from his captors.

In Russian, Alvar gave a command to one of his killers. The man drew and cocked his machine pistol, casually pointing it at Owen's head. There was no mistaking the man's intent. He planned to make an example of Owen.

Desperately, Mitch lunged from his chair, clumsily grabbing for the gun. He was much too slow. The gunman simply adjusted his aim and released a burst of bullets into Mitch's chest and shoulder. Mitch dropped to the floor, writhing and twisting.

"Goddam it, Owen!" screamed the panicked Flexx. "Stop it! Just fix the damn program. Please! There might still be time to save your friend!"

Dogg looked to Owen for instruction. Mitch would die without immediate help. They needed a plan but had none.

As Owen wracked his brain, the stairwell door in the common room clicked open. No one in the programmer's area could see the intruder, but they all heard steps approaching.

"Owen?"

At the sound of Astrid's voice, Flexx's eyes bugged out. Alvar caught Owen's attention and shook his head as a warning.

"Hey, Astrid," said Owen urgently. "You should go back to the party, OK? We're doing… we're having a stag party. You know. Guy stuff. No girl's allowed. Don't look."

"Oh, please," said Astrid, dismissively. From the common room, she approached the open doorframe and looked beyond. Glancing down, she saw Mitch suffering from his wounds.

All three gunmen had their pistols out, but once they realized the interloper was actually a beautiful woman in a shiny, blue satin party dress, they relaxed. Alvar made a rude comment in Russian and his comrades all chuckled.

Her pale eyes glowing in the dark, Astrid swiftly raised a weapon. It was a matte black machine gun, identical to those carried by the hit squad. With precision, she fired a single bullet through the forehead of Mitch's shooter, killing the man.

While the Russians had underestimated Astrid, Owen had not. As the killers gaped in shock, Owen threw himself at Alvar, grappling for his gun. Flexx moved to pull Owen off the scarred man, but he hadn't counted on Dogg. The huge programmer grabbed Flexx and rammed him head-first into the back of Jenn's old desk, stunning him.

The third gunman recovered from the shock of the surprise attack and focused his attention on the greatest threat—Astrid. Panicked, he sprayed the room with long, poorly aimed bursts. Astrid ducked back into the common room and Dogg dove for cover behind Jenn's corner desk. Bullets tore through the office's drywall, furniture, computer monitors and mint-in-the-box action figures.

Owen put all his effort into stripping away Alvar's machine pistol. Face-to-face they wrestled.

Owen pried the gun free and dropped it to the floor, but he'd underestimated his opponent. Entirely focused on the pistol, he hadn't noticed the combat knife in Alvar's left hand until its point had punctured his side. Crying out, Owen fell to the floor beside Mitch.

Alvar jumped on top of his victim. Holding the knife's pommel with both hands he pressed the blade downward toward Owen's heart.

Fighting back, Owen grasped his assailant's wrist with both hands.

"No more games," gloated Alvar.

Owen resisted, but inexorably, the knife descended. All was noise, smoke and chaos. Then suddenly, there was silence.

At the room's center, an armed thug looked fecklessly at his worthless machine pistol. In his desperate firing, he'd emptied it of bullets. The gunman looked back toward the doorframe. He saw Astrid in classic firing stance, arms extended, two hands wrapped around her pistol's grip. The gunman thought about dodging but knew it was far, far too late. Astrid pulled the trigger and two bullets passed through the man's heart. The third went astray, smashing a large hole in the office window.

Recovered from his collision with the desk, Flexx crawled across the room on all fours, staying low beneath Astrid's fatal volley. He'd seen Owen wrest the machine pistol from Alvar and in just a few more feet he'd have it.

Dogg saw Flexx's move for the gun. In a fit of rage, he grabbed Flexx with both hands and lifted the hacker above his head as if he were a barbell. With a roar, the giant turned and heaved the hapless man through the blacked-out plate glass window and down one floor to the sidewalk below. Flexx hit the concrete like a sack of wet cement.

Meanwhile, Owen was losing his fight. Unable to resist Alvar's strength and weight, he felt the point of the knife pierce his chest. In desperation, the wounded young man released his right hand from Alvar's wrist and reached out to grab anything he might use as a weapon. He groped under his desk, and his hand landed on a large, irregularly shaped object. Owen gripped it as best he could and swung at his attacker's head. The makeshift bludgeon connected, shattering on the man's face, cutting him.

It wasn't a powerful blow, but it was unexpected. Alvar leaned back, reflexively. Lifting the knife from Owen's chest, he looked around. He'd been struck with a toy NERF gun made of blue plastic and foam. Alvar laughed and raised his knife to impale Owen with one final, heavy blow.

Astrid didn't give him the chance. Firing her last torrent of bullets point-blank, she blasted Alvar Morozov backward where he lay dead, twitching on the blood-stained carpet.

Owen sat up, holding his side.

Frantically, he called to Astrid, "At the party! There was a fifth man!"

"He's dead. I put his body under the porch," said Astrid.

"Good," Owen whispered, then fell back and passed out.

* * *

March 5, 1994
St. Petersburg, Russia

Dr. Ilizarov's security detail of three preceded him as he left his townhouse. Descending the short staircase, they blocked the sidewalk to clear the doctor's path, preventing a pair of babushkas in shawls and headscarves from crossing his path. The old ladies waited in the cold while Ilizarov made his way distractedly down to the street.

He was lost in thought, considering his situation and his options.

"Flexx missed his deadline. He can't say I didn't give him a chance. When I reach the office, I must give the order to kill his sister. Then there is the problem of the Stingers. I must deal with that quickly. No doubt, some of my customers are already plotting my assassination. But in my experience, few problems can't be solved by a large check…"

Upon reaching the bottom step, Ilizarov woke from his thoughts. His foot kicked something soft. Looking down, he found his men flat on the sidewalk, each with a single hole through the head. He then noticed the babushkas for the first time. To his surprise, their faces were young and serious and their eyes blazing. Each carried a silenced semi-automatic pistol; smoke still curling from the barrel.

Overcome with sudden terror, Ilizarov gave an involuntary shriek and turned, running clumsily back up the stairs. The women aimed carefully. Each fired several shots into Ilizarov's back.

Leaving their victim dead on his doorstep, the assassins crossed the street and escaped in a waiting car.

CHAPTER FIFTY-ONE

PHRENETIQ

The emergency medical technicians stabilized Owen and Mitch as best they could, then drove them by ambulance to Marin General. Simultaneously, federal agents invaded the Nickerson wedding reception, clearing the distressed and bewildered partygoers from the mansion.

The Feds also arrived at the scene of the Coliseum Arts shootings, surprising the San Rafael Police Department by taking charge of the investigation.

The incident, in which four Russian nationals had been killed, was declared a burglary gone wrong. It was also reported that a fifth man had fled the crime scene and was still wanted for questioning.

Saving Mitch's life required multiple surgeries. Owen needed just one.

Though his wounds were serious, Owen recovered steadily and was allowed visitors only a few days after his admission to the hospital. Viv was first to visit her husband and stayed with him as long as was allowed each day.

Wedding guests rearranged their travel plans, staying several days longer to visit Owen with flowers, gifts and careful hugs.

One evening, after the nurses had chased the last well-wishers from Owen's bedside, a young woman slipped into the room.

When Owen saw her, he said, "Hello, Astrid. Or is it *'Phrenetiq'*?"

She just smiled and took his hand.

"Any word on how Mitch is doing?" Owen asked.

"It will take many months for him to fully heal," she said. "But there is good news. He will recover."

"And Dogg?"

240

"Fine. He agreed to back up the cover story," she answered. "How do you feel?"

"If I'm honest, Astrid," replied Owen, "I'd have to say that I'm a little disappointed in you. It looks like I still need to find a new writer."

"Yes," she replied. "I'm afraid I already have two jobs."

She smiled again, her blue eyes luminous in the dim light.

"You're a reporter and a spy?" he asked. "That's pretty cool, Astrid."

"Thank you," she said.

"What was your business with the Stinger missiles?"

"So many had escaped your country's control. It fell to me to neutralize their threat," she answered.

"Couldn't you just buy them back?" asked Owen.

"The C.I.A. tried. They offered $100,000 per missile, but that just drove up the black market price. That's when I came up with my plan —selling a Trojan horse to trick buyers into destroying their own weapons."

"How did it work?"

"Acquiring rigged missile software was simple. I just told my plan to the CIA and in a few weeks, I had it," she answered. "The hard part was getting it released on the black market. For that, I had to find an established hacker. So, I convinced *Pelit Magazine* to sponsor my game piracy story."

"That's how you met Flexx? You told him he'd be featured in your article?" asked Owen.

"Yes," answered Astrid. "Pirates like Flexx steal for glory. He bragged so much, I couldn't help but learn all about his underworld ties. Then I created my alter ego, *Phrenetiq,* to sell him the goods. It all worked perfectly until—"

Owen completed her sentence, "—until I came along."

Astrid spoke with regret, "When I brought you to Flexx at the Kruunuvuorenranta villas, I lost control of the situation. I will always regret that decision."

"What happened to Flexx?" Owen asked.

Astrid shrugged, "He must be badly hurt. But somehow, it looks like he just crawled away."

"The man is a chaos magnet," declared Owen.

"Flexx was almost the perfect puppet for my operation," said Astrid. "*Almost* perfect. But I didn't foresee him coming for you when his deal fell apart. I'm so sorry for you and Mitch."

"Don't feel too bad, Astrid. Any complex program has bugs," Owen replied. "You can't be expected to keep track of every variable. I'm actually very impressed—you were only off by one."

EPILOGUE

An anonymous tip caused the Nevada Bureau of Mining Regulation and Reclamation to examine the U.S. ventures of the late Leonid Morozov and his partner, Dr. Ilizarov. This resulted in a full-scale investigation of the Sourdough Mine site near Las Vegas. The locals assumed that the Bureau had found something important because they reported seeing teams of scientists, all wearing radiation-resistant suits, combing the property with Geiger counters. Whatever the radioactive discovery, it was never disclosed.

It took weeks more before the Coliseum Arts team could even think about returning to the office and some time after that before they felt ready to work on a new game. Owen suggested that they abandon the 3D shooter genre, given the events of the past few months. Besides, *Apoplexy II*'s sales had been mediocre at best.

Owen suggested they try making a cartoony console game for kids, maybe something for the Sega or the newly-released PlayStation. CEO Ryan supported the idea and told the team that with the right pitch, he'd find the platform.

Owen gathered the team and they brainstormed some ideas. This time, Vivian didn't participate. She was busy with her law-school preparatory courses.

The team's new pitch was for a cartoony 3D platfomer. Its main character, Sebastian Sugar Glider, jumped and soared through a colorful world filled with pinwheel flowers and monsters called "Pinchers." Stevie created the first drawings of the Pinchers by tracing his thumb and index finger, then adding googly eyes.

While the team loved Stevie's artwork, they lacked confidence in their own concept. No one at Coliseum Arts had ever created a game without blood splatters.

Regardless, Ryan declared that brainstorm time was over. They needed to start development before the company ran out of cash.

"This idea," said Ryan, "sucks less than the others."

Unbelievably, the rookie CEO booked a pitch meeting with Nintendo at the Computer Games Developer's Conference. Impressed with Coliseum's slapped-together demo and needing another triple-A launch title for their new *Project Reality* gaming machine; Nintendo bought the game and funded its development.

Ryan, Owen and a mostly-recovered Mitch spent a month planning the development strategy. This time around, they would staff and schedule correctly. There would be no crunch mode.

"We will need more programming firepower," warned Mitch.

"I have an idea about that," Owen replied.

"Irma?" asked Mitch, laughing.

"I wish," lamented Owen.

A week before, they had read an article in the San Francisco Chronicle's business section spotlighting a brilliant young Bay Area tech entrepreneur, Irma Fournier. Cole's secret subcontractor had taken her new online auction company public, making her an instant millionaire. A few years later, she would become a billionaire.

Owen replied, "I hope Irma remembers who gave her her first break in business. But no, I have someone else in mind."

Dogg had picked up the phone on the first ring.

"I could use the work," said Dogg, dryly, "You may not believe this, Owen, but I haven't pursued any new military contracts recently. Wait. We *are* just talking about making a game, right?"

In 1996, *Project Reality* was launched under its new name, *Nintendo 64*. Sales for the game platform were strong and at first, consumers had only three games from which to choose: Super *Mario 64*, *Pilotwings 64* and *Sugar Glider 64*. Sales for all three were outstanding. Coliseum Arts had another hit on its hands.

If Owen went on to make a hundred more games, *Sugar Glider* would always remain his favorite. He took the most pride in the fact that none of his team had ended up exhausted, sick, hurt, or angry.

Astrid returned to Helsinki, but visited Coliseum Arts, and Miles, as often as possible. After *Sugar Glider*'s launch, Miles took an offer to compose ringtones for Nokia, moving to Finland to be with Astrid. When she'd finally told him her true profession, he'd taken the news surprisingly well, although the poor timing of the revelation had caused Miles to spray coffee across the breakfast table.

The following summer, Viv convinced Owen to travel with her to Italy on an extended, belated honeymoon. Their epic vacation began in Naples and then headed north through Rome, Florence, Bologna and Venice. From Venice, they took a day trip to Verona, where Owen gave in to temptation. Passing an Internet café, he slipped inside to check his work email account.

To his relief, all was good back at Coliseum Arts. As Owen prepared to log off, a new message came through, but not from work. The email's subject line read, "Life or Death."

"Pretty dramatic," thought Owen, opening the message. It looked like it contained just a bunch of weird characters.

0\ / \ / 3 I V. 1 4 I \ / I 0 I V I \ / I 7 \ / \ / 47 70 533 70(_) 4 I V[) \ / \ / 111 4221 \ / 3 70 I V19 I - I 7. \ / \ / 3 423 807 I - I 1 I V [)4 I V932 4 I V[) 1 I V33[) 70(_)2 I - I 31 I *. I *4(X 70(_)2 8495. 83 234[)7 70 134 \ / 3. 1 \ / \ / 111 3>< I *141 I V \ / \ / I - I 3 I V 1 4221 \ / 3.

"Not this again," laughed Owen to himself. "What was it that Mitch had called hacker writing, 'Leet'?"

He studied the text, reminding himself how the symbols combined to create letters from the Latin alphabet. In a few minutes, he had deciphered it.

> "Owen. I am on my way to see you and will arrive tonight. We
> are both in danger and I need your help. Pack your bags. Be
> ready to leave. I will explain when I arrive."

"This has got to be a joke," thought Owen.

From outside, Viv tapped on the café window to capture his attention. He held up his open palm, mouthing the words, "Five minutes." She waved and nodded. He turned back to the puzzling message.

The author had signed his name in code. Nevertheless, Owen recognized it on sight.

I =13><><

The message was from Flexx.

"*Paskiainen,*" *whispered Owen.*

Stunned, he paused for a moment before deciphering the postscript. It read, "Don't even think about double-crossing me. Also, Maxine says, 'hi.'"

ACKNOWLEDGEMENTS

Thanks to my brilliant wife, Casey for her support, advice and editing.

I also had the unbelievable luck to be born into a family of writing and editing professionals who were kind enough to bring out the "Red Pen."
Thank you to my Sister Laura, Father Michael and Mother Nancy.

Finally, thank you to all my wonderful test-readers who gave generously of their time and insight.

Ryan Donahue
Sander Temme
Mark Petersen
Larry Ahern
Jay Baird
Kit DeGear
Candi Cooper-Towler
Seth Mendelsohn
Prudence Fenton
Seth Gillum

Made in the USA
Middletown, DE
22 January 2022

59370267R00139